M000316809

In the Land of the
LOVERS

Sakoon Singh studied English Literature at the
Jawaharlal Nehru University (JNU), New Delhi
and Panjab University, Chandigarh. She has been a
recipient of the Fulbright Fellowship and currently
teaches Indian Literature and Cultural Studies in
Chandigarh. She has published her academic writings
extensively, and contributed to *Cultural Studies
in India* (Routledge, 2016). She has served on the
editorial board of *Dialog* and edited a special South
Asia section for *E3W Review of Books* (University of
Texas, Austin). She has written pieces, articles and
op-eds on literature, art, culture and aesthetics for
The Tribune, Hindustan Times, DNA and *The Quint*.
She is currently doing a stint at the Indian Institute
of Advanced Study (IIAS), Shimla.

In the Land of the LOVERS

— A PUNJAB QISSA —

Sakoon Singh

RUPA

Published by
Rupa Publications India Pvt. Ltd 2020
7/16, Ansari Road, Daryaganj
New Delhi 110002

Sales Centres:
Allahabad Bengaluru Chennai
Hyderabad Jaipur Kathmandu
Kolkata Mumbai

ISBN: 978-93-89967-03-6

First impression 2020

10 9 8 7 6 5 4 3 2 1

The moral right of the author has been asserted.

Printed HT Media Ltd., Gr. Noida

To my father,
who taught me to look over and above,
below and beyond

'I know the world is bruised and bleeding, and though it is important not to ignore its pain, it is also critical to refuse to succumb to its malevolence.'

Toni Morrison

Contents

I

No Traveller Returns

The October afternoon abruptly changed complexion. The sun, radiating just the right warmth to get you by on a reasonably cold day, was suddenly eclipsed by raucous grey clouds—unruly kindergarten boys kicking up a ruckus. It could be inconvenient, but Nanaki did not mind them in the least— these sudden downpour days that came without warning, like a piece of unexpected good news. Each time the day plunged into sudden darkness owing to the rain-filled clouds, the remains of the day illuminated by naked yellow bulbs, the mild chill filled her with an unknown anticipation. Now a sudden burst of cool spray brushed her cheeks and before long, a steady rain had set in. The hitherto clear line of houses and moving cars became indistinct behind a watery screen. She quickened her pace as she entered the lane of her house, which was the farthest in a leafy neighbourhood.

The house lay hidden behind dense foliage set off by a row of tall areca palms, their fronds and panicles making for dark silhouettes at twilight. On a day like this, the trees would sway noisily in the breeze, creating a loud rustle against the turbulent sky. There was always the danger of a gigantic leaf coming crashing down on the row of clay pots. A hardy shrub had been clipped over the years to make for a low hedge skirting the outer wall, and a three-decade-old guava tree stood at the entrance, shielding the wrought iron gate, sprawling into a canopy over the garage driveway. On a shady, grassless patch at the other end of the lawn was an old, gnarled mango tree. It bore fruit every alternate summer, speckled with a pale golden frizz by spring, gradually morphing into tiny plump paisleys—miniature mangoes, which, if fate, weather and the goodwill of the neighbourhood colluded, would, by summer, turn into full, ripe fruits. The girth of the tree had considerably widened over the years and, owing to its annual pruning, had started shooting upwards, with many of its branches cutting with vitality through the facade railing, depositing a stray harvest of mangoes in the nooks and crannies of the terrace, especially in the monsoon months. Sometimes the tree hid winged creatures: parrots and mynahs were common enough sights, but once Nanaki had been stupefied to find a lone hornbill, its grey form perched on the highest branch, from where it smoothly glided to the adjoining green stretch, the Leisure Valley.

The little verandah skirting the front yard led into the garden when its wall-sized window panels were thrown open. In winters, one could slump there on a bamboo chair, or better still, sprawl on a charpoy to soak in the sun, with a book in hand. On the facing wall hung a long panel of phulkari framed in solid wood. Nanaki had seen it here for as long as she could remember. The rust base had become somewhat discoloured through the many summers of harsh sun, but the threads still shone with their original lustre. On lazy summer afternoons, looking up from a book, she would examine every inch of it. Geometric patterns in ochre silken thread filled the two ends of the fabric. On closer inspection, it was a procession of carriages: women and men marching, riding horses, a caravan filling the other end, a peacock perched on a tree; its branches filled the body of the tapestry. There were some travellers. *Where could they be going?* Nanaki would think. *Are they happy? Are they sad? Could they be in exile? Or, wait, no—it looks like a wedding procession. Something ceremonial.*

From the main road, through the gaps in the foliage, one could glimpse the brick house. On the outer wall, next to the gate, was a kota stone slab with the brass letters 'Brig. Arjan Singh, Infantry.' It concealed a concrete letter box on the other side. Nanaki made a dash over a puddle and entered the house with her kurta soaked to the bone, her hair sodden, letting out meandering streams that went all the way down to her, by now ruined, jutties.

She changed into her worn-out white tee and cotton wraparound. Beeji instantly emerged, bearing two cups of tea. That both of them were tea lovers only helped matters, and it was a time of the day they both looked forward to. For Beeji, tea time was a bit of a ceremony. She would spread a cross-stitched cover on the tray and use the old porcelain mugs. She would then empty out atta biscuits from a fresh packet, or if there were supplies, place home-made *pinnies* into a bowl. And she would do it patiently, each time with the same amount of fuss. Nanaki would often get impatient with her, half cajoling, half complaining, urging her to come fast. At times, Beeji's coarse hands and the blackened end of the tea pan would trigger a strange restlessness within Nanaki; she would want to steer her clear of all household drudgery. On occasions, she would storm into the kitchen and walk out with the containers, 'We'll just eat out of the dabbas, Beeji, who cares...*tussi aa jao* (you just come).' Beeji would then give multiple shakes to her salt-and-pepper hair and hobble out of the kitchen—'*Kamli jehi* (silly girl). Coming! Just coming!'

Since her college was at a walking distance, Beeji would get the tea brewing around the time when Nanaki's last lecture winded down. The practice had led to such precision that Nanaki ringing the bell would invariably coincide with Beeji straining tea into the cups. Like clockwork, she would emerge into the sitting room where Nanaki sprawled herself on the bed next to the window. Her dupatta would be carelessly dropped on the armchair and her jutties would be discarded near the door. Without wasting a moment, she would take off her silver earrings, relieving the lobes of the weight of the chunky things she had carried around the whole day. She would remove her watch, keeping it clutched in her fist before absent-mindedly depositing it on the nearest available surface—a table, a shelf or a niche. The two women would then catch up on the day's events. Nanaki would go over her college, colleagues and lectures, and Beeji, over the mali, the harvest of the seasonal vegetables from the kitchen garden and some fixed deposit or the other that needed to be reinvested because the maturity date was fast approaching. At times, she would be excited about a column she had read in *The Tribune* that morning. This was a daily fix.

Brig. Arjan Singh was Nanaki's maternal grandfather (nanaji). Nanaki had lived with her grandparents since she was a toddler, having moved in with them after the death of her parents in an accident. Her father, a professor of Computer Science at the newly set up Regional Engineering College, had been driving back from a conference in Delhi. His wife had accompanied him while the child had been left with her aunt—her father's sister—in Jalandhar. Their car had collided head-on with a trolley truck on the highway and the two lives had been instantly snuffed out.

It was in April, the week after Baisakhi, the harvest festival, when highways frequently teem with tractor trolleys overloaded with produce. At times, in their greed to pack in more and more, they load up enormous volumes, spilling out of the edges of the trolley, blocking the view. Insolent drivers blare screeching horns while speeding trucks and private cars cruise at dangerous speeds and manoeuvre any which way, just to get past.

Nanaki was not yet three when her parents died. Not that she was a stranger in her grandparents' house, but when she arrived a day after their death, it had an enormously fatalistic ring. She had stood there in the outer verandah, in a white home-stitched frock. With her enormous brown eyes, she had appeared very tiny that day. Way smaller than how Beeji remembered her. One look at her through the window as she alighted from Nanaji's old Fiat and stood motionless in the driveway, waiting to be led inside, had created a void in Beeji's stomach.

∞

Beeji lay in the darkness of the morning. She thought about her husband's breakfast porridge. She would add some figs to it today. Figs are good for his blood pressure problem. And there were old winter clothes to be given to Sadashiv. She will get the back store cleared, it smelt dank the other day, and have him sun the woollens for a good day or two. Winter had long passed. Passed. Passed away. Last week her daughter and son-in-law had passed away. Killed in an accident. They had been cremated. Yes, that was true. It was a finality she could not argue with. She started. Yesterday, at this time, they had arrived in a Red Cross ambulance, cold in strange blankets. They had died on the highway. There was no chance to take them to the hospital. Their bodies had lain cold on the highway in the receding night. Death was final. She tried not to dwell on these matters. But then, whose blankets were those? They smelt of wheat husk. Maybe some passing farmers. Generous that these village people are, they must have covered the dead strangers with their blankets. She went on an involuntary train of thought that she had to sit up and put a stop to. The details were jumping at her. She did not want to think about it. The kid lay on the bed next to her. The child still curled her fists while she slept. Her lips quivered intermittently even as she lay fast asleep, and made a little pout. Scales of her persistent dermatitis had not yet completely gone. She had come down with a nasty outbreak, with crusty scales on her cheeks that would get particularly worse after a bath. She had been put through a three-week course of ointments by the dermatologist. The doctor had advised complete abstinence from chemicals—so her soap had been replaced with curd. Yet the scaly remains of the outburst were visible on the hairline and the temples. And that mango stain on her muslin frock looked very obstinate. There were little crescents of dirt beneath her nails, which needed to be clipped. Days of neglect showed. Her hair needed a good round of brushing. These practical matters were very comforting. She could do something about these. She could start with the nails.

℥

There were days Nanaki would persistently ask for her mother. It would be a constant 'mama, mama,' punctuated with sighs. She would be in no mood to listen. By and by Beeji would calm her and, when better, prop her on the marble slab of the kitchen. By the end of it, Nanaki would give up, not because she understood any better, but out of sheer exhaustion. Beeji would repeatedly prompt her to finish the contents on her plate while rolling out more chapattis and telling her some winding story, all the while adding new details. She would keep the story moving, adding imaginary details, because each time she paused, Nanaki would, by default, stop chewing. And so Beeji had to go on and on, quite like Sheherzade. She would sometimes make little figurines of dough—a bird, a car or a ball, and that would get the child interested.

Some days, she would make a special roti for Nanaki—a *chikdi* roti. She would take a ball of dough and roll out just a little bit and put it on the tawa. When it got just a little warm, she would take it off and roll out the now warm dough. This done, she would add desi ghee, some salt and hand-ground pepper and ajwain, and give the dough a fold and a twist so that a layer or two was formed. She would then roll out this ball again and put it back on the tawa and cook it on a very low flame. The roti would come out golden and flaky. Her mother used to make rotis like that, back in Okara. Beeji had learnt it from her.

In summers, Beeji would cajole Nanaki to lie down with her for an afternoon nap. A typical lunch, accompanied by cucumber salad and tall glasses of lassi, with the bellowing heat wave outside, was hugely soporific. As Beeji got up from the table and cleared the last remains, her eyelids would become progressively heavier. She would draw the curtains of the bedroom and make Nanaki lie down too. Nanaki, however, would steal out of the room as soon as she felt the vibrating rumble of Beeji's snores. She would amble into the garden from the verandah and get on with her little private escapades. Her mother had taught her to dig her feet into a little mountain of sand and then pat it till it looked smooth, without the cracks. Upon gingerly removing the feet, a mud cave would be left standing. But one had to be careful. This was also the time it could all crumble into a sandy heap. Each time she made one, a gasp escaped her lips. She would then go about embellishing it with odds and ends from the garden. A stick insect on the rose shrub would be pinched between the fingers and put in the entrance as the woody 'door'. This was almost always her favourite catch. It was another matter that the 'door' would move by itself, necessitating an 'adjustment' every few minutes. A couple of snails would be dug out from the cool edges of the garden and placed in the 'yard' of the cave, where they would continue to slither at dreadfully slow speed, at times becoming almost immobile, upon which Nanaki would nudge them with a twig to keep the circus going. She would suck the nectar from the ends of the tiny white blossoms of the hedge shrub, before planting them in front of the cave to create a garden of 'white trees' like peach trees with blossoms. At this scale, the flowers could be passed off as trees. She had saved a piece of her old school ribbon, which she mounted on a stick to make a miniature flag; matchsticks for a picket fence that hemmed in the cave and a dinky car parked at the entrance completed the picture.

She would then have winding conversations with people 'visiting' her in the cave house. These were real people, mama—papa, sometimes superheroes and at times characters from books that had been read to her by her father. She would remind her father of the new Lego he was supposed to buy her. 'Too late. You have till Monday,' she would end the matter conclusively, aping her grandfather. Moving on, she would enquire of 'Alice' if she had eventually found the right keys and cards. She would enquire of an imaginary villager if Guru Nanak had indeed bought anything else with the twenty rupees his father had given, apart from feeding the hungry sadhus in the forest. On other days, Dorothy and the Tin Soldier would be hauled up for breakfast while on their way to the Emerald City, or Pinocchio would be asked in all earnestness if he was having trouble blowing what was an inordinately long nose. It was a non-stop soliloquy emanating from the fag end of the garden.

There were days Sadashiv's son Mohan would bend over the hedge and troop in to join her. Once, he brought his newly acquired treasure: a box full of buds collected from under the eucalyptus trees, which he was too proud to part with at first but eventually gave away in exchange for something more alluring that Nanaki offered. Sometimes he would carry little baubles, like a string or two of those shiny plastic beads in black threads—hanging decorations from his uncle's new rickshaw— that he would stealthily pluck on a ride and keep hidden. At times he would bring a firefly or two that he had captured in a matchbox. As a precaution, he would make tiny perforations to keep the air supply going. Not so much out of sympathy for the wretched creature, but out of a purely selfish motive to keep the thing alive. He would gingerly push the tray of the matchbox and deposit the flighty creature into Nanaki's cave. They would then lie on their stomachs, expectantly longing for the firefly to flash, with their faces perched on their palms, with elbows digging into the earth. Each tiny flash was greeted with applause. Electricity would thus be introduced into the cave. Hours would roll by. Nanaki would then hear Beeji call out to her for her Bournvita, when activity stirred in the house once again in the evening. This was a cue for Mohan to make a dash back to his own house.

๛

On cold winter evenings, the two would sit up in a razai after Beeji had had a long day. She always kept a little bottle of Hamdard almond oil next to her bed. She would pour a coin-sized helping and spread it on her palms and give Nanaki a good massage on the legs. Her legs looked dreadfully chapped in the winters and as the oil spread, it smoothed out the unseemly flakiness. There was invariably a scab or two on her knees, testimonies to the everyday rough play—escapades with Mohan; climbing the jamun tree to quell the craving of a quick bite; getting under the prickly hedge to pluck the white tubular flowers, the ends of which they would endlessly suck for its sticky sweet nectar.

Nanaki always demanded to play 'Who-laughs-first'. She and Beeji would face each other, perfectly still. With all movement frozen, they would just look at each other, and whoever laughed first would lose. So, one had to contain their laughter. That was the game. Beeji thought it was easy. So easy, it was no game at all. Nanaki, on the other hand, would become particularly ticklish. No sooner would they sit facing each other, holding their smiles, than Nanaki would be seized with a terrible urge to break into guffaws. She would have to make a herculean effort to contain the waves of laughter threatening to break out any time. She would clench her teeth and calm her quivering lips to fight it but, despite her effort, laughter would erupt, slithering, spluttering at first and then, and when she gave way, a whole flood of it gushing out. Her cheeks would be flushed by the end of it and her eyes watery. Beeji would be exhausted with all this, in a good way. First, the effort to laugh when even smiling was a herculean task, and then to feign containing laughter that was non-existent to begin with. But to succumb to this no-laughter state would also be such a dampener. So she would bring on peals of feigned laughter to humour Nanaki. The exhaustion came from the pretence involved. But Beeji had decided that it was worth the effort.

Once, the child had to be taken for her vaccination schedule the following morning, an ordeal repeated every few weeks. In preparation, Nanaji pulled out her vaccination card from the vault in his study the previous night and, first thing in the morning, drove her to the Sahib Singh and Sons Pharmacy in Sector 17. Entering the humungous space, their senses were hit with a spiky antiseptic odour. The passage leading into the inoculation area was a dark and dingy one. The walls on either side were lined with dark wooden shelves filled with hundreds of glass bottles and tiny decanters with corks. Each time she entered the space, a cloud of dread seemed to emerge from the aged tinctures stored in the bottles, most of which had, by now, become viscous and cloudy with age. In some, a rainbow-coloured film seemed to swim over the top layer. On each of these occasions, Nanaki would feel her steps becoming laboured, as if somebody had poured molten lead into her legs. The fag end of the passage was lit up with a yellow bulb peeping from an aluminium downlight. The man who delivered the shots had a curly mop and wore a viridian green hospital apron with an identical mask. His eyes emerged from under the bushels of his unusually thick eyebrows. He had a summary manner: he would make Nanaki lie down on the wooden bench and transfer the vaccine from the vial into the injection after duly noting the expiry date and batch number in the old, frayed register. He would take a blob of antiseptic-soaked cotton ball, rub it on Nanaki's thigh in circular motions, and then in a split second, feel for her vein and deliver the shot. The ritual was known to all by now. Nanaji, for all his military experience, would look away at that precise moment when he jabbed the needle into the thigh. After it was done, Nanaki would jump down from the bench and then, adjusting her skirt, troop to the other part of the pharmacy where children expected to be treated to an ice cream as compensation for their 'bravery'. Nanaji would pay up at the counter, which was manned by the owner himself—an old Sikh gentleman with silver beard, who always tied a navy blue turban. Nanaki thought of it as a uniform of sorts. His pince-nez would gleam as he meticulously arranged the received cash into the wads lying in the drawer. There would be 100s, 50s, 20s, 10s and coins in plastic sorters—the kind you have for pills—with Monday to Sunday written on them. Nanaki would keep looking at the filigree of veins under his unusually fair hands as he arranged the cash and, more often than not, handed over two Cadbury Eclairs to her in lieu of change. He would exchange pleasantries with Nanaji in his Rawalpindi Punjabi and always have some story to relate of the bygone days. Out Nanaki would walk, with a dribbling vanilla ice cream in one hand and two chocolate éclairs, like gold guineas, secure in her skirt pocket. She would forget all about the injection till the evening, when the soreness in the bum returned.

∾

Sundays meant a late start. Nanaki would leisurely emerge from her room and amble around the house in pyjamas. With the curtains thrown open, sunlight from the lobby window would flood the whole house. Every month, Beeji, with the help of Sadashiv, would get the monthly wheat washed and spread out on a cot in the backyard. They owned a little farm in Barwala on the outskirts of Chandigarh, which they had leased out to a marginal farmer. He would sow his crop on their land and in turn pay them in kind—three quintals of wheat in one season and two big drums of rice the next. It saved them many a hassle in old age. In their backyard there was a kutcha shed with a clay-tiled roof, where grain was stored in large metallic drums.

The monthly share of wheat was scooped out and given a thorough wash. It would be submerged in a large metal tub till impurities and loose husk and weevils swam on the surface, and then drained out. It would then be run under tap water several times, till the water ran clear. Beeji would then have it spread out on the cot and leave it in the sun till it was shell dry. Every now and then, she would comb through the wheat with her fingers to air it and feel for any traces of moisture. The dhobi would then load the sack on his bicycle and take it to the mill, where it would be ground to fine atta flour. At times, Nanaki would drive the dhobi in Nanaji's old Willys and get the work done.

To say that Beeji was frugal in her ways would be an understatement. She liked to first extricate as much as she could out of things and when done, if possible, pass them on to needy acquaintances—and if not, then the poor. To throw away food in that house was sacrilege and there was a tacit agreement in this regard. Her dinner plate would be speckless before going into the sink. Let alone the food, even the leftovers were managed very efficiently—arranged in appropriately sized katoris presented promptly at the next meal despite Nanaki's screwed nose protestations. The leftovers of leftovers were passed on to Usha and the food that fermented or expired or developed a layer of mould despite the care were fed to the stray dogs outside or put, in portions, in the bird house hanging from the mango tree. Her clothes would be completely worn out when she discarded them; the edges of her salwar *pauncha* become frayed, the mulmul of her undershirts sheer with use. She would get refills for her ball pens from the stationer, Nanaji's waste papers would be cut into note-sized wads held together with a kitchen clip and used to jot down 'things to do', old newspapers would be meticulously stacked, old pillow covers would be cut and edged with lace to make duchess sets for the dressing table, old yokes would be reused on new cotton kurtas and laces would be gently pulled out from old shirts if they were good enough to be rescued. Sarees would be made into salwar kameez or cut into dupattas, old dupattas would be made pretty with little tassels and transformed into bathroom curtains. As a result of this frugality, Nanaki would always be bought school skirts that were a size too big for her. To begin with, Beeji would hem in the extra length and the following year, when it would be a tad short, going precariously above Nanaki's knees, Beeji would sit down with the skirt to open the hems, so as to make it longer. The newly opened part of the fabric would look unnaturally unused and two shades darker against the faded skirt, making for a two-inch visual border going around. In her eyes, it was just a small price to pay; what was vanity against wisdom? In retrospect, Nanaki cringed at the thought of having been made to go through all that and held it against Beeji for the most part. Nothing went down the drain if it was edible, nothing discarded if it could be worn, nothing thrown away if it could be recycled or passed on. Broken? Repair it. Faded? Dye it. Torn? Sew it. There was a fix for everything: Watches to the watch repairman behind the wooden counter, bending over time pieces with his magnifying glass; shoes with soles coming apart to the cobbler sitting under the *amaltas* tree on the bend; cooker with a broken rubber ring to the man in Rehri market; old brass karahi for polishing to the *kaliwallah* in the old bazaar of Manimajra; the quilt stuffed with cotton, depressed with use, to the itinerant quiltmaker who came only in the 'season' with his wooden tools that could pass off as musical instruments. On Mondays, it was frugality of a different kind. Beeji fasted every Monday and refrained from consuming grains. It was a habit from her youth. It was not a religious fast, which had then been popular amongst young girls who undertook it to appease Shiva in order to get a good husband. It was a fast Lal Bahadur Shastri had ordained for the people in the years after Independence to make up for the severe scarcity of grains in the country. She had listened to his fervent appeal on radio. She had been adjusting to a new life in the cantonment with her husband and a grieving mother who had lost her home and husband in the Partition. In the face of so much helplessness, somewhere Beeji had wanted to be able to do something. So she had begun to fast. She had continued with the practice even decades later.

Of all these pet activities, Nanaki liked to watch the quiltmaker at work. No sooner would he come around to Beeji's haggling machinations and motion to his assistant to start work, than Nanaki would sit cross-legged on the verandah floor and watch the proceedings. He would spread his paraphernalia and, together with his young apprentice, work on razais—scooping out the clumps of old cotton and stretching them taut against the wire of his instrument, and then plucking them with jerks so that the clumps would loosen, and one by one they would fill the verandah like clouds, like autumns' breath had been blown into them. The fresh cotton would then be shoved into old velvet covers with prints of big flowers, and sewn on both ends. Once filled with fresh cotton, these would finally be stitched with big needles and decorated with flowery thread patterns. This exercise was repeated every two years or so. A substantial part of Beeji's effort went into keeping the household thus 'maintained'.

❦

On Sundays, Nanaji, too, would emerge after a protracted early morning session in the study. Both he and Nanaki would stretch out on the low bed overlooking the window. Beeji would emerge after a head bath with water still dripping from his hair. The hair dye mark left little dark clouds on the outer edges of her hairline. Nanaki would sit with the Sunday papers with her back to the window. She loved the sensation of the mild sun shining on her back through the window while she pored over the local news and the household help Asha swept and mopped the house. Asha would apply the mop with brisk, arc-like movements and the wet trail it made would evaporate in no time, leaving the old Terrazzo floor gleaming like new. In summers, cuckoo birds would intermittently let out hollow, plaintive calls from the frontyard mango tree. A shaft of sunlight with floating particles fell on the floor. Beeji would constantly keep passing instructions to Asha to not leave out the nooks and crannies, and this would really exasperate Nanaki. Nanaji would be sitting across the room on the armchair, absorbed in his Urdu newspaper. This was his Sunday special. On weekdays, it was the standard *The Tribune* but on Sundays, it was the added indulgence of the Urdu newspaper. It gave him a chance to renew the old connection he felt with the language and its idiom, a material remnant of his childhood and youth that had progressively been shoved to the margins of existence.

'You take their lands. Then you want to take language also. Nobody even got a whiff of it. How does it help anyone?'

This was a common refrain.

Beeji would sometimes join in on Nanaji's harangue. 'Big questions.' She would give her pronouncement, conceding her sheer insignificance in the scheme of things. On other occasions, she would be more interested in Asha scrubbing the floor well. After partaking in the discussion, she would amble into the kitchen.

Of late, the otherwise staid Urdu newspaper from Jalandhar was seen to be carrying rather salacious coloured images on one quarter of the last page. These images of white, semi-clad women, in colour, were very conspicuous in an otherwise unintelligible newspaper to Nanaki. It was somewhat incongruous to see little pictures, sourced from foreign news agencies, of white women in bikinis, sun tanning on a beach in Zakynthos or a procession of revellers in Sao Paulo complete with exotic costume regalia: trailing pheasant feathers for tails, operatic masks tantalizingly revealing pouty red lips, breasts protruding out of sequinned two-pieces, toned derrieres jutting out of glitzy G-strings vibrating animalistically to the samba, shapely legs fitting snugly into gold stilettos. Others showed women walking down the ramp in skimpy lingerie at a Missoni fashion show in Milan. At times these sights would intrigue

Nanaki. To her, Urdu was unintelligible, just black marks on paper. *Who reads this newspaper? And who are these pictures for? Whose reality is this? So very discordant.* She could just gaze at these images while Nanaji pored over the news and other contents. He would not realize the incongruous sight he made for as he intently read the inside pages, and out of habit, would so fold the newspaper that the particularly salacious images would always appear in line of Nanaki's vision. One particular morning, the sight made her laugh so hard that a spurt of tea sprayed from her lips. She discarded the cup, then burst out in uncontrollable laughter, rolling on the bed with legs kicking in the air. She clutched her stomach and doubled up for a good while before getting a grip on herself. The joke was totally lost on Nanaji, who looked up from his reading glasses and kept punctuating his reading with a nonplussed 'What? What?? *Sanu vi dass deo*—tell me, tell me also.' By this time Beeji realized what an odd sight Nanaji made and she joined Nanaki, both like schoolgirls bursting into uncontrollable guffaws at his expense, who, by now, would be utterly bewildered at the goings-on.

∾

Each meal saw Nanaji seat himself at the head of the table and plant himself there to be served. He moved very little through the proceedings. He would demand to be served water or would show his severe displeasure if the napkin went missing. His entitlement was complete. Beeji hovered over him, adjusting his plate, glass and napkin, and serving him daal and sabzi. Chapattis were served fresh off the tawa. They were both big on desserts, a habit picked up and solidified in army messes where a meal was inconceivable without being rounded off with some sweet. Why, Nanaki could imagine Nanaji in his fatigues, perched precariously on a rock, digging into the crusty dehydrated viands from a vacuum-sealed packet of MRE (Meals Ready to Eat)—war food diet—and that done, rounding it off with dehydrated marzipans from his backpack. In the days when he went to battle, the soldiers were made to carry *shakkar paaras*, which could last for days on end. Some sugar was mandatory. That was how meals on good (and not-so-good) days would end.

Nanaki, however, would be struck by this dining clockwork and this order that eschewed surprises of any kind—or even a departure from the given. Departures could be delightful. Pregnant with possibility. Perhaps this urge had something to do with having witnessed a very eccentric professor father who would be so preoccupied with his internal life, that these daily chores and routines just existed in the margins. One did not have to feed them, they had to feed one's life—a life that added up to being more than a succession of everyday banal routines. A session in her father's study could go on longer than anticipated, and he made allowance for that. But it was also about how unproblematically Beeji put herself in the singular role of the nurturer, the wife. Nanaki could not imagine herself in that space. She could not fix herself in roles of that kind. It was inconceivable for her.

❧

Winters in Chandigarh were pleasant for the most part, with only a fortnight, at the most three weeks, of what could be described as really harsh cold, complete with fog and temperatures almost hitting zero. In the chilly nights they would be done with dinner by 8 and then have the whole long evening ahead of them. It was on these occasions, with both women sitting under the razai, that Beeji would talk of her Pakistan days, their old house, the days before Partition. Beeji would invariably be tatting and Nanaki would be sorting her file of art prints. At times she would be sifting through the digital print collection on her iPad, preparing for her lecture the following morning.

In the bedroom, there hung a painting of Guru Nanak, 'The Pilgrim' done by Jaswant Singh. They had bought it from the museum shop. It was one in which only Guru Nanak's legs and feet in wooden sandals were visible, traversing a barren mountainous landscape complete with obscure passes and water streams. All that was in view in the foreground were his muscular calves, emerging from below a partially visible ochre tunic, and just a part of his rosary dangling from his hand. It was this avatar of the Guru that she liked the best: Guru Nanak, the expeditionist, the adventurer, who went beyond the small world of his village, Rae Bhoe ki Talwandi, his glow and his rebellion enabling him to leave the confines of his limited existence to traverse alien landscapes in a seer's clothing. He had set out, on foot, on long journeys, *Udasis,* in four directions with his friend and companion, Mardana; North as far as Tibet and China, South as far as Ceylon and East as far as Assam and Burma. In Mecca, the Guru and his companion had donned a blue tunic called *bekh*, which was the dress of the hajjis. According to lore, the Siddhas, intrigued by his journeys, had asked him:

Kiss karan greh tajeo udasi?
Why have you left your house and become an
itinerant Udasi?

Kiss karan eh bekh nivasi?
Why have you adopted these religious robes?

Gurmukh khojat bhaye udasi.
I became a wandering Udasi, searching for the
Gurmukhs, the speakers of truth.

Nanaki felt an affinity with Guru Nanak, probably because she
was named after the Guru's sister Bebe Nanaki, whose love for
her saint brother was the subject of many *saakhis* or the Guru's
life stories. She had been instrumental in many of the Guru's
important life decisions. She was the one to look above and
beyond what were seen as his errant ways, his ineptitude for
instruction and business. She was the one who was convinced
of his great bearings and prodded him into moving out of their
parents' limited existence. Nanaki's grandfather had bought her
dozens of these comics. She had read these stories. Nanak and
Nanaki: a nice jodi, a brother sister pair with similar names.
Nanaki was the elder sibling and named thus because she
was born in her *nanake* or maternal grandparents' place. In
Punjabi, there is a special word for grandparents on either side:
nanake, or mother's parents, and *dadake*, or father's parents.
The culture necessitates this sharp demarcation in two sets
of grandparents. The role of *nanakas* is defined, decidedly
subservient, their 'contribution' in each of the child's several
milestones spelt out; their role starts with the birth of the
child, at which occasion the *nanakes* are supposed to act as a
kind of sanctuary for the 'daughter of the house' who repairs
to her parental house as a more comfortable dwelling where
she is allowed a few month's rest, post-natal care and freedom
from the bondage of the several daily codes that make for the
traditional role of the daughter-in-law. So Guru Nanak Dev Ji's

mother had followed a well-wrought tradition by proceeding to her parents' place, to see the child born and the infant reared for a few days. Therefore the name Nanaki—the one born in the *nanakas*. Nanak followed, his name derived from that of the sister, as he completed the picture of the family—a pair of children for the parents. This connection with Guru Nanak felt homely to Nanaki: very intimate, devoid of the wherewithal people generally attach to the Guru. In this particular painting, the Guru seemed to embody a quest, a lifelong adventure.

On the wall next to the wooden niche, there was a collection of photographs of the family. Black and white with an acquired sepia wash. The glass on the photographs reflected the amber of the old Murphy family heater, which had begun to emit a crackling sound as it heated up. It was issued to Nanaji when he was a Captain and had travelled to all the stations with him. Each winter, it was taken out of the loft where it would hibernate in summers, tied up in an old bed sheet. Beeji's mother had shoved these old photographs inside the white cloth bag with her other possessions when leaving Okara for good.

There was one photo in which the Nanakshahi brick facade of the Okara haveli was clearly visible in the backdrop. The photograph had developed discolouration at the edges; indistinct clouds of mildew spread like Rorschach ink blots on the prints. Sardar Gurbaaz Singh, Beeji's father, stood in a kurta and lungi with a turban framing his broad face, while Beeji's mother, Maanji, sat on a chair, holding the infant Beeji. She wore a salwar kameez and her head was covered with a sheer voluminous dupatta through which sizeable gold jhumkis could be seen. She looked somewhat diffident and unsmiling, reacting perhaps to the stranger photographer who must have entered the house with his alien contraption. It was a black-and-white photograph. The couple looked pristine to Nanaki, otherworldly creatures rising in a hallowed space above the monochrome collage of the many textures that crowded the background—the narrow Nanakshahi bricks, the clunky wooden doorway with discoloured brass knobs, the stacks of dry branches of cotton plant, which were used as fuel in the tandoor. Only Beeji knew that this innocuous stack would one day be used for Gurbaaz Singh's pyre. Nanaki would invariably ask something out of curiosity, but for Beeji, answering her questions was never a simple affair. It would mean a walk down an old path—a very old, winding path. It was revisiting a land that her mother's desperation and inability to visit made all the more agonizing. Agonizing, because it had been so unjust. So damn unfair. Beeji would talk about the trudge from Okara with her mother to reach Amritsar. By some strange stroke of association, each time Beeji revisited the episode in Okara, which was now a phantom land that you could coax others into believing existed just because you said it did, involuntarily, an image of her black *bosky* salwar drenched in urine and rain would flash before her. She could see it clearly, the sheen and the texture of bosky. It had initially kept her warm on the trudge, but in time had become so soggy that with every step she took, it had begun to cut into the folds of her inner thighs. When mother and daughter eventually reached Amritsar and she changed into a fresh salwar kameez, she noticed on closer inspection flaming red eruptions on her inner thighs. The frequent urine leakage because of incontinence had stung her at these points so sharply that it had made her flinch for every step she took.

Nanaki could never understand Partition. She felt nobody really had the answers to her questions: Even if one accepted that Partition was inevitable, was there no better way to divide the country than such a blunt perpetration of injustice? Why were people just left to fend for themselves, exposed to the elements and brutal human savagery? Were they nobody's people when mass killings took place in every nook and cranny, every mohalla of Punjab? More than anything else, she would be struck by its sheer absurdity—one fine day you are told to just move, to leave your house and move—lock, stock and barrel. Actually, no, you are not even properly told—you are threatened and made so vulnerable that there is no choice. And then you begin to move in the opposite direction, to a place where a family just like yours is ousted and is now headed in your direction. They end up in your house; wild creatures, like Goldilocks, trying out your chairs, your tables, your beds, your porridge. They take what suits them. The rest is discarded. At the other end, you end up in a strange house too. Secrets long buried, leaping out of cupboards. You kill their people, they kill yours. Blood flows. Collateral damage. Dislocations and settlements. Goings and comings. I am coming, you go. We are going, they are coming. They are waiting. Nobody comes, nobody goes.

By some stroke of association, it also reminded Nanaki of her own parents. It was mostly in the realm of abstraction, but the violence of the accident leaped at her. Did the trolley take them from the side, or was it head-on? Did the glass splinters come flying like tiny projectiles and pierce them? Did the metal feel cold? Did their faces twist in unimaginable horror when they realized they were in the jaws of death? Did they smile at each other or cry? Did they think of their child back home? Did they feel helpless for that fraction of a second when all these truths came home, just before the inevitable? How would it be to have them around? The answers to these questions she would never know.

ॐ

Within a year of passing out, Nanaki had joined the Government Arts College as Assistant Professor with specialization in Textiles. It was now her second year of working here. She was mulling over working towards a PhD eventually on *Chamba Rumaal.*[1]

The college was a sanctuary in ways more than one. It was a low-roofed, brick and reinforced cement concrete (RCC) building, with a shallow lotus pond at the entrance. The foyer of the college was offset by stone rubble walls that enclosed cement jaalis, so as to let in daylight. The main building had an unusually high ceiling and part of the inner courtyard was roofless, so that the walls framed in a neat piece of sky. Unlike the rest of the foyer and corridor, this part of the building did not have a concrete floor, but sod, with huge monsteras. The long RCC corridor that led to the academic block was lined with massive oil paintings done by renowned contemporary Indian artists.

That day, while inside the academic block equipped with cavernous classrooms, over the cyclical din of the slow

---

[1]Literally, 'rumaal' is a handkerchief and Chamba is a region in Himachal. Chamba is known for its exquisitely hand-embroidered handkerchiefs. These are used ceremonially, gifted in trousseaus and have a wider cultural significance. It is also worth nothing here that Bebe Nanaki, Guru Nanak's sister, was also said to have embroidered a Chamba rumaal. It is preserved in a gurudwara at Hoshiarpur today.

screechy fan, she heard the familiar booming voice of Prof. Neil Sengupta. His passion was unmistakable as he harangued on the finer nuances of Indian sculpture. Each time she walked past the corridor, Nanaki would be tempted to stay put to catch snatches of his lectures, which were circuitous, like stories, seemingly not progressing anywhere—with the students hooked to his animated, voluble manner, knowing he was forging connections between seemingly disparate things that they were sure to understand at some moment in the near future, but were currently lost on them. He was explaining the twin, opposed forces that embodied the spirit of Bodhisattva. The push and pull. Here and there. The push of the earthly and the pull of the spiritual, one threatening to suck him into banalities and the other promising nirvana. '*How much he speaks. What capacity!*' Nanaki thought to herself. The class was under a spell: on a roller coaster ride, just about to touch terra firma but unexpectedly swooped into the sky over and over again. Neil was from Kolkata. Nanaki counted him a friend on campus.

She was waiting to accompany him to a special lecture on colonial art by the veteran art historian, Prof. C.N. Nagar. Nanaki had helped put it together; she had collaborated with the museum to help throw it open to the public. On such occasions, the museum would circulate the information to interested people through their email list. A snug group had gathered in the mezzanine lecture theatre. To reach the venue, one had to cut across the small museum library and book-lined teak shelves. Musty old books and the grainy smell of wood created a heady concoction that instantly enlivened Nanaki. Prof. Nagar started the lecture without any fanfare and went straight to running the audience through a plethora of slides he was carrying. The constant tick-tock of the changing slides, along with Prof. Nagar's winding manner, had a soporific effect on the gathered crowd, so much so that when, in medias res, Nanaki threw a casual glance at the audience, she saw at least a score nodding and many staring balefully at the professor. On two occasions, Nanaki found herself losing the thread, falling uncontrollably from her hands like a slippery eel, and tried hard to net it like a prized catch. She silently admonished herself to come back to the presentation. *Wake up, Nanaki!* Thankfully there was no major damage done, and like it happens in most lectures, by the end even issues of earth-shattering magnitude were patiently netted in a fine web of words. A prized catch. Slowly but surely, a consummate professor, one at a time, catches all the unruly, slippery creatures, the arguments and counterarguments, in this web where they beat violently and resist for a while but eventually succumb, overpowered and contained, to the satisfaction of all. Not that it has any immediate bearing on real seas, real creatures, or for that matter, the real world at large. But yes, it is singularly magnificent to witness the spectacle of the power of words. Creatures are slayed and reputations are made and unmade in the flickering throws of these gossamer webs.

At the end of the day, the sky suddenly became overcast and Nanaki quickened her pace on her way back home after the lecture. The sudden downpour, not the lecture, became the high point of her day.

༄

Across the road in their neighbourhood was the Gill mansion. The senior Gill, an agriculturalist from Faridkot, had sold part of his land and constructed this house way back in the 1950s when Chandigarh was still developing, and had moved here with the sole motive of educating his two sons. The elder one, after completing his degree from the local Punjab College of Engineering, had secured a government job and was leading a predictably itinerant life of postings and appointments, marked by relative stability. The younger one could not get a professional footing and had spent some ten years in Calgary in Canada where, after driving a taxi for a couple of years, he had set up a transportation business. Now he had returned home for good, and his wife Navneet, a Ludhiana girl, affectionately called Neena, had set up a boutique in the garage of their house. He had returned with considerable foreign exchange and the wife's boutique, too, had had steady customers for years now. He was stepping into the real estate business and was successfully able to seal two deals to the satisfaction of the parties involved. His entrenchment in the property business began in right earnest. Very soon, as if it was the next logical thing, their house began to witness frantic construction activity. The old, austere structure of the house built by senior Gill soon began to be viewed as 'not upto the mark' by the son. Like it is a given that every successive brave new world has to leave a signature in concrete.

Vast portions of the old structure were pulled down, and soon a mountain of debris accumulated at the edge of the road. In no time, the house had been replaced by a monstrosity fashioned out of granite, aluminium and reflective glass. It was said that on the top floor they had created a home theatre complete with the latest surround sound system, with faux leather recliners and posters of old films in gilt frames on the walls. A marble half-wall, fitted with hidden LEDs, occupied substantial real estate in their new drawing room. Goblets of varying sizes hung from the corner ceiling like gallows. The bar, gleaming in white sunmica, was stocked with a range of foreign liquor picked up in tax-free airport outlets and proudly displayed here as some kind of proof of their 'having arrived'. A hidden shelf was stocked with Om Bikaneri bhujiya and spicy besan peanuts—drink accompaniments. In times of crisis, when her husband's friends landed up unannounced, Navneet would disappear into the kitchen and rustle up an omelette studded with onions and chillies and present it to the drinking party.

Apart from that, the golden fixtures in their bathrooms were already the subject of lore. Some reported that the imported bath had already begun to accrue a layer of mineral deposit in the crevices, and the glass panes were looking clouded. An ornamental chandelier with numerous crystal blobs hung from the roof of the house and threw patterned beams of coloured light when switched on. Not to be outdone by their industrialist Inder uncle in Ludhiana, they had specially added two gothic pillars to prop the high elevation, where they rubbed shoulders with Taj Mahal-inspired grills in the old *roshandaans*. A decorative bunch of grapes and two angels in plaster of Paris, perched at the upper end of the pillars, stonily espied the Punjabi mortals and their hubris. The Gills, blissfully unaware of this reproach, gave a nod of satisfying affirmation each time they pulled up their Land Cruiser right up to the swanky foyer of the house.

Neena would often come home to chit-chat with Beeji, who would be interested in her goings-on and would at times rely on her for embroidery threads, buttons and laces. As Nanaki made her way in from the front entrance, she was greeted by the sight of the two sitting in the lobby. Neena sat there, her voluptuous frame swathed in metres of fine embroidered crepe. She was a well-endowed woman and her bust line was bursting through the seams, the detailing of her lacy bra protruding from under the gauzy fabric. The edges of her kameez were trimmed with a fine coordinated lace. When Beeji customarily complimented her on her outfit, little did she realize that she had got the lady started. In such circumstances, Neena's eyes would come alive and she would flash the most radiant smile. These laces, she animatedly explained, had been procured and dyed the colour of the suit material and then joined so cleverly that you could not see the seams. 'See? You can hardly tell,' she upturned a part of her shirt for Beeji to take a closer look, like it was a coup of sorts. She waited for a fraction of a second to spy on me 'you-got-me-totally' looks on the faces of her audience and then continued with the details: On the kameez, she had especially got the embroidery man to create a considerable panel of thick needlework flowers in bright contrasting colours so as to make them 'stand out'. The dupatta, which was inordinately flowy and two inches longer at all four corners, was 'pure Binny chinnon chiffon' (a self-respecting woman would not accept any lesser) and had been custom dyed in three colours to pick up the exact shades of the floral creations on her suit material. The kameez had an inner lining with a meticulous gold finish. Neena offered this detailed explanation and Nanaki, tired that she was, found it hard to concentrate and felt a constant hammering inside her head. Involuntarily, her eyes hovered on Neena's beaming diamond studs, which moved forward and backward like pistons as she excitedly spelt out these details, not realizing that there could be people who didn't care for them. Nanaki, however, snapped out of the reverie and nodded in affirmation when she felt Neena's explanation accompanied by that unique triumphant lilt in her voice. Nanaki waited for a let-up, and at the earliest opportunity, butted in and excused herself. Before she left, Neena had shot an open offer to Nanaki to visit her boutique in order to spruce up her wardrobe, which was rather 'simple', and make it 'fancier' and more suitable for an eligible young girl like her. Neena screwed her nose, jerked her head on one side and offered to make Nanaki a really fine crepe salwar kameez, like the one she was wearing, complete with the accents. Nanaki only had to pay her one visit for measurements.

'*Hain,* Nanaki... The masterji will be there and we have a good collection of fancy buttons and designer laces. And yes, you must get an evening gown done. *Must have.* It's really in,' she reiterated it like a prescription.

At this suggestion, images of big, voluptuous women in leopard prints, bleached hair and false eyelashes dancing to bhangra numbers swirled before her.

An assault.

Nanaki blinked.

'Think I will be busy with juries till May, but will surely visit you sometime.'

'I see you really need to get some new variety.' Neena's gaze travelled up and down Nanaki's vulnerable, petite frame, hitherto at ease in a regular Fabindia cotton kurta. She felt the older woman tearing her to bits and her reaction was a hasty flight. Neena promised to transform her looks, at which suggestion Nanaki almost recoiled, and then making no further show of courtesy, shot inside.

It was a familiar discomfort. Nanaki hastily took refuge in her room. She collapsed on the bed and marvelled at her capacity to nurse bygones. Neena's arbitrary comments had triggered it all. And come to think of it, there was no need really to hold it against her. How many more such unwarranted occasions, before she could make a neat bundle, tie the knot and get rid of it? Throw it somewhere, unburden herself. The problem was not Neena aunty. Hardly. She was but a trigger. The Gills' nephew Yadwinder—the summits and the depths she had experienced on his account, way back as a sixteen-year-old. Yadwinder, son of Neena's elder brother-in-law, who was posted in Ferozepur at that time, had moved in with his uncle's family in order to take his Class X board exams. This made it possible for him to take good tuitions in Maths and be in the comfort of home. Nanaki was then a somewhat awkward teenager; Yadwinder, on the other hand, was nothing like her. Tall, athletic, he was into squash. He had just begun to tie the turban, with somewhat clumsy folds, and a soft beard had begun to sprout, framing the sides of his still baby face. They ended up in the same Maths tuition. Nanaki's sixth sense warned her that there was going to be trouble.

One day, as they walked home together, holding their cycles by the handles, Yadwinder, clearly perplexed and not saying anything, thrust a brown paper bag and an envelope into Nanaki's hands and hurriedly cycled away, mumbling a quick bye. Nanaki began trembling. She put the contents into her backpack and slid the envelope in her *Wren and Martin*, shot through the door and went straight to her room. She ripped open the envelope, impatiently pulling at the sparky cellotape. Her hands were unsteady. She started just as Nanaji called out to her.

Nanaki had scarcely gone beyond the well-put tape when

she hastily shoved the envelope under the mattress and went down to meet her grandparents' old friends Col and Mrs Harinder sitting in the lobby. The courtesy visit lasted longer than anticipated. Bite-sized tandoor tikka was first circulated, mounted on a tray, complete with the usual drill of tooth picks, paper napkins and two chutneys—green mint and red tamarind. This was followed by the staple peanut masala. Nanaki was palpably distracted. All this was tedious. The usually sprightly girl, who loved to participate in the ritual of entertaining guests, was considerably lost.

Dinner was laid. Nanaki volunteered to run fresh chapattis from the kitchen. She stood there, wrapped in a reverie, when the chapatti on the tawa was puffed using a muslin napkin. Brown spots on the roti became large indistinct shapes. When it was visibly done and crisp, it was tossed onto a quarter plate. With a deft hand Beeji scooped clarified butter with a spoon and made a quick swirling movement, glazing the roti—the final flourish before it was brought on the table. Nanaki, in her restlessness, began to notice all these innocuous details. Not that it helped matters—everything seemed to drag. When would they go? The meal was rounded with *gud shakkar* and finally the prolonged goodbye session at the gate. Nanaki was spilling over by now. Scarcely had the guests' old Maruti-800 purred when Nanaki said a hasty goodnight and shot through to her room, bolted the door and sat herself down. She then pulled the envelope from under the mattress, her heart pounding, and in her impatience to take out the contents, ended up tearing one end of the envelope. She was panting. On to the bed tumbled a Cadbury roast almond chocolate bar, a sheet of M&M stickers and a card. She opened the card with shaky hands. A vintage image of a cherub looked out, framed with vines of roses running across the borders. An 'I Love You' scrawled in a decorative, albeit awkward cursive. A few miniature red hearts, impaled with arrows, sprayed here and there. Too much effort. A wave of thrill shot through her body.

The first practical problem was to consume the entire bar of chocolate without leaving a trace. Second were the diminishing prospects of seeing Yadwinder, now that tuitions were over.

The nippy days were changing colour. The air had become crisp and the trees, after the turmoil of autumn had, by these months, started growing anew. Nanaki's senses came alive. She had begun to notice things: the winter spray on the neighbourhood simbal tree. Everything was oddly exhilarating. She decided she was in love.

It was their classmate Gurbaaz's birthday party at the Defence Club. Nanaki sat at arm's length from Yadwinder. They were both palpably distracted. While the others got busy with pass the parcel, Nanaki moved into the garden. Yadwinder was prompt in following her. They climbed a flight of steps at the other end of the garden to arrive at a small terrace that would usually accommodate a pipe band on formal occasions. It needed a coat of paint, what with chipped paint on the walls and a woody vine of ivy trailing all over the leaky water tank. Yadwinder placed his hand over hers, resting on the balustrade. He held on to it. There was a little enclosure with a door next to the water tank. Yadwinder shot a quick look inside. A motor pump was installed there. Just enough of an enclosure to save it from sun and rain. Yadwinder pulled her in. It was dark and dank. A steady trickle engendered trails of moss on the narrow wall. With the door shut behind them, they were plunged in darkness. He felt for her face and could sense the depression in her neck. He pulled her close and the stiff threads of his tweed jacket brushed against her bare neck. He traced a lingering kiss from her neck and planted it on her lips.

ജ

Before she realized, months on end had passed and the exams were upon them. Nanaki gathered herself and began to discipline her day. Nanaki's upbringing had been different from average kids in subtle ways. She did not have young, energetic parents who, like knights, could swoop down on the difficulties and irritants of her daily existence. In some ways, Nanaki was not directly in touch with the outside world. A link in the chain was broken, a page missing—things appeared to her through the butter paper of her grandparents' perspective. Somewhat hazy but pleasantly diffused. There was an austerity about her that she had internalized from her grandparents, a trait of their generation.

While children her age would be fussy about food and force their parents to pack a new tiffin every day, Nanaki's standard parantha-achaar would instantly invade the nostrils of the class at lunch hour. Beeji had also regularly fed her fresh malai—milk cream, mixed with Bournvita—since she came to live with them. Nothing gave Beeji more satisfaction than to see baby Nanaki lap up the malai-Bournvita and then be lulled into a siesta. Now, as a teenager, Nanaki nursed a major grouse against her Beeji for having done this. 'See, it's all got stuck here and here and here...' Nanaki would alternately point at her cheeks, stomach and forearms. With her indulging ways, Beeji could never see any flaw in her. She would just shake her head and with an exaggerated frown, say, '*Kithe*? Where on earth? High school girl's drama.'

Again, not for her were clothes that mothers bought their teenage girls at Kapsons and the new Benetton in Sector 17. They were all the rage with young girls. Beeji had no such notion and had continued to buy her standard smocked cotton frocks. Now, as a teenager, Nanaki had graduated to jeans and tees. Beeji would stitch blouses and shirts for her. She would buy cotton prints by the meter and at times use the leftover cloth from the material she bought for her own salwar kameez. At times, Beeji and Nanaki ended up having the same print. Lately, it had been a white cotton shirt with bunches of tiny cobalt flowers sprayed on the entire length of the cloth. Beeji ensured that Nanaki, without fail, wore a slip inside. Nanaki wasn't attractive in an immediate way, but subtly, her beauty grew on people. She wasn't of the fair complexion that people were partial to in Punjab. Beeji ensured that her long unruly hair was braided neatly and held on the end with a beaded rubber band. Her somewhat big, brown eyes continued to carry that wondrous expression from childhood that was half-delight and half-question. Of late, she had started using kajal to highlight the lower ends. Beeji's one indulgence was buying Nanaki studded pins and bands. She dressed mostly in jeans and bellies and wore a fine gold chain with a dainty cuboid amethyst—her mother's memory constantly brushing against the little depression in her neck.

Exams over, Yadwinder's parents drove down from Ferozepur to take him back. He had been inordinately uncommunicative for the past few days. The parents drove him back with all his stuff. Nanaki saw their burgundy NE 118 turning on the bend. In the days that followed, she was desperate to get some news, but was clueless. She thought he had only left for a few days, but there was no word. She did not know what to do. One day, summoning courage, she asked Yadwinder's cousin, Neena aunty's son Karanveer, if he could pass on his phone number. He told her that Yadwinder had left for the US for his undergraduate studies and passed on his email ID to her. This was news for her. She took two days to set up her email account and get a hang of how it worked from Priyanka, her school friend, and every other day, spent a couple hours at her house, bent over the computer. Nanaki was so conscious of being found out that all the while, a deep red flush spread on her cheeks. She was eventually able to send Yadwinder an email. She would expectantly drop in at Priyanka's place to check the email account for any reply. But it eluded her. Mail after mail elicited no response. It was as if she was talking to a wall.

She had known this demon of loss before. And in desperation, she morphed into the bewildered three-year-old who had had her tryst with it. What was worse, she could not share this with anyone. It was eating her hollow. Not with her beeji, not with her nanaji. This loss was bewildering in a different way. She alone had to muster her resources to deal with it. The break after exams turned into a bleak whirl of indistinct time, with days melting into days. For some reason, she continued to nurse a vague hope. She would climb up to the terrace, spread the old coarse mat with one end of the water tank as a backrest, and repeatedly read Yadwinder's card. At times she would part the curtains of her room and stare at the Gill mansion for a long time, wildly hoping to see him at the front gate. It did not happen. She would go on a trip, thinking of him, and end up struggling to push these thoughts out of her mind. Nanaki knew she was losing her sense of proportion. She was spending too much time thinking of him.

But then, this treachery is at the heart of love. That two people's needs are never the same. That while it involves fulfilment through another, you understand more about sovereignty. That your desire will always be in an elusive chase with the other's independence of will. That some might just be transiting through love because they are conditioned to do things in appropriate stages, like other life activities, while others might be totally transformed by it. That two in love might be looking in one direction but never at the same thing. This struggle to get the lover to see what you see is futile, and yet a deep desire remains. Much later, she would grow up and learn more. And even though Nanaki felt bereft of love, heartbroken and utterly abandoned, even someone seemingly seeped in love could experience heartbreak—when that basic urge to be understood by the lover remains unfulfilled. The desire to be understood is primeval too. It might be forgotten for a while in the euphoria of new love. But it resurfaces like a lost child come home. You can't shut the door. You have to take it in. The tussle then begins.

And even though body has entwined with body, vows have been whispered into the lover's ear in the throes of unimaginable passion, there's a pang still. One has not felt understood by the lover. And that is a different quality of loneliness. A constant dull hammering. Like a static hum. Dissonance. Ultimately it translates into a plain inability to see the other's view. We shout betrayal. We shift blame. We feel inadequate. When it is just plain inability. So the intimacy has a narrow gap running across, like a rift between two continents, and it's only when you examine it from above that you really see it. You realize that the gap might have the breadth of a hairline, but it is deep. Its darkness stretches all the way down into a free-falling abyss.

❦

August was a deluge. It turned out to be an unusually rainy month. Days became hot and sticky. Mosquitoes were a menace. They were copiously breeding in the Leisure Valley nullah. And ants appeared. Out of nowhere. Minute, red ants. The big black ones on tree barks are like gentle giants in front of these deadly minuscule ones. You just have to brush the bigger cousins off and they drop on the ground, scampering for cover. But these little ones, now they can be noxious. For one, they are hard to detect, and on top of that have the ability to dexterously enter unknown zones: folds of skin, the viscous swamp in tubs of Vaseline, and biscuit packets, making tiny perforations.

They first emerged from the corners of the chipped floor in Nanaji's study. They entered the kitchen in well-orchestrated moves. After lunch every day, the kitchen was cleared, the marble slab cleaned with a phenyl-dipped mop that left a spiky trail. The leftovers were transferred from big vessels into Tupperware containers and stored in the refrigerator. God forbid that a grain or two of rice or a shred of potato from the day's curry or a drop of banana custard be spilled on the marble shelf. They would materialize out of nowhere, in big battalions, on two minute's notice. If you came back later in the night to fetch a glass of water, it was not unusual to spy a long black quivering trail behind a grain of basmati. In a fortnight they had become brazen enough to attack even medicinal syrups lying in the chest. Silly creatures. Crusty remains of their shiny coats were found stuck, lifeless, in the grooves of jam bottles. Some had the guts to even withstand the freezing temperatures of the cheese tray in the old Kelvinator. A trail of haldi was duly sprinkled to deal with the escalating problem. But the insecticidal powers of the spice seemed to have no effect whatsoever on the pests. Soon the house was teeming with them. From the corners, moving in a procession, leading up to the bathroom, attacking nuts in the containers—so much so that a loud shriek was once heard from Beeji's bathroom—a particularly nasty one had entered her underclothes while they had been flapping on the clothesline and had now bitten her sore in her lady parts. She flapped her kameez hysterically for some time to shrug it off, but the sharp sting only dug in more sharply.

'*Pare hatt…* Get off me… *Pare hatt.*'

Nanaki knew Beeji used that turn of phrase only when she was hugely agitated. She banged on the door frantically, not knowing what to make of it. Beeji had shed the last shred of clothing to eventually find a couple sticking to her inner thigh. She pinched them between her thumb and forefinger before disposing of them in a watery grave in the sink. She emerged, hassled with all the unwarranted trouble, cursing the pesky creatures and yet not clearly announcing where exactly she had been bitten. They were getting gutsier, exploring newer territory—they were getting out of hand.

Eventually, a pest control team had to be duly summoned.

ఴ

The grandfather-granddaughter duo became regular golfers. Nanaji would be dressed for the occasion in his collared tees and khaki trousers. His turban was always well turned out, with the pleats carefully wound in an oblong manner that framed his face. By now it was part of his bearing. He would affix his big strappy military-issue sunglasses over his turban. He had owned them since his service days. Nanaki liked him in them. He looked every inch an expeditionist. His beard was now snow-white and was always dressed in two knots under his chin. Deep furrows criss-crossed his otherwise broad forehead, and scores of crow's feet erupted like firecrackers at the edges of his eyes. Nanaki did not mind caddying for him. In the bargain, she got to spend some time with him on the fairways.

Sometimes the sight of caddies at the entrance did bother her, the disparity of status in the place etched on their beseeching faces and more than the utter apathy of the haves, who flaunted privilege like their membership cards. Entitlement here was like a scientific dictum: sufficiently proven, demonstrated and accepted without question. She was never at home in the clubhouse teeming with wannabes, kakajis whose lives consisted of spending a decade and a half in boarding schools and colleges and then living off the land, spending days recounting the exploits of their grandfathers/ illustrious uncles and catching up over beer with buds from days of yore in school, if not attending weddings and bhogs. Sometimes, to Nanaki, people lounging in the clubhouse transformed into giant spiders emitting webs of network, transmitting privilege like high-voltage current.

It is said that one such strapper came face to face with a distant aunt after many years. They ran into each other in Sector 17. She was naturally curious to know of his preoccupations after college, to which he replied with a poker face, 'MBA.'

She was impressed. Few in her orbit had gone further than a suppli-riddled BA or at the most an LLB. But he quelled any doubts about his being more than an absentee landlord by expanding the fancy-sounding acronym as 'Marriage/Bhog/Akhand Path'—much to the aunt's dismay, who, in the span of the ten minutes she spent chatting with the young man outside Empire Stores, had imagined him potentially married to at least three of her nieces. Her matchmaking expedition came to an abrupt end.

The expanse of the greens was what Nanaki loved. And she could listen to Nanaji endlessly. He often recounted the story of his joining the army as a sepoy almost a decade before India's Independence. His family belonged to Gujranwala District, now in Pakistan. Barely a year into service, he was picked up for the British expedition in Burma during World War II. The Japanese were already in Burma and there was a real threat of their crossing over from Kohima any time. It was a strange feeling. Although they were fighting for the gora sahibs, the Burmese people filled up the sidewalks to see the spectacle. It was pageantry of the highest order. The soldiers parading in starched uniforms stretched over their sinewy limbs. The pageantry signalled gravity, the jangle of the Captain's medals and decorations inspired awe. For a teenager from Gujranwala, who had not ventured beyond his district, this was strangely thrilling, but also terrifying—this feeling that he was a part of one of world's mightiest armies and was exhorted to be proud on this account. But then, errors, human errors, could be fatal. Errors that could be forgiven and forgotten in his village with a pat on the back from his elders would find no such compassionate forgiveness here. No, these could mean death. The thought was terrifying.

Jemadar Joginder Singh was from the village Dauli in the district of Jallandhar. In this brave new world, he was the one comforting presence for nanaji. For the time they were in Burma, the army had camped at the western end of the river. Joginder Singh, who was then a sepoy, had his tent just a stone's throw away from Arjan Singh's. A strapping teenager whose beard had scarcely sprouted, Sepoy Arjan Singh would get teary eyed and terribly homesick on some days. At twilight, this sinking feeling would get worse. He would invariably end up in the Jemadar's tent.

'When will this end, sa'ab?'

'Kakaji, it has barely begun—*tagde raho*—got to be strong.'

There were days when he was put on night-sentry duty around the camp area. It was his duty, along with another young jawan, to report if they saw anything untoward—any movement or presence. The camp area was circular, so Arjan Singh was expected to recce along the arc that partly touched a dirty stream and a thick bushy tract. To him, this was the hardest part. As other jawans of the party would retire by and by, and the kerosene lamps would also be put off early due to paucity of oil, Arjan would feel utterly vulnerable on such dark, inhospitable nights. His heart would leap to his mouth and his lips would go totally dry. He would keep sipping from the water flask that perennially hung from the loop in his belt. However, that would hardly help. It wasn't thirst, but fear. Fear of the unknown, of an enemy assailant who could get you from behind. Fear that read meaning into innocuous shadows or a furtive lizard slithering on dry leaves. Fear that leapt inside him like a yelping dog. He was but a boy. And then the inescapable happened. He became a reluctant witness to the sudden death of a fellow jawan. The young man, Abdul Razak, like him barely out of his teens, was manning a post when the Japanese began heavily shelling the area. Arjan saw, with his bare eyes, the young man's torso flying in mid-air, disjointed from limbs, and falling into the inhospitable thicket beyond the river. Arjan's insides had revolted and he had thrown up and fallen unconscious.

The dread progressively became more acute. It became a free-flowing anxiety. God forbid that he had the urge to go to the loo. For the purpose, a temporary standalone structure had been erected overnight, a few meters from the camp area. Hardy stalks of cane grass were used to thatch the roof. It was already giving way owing to the particularly incessant rain one night. So when Arjan would perch himself on the two bricks used as footrests on either side of the hole, he would look at the shaft of the blue sky visible through the grass roof. Nights were worse; the intermittent rustling in the dry grass would not allow Arjan to concentrate on the task at hand and he would end up feeling miserable. A simple piss would take him inordinately long. And if he sensed a fellow sepoy waiting in queue outside, the very thought would throw his insides into a clump of knots. On many an occasion he would come out without the job done.

On some days Joginder Singh would do what he could to comfort him. He would narrate to him a tale or two about his adventures since his induction days or some anecdote about his village, and then enquire about Arjan's family. He would take out the cloth bag he had kept deep in his uniform pocket, and using his deft fingers, eke out a couple of almonds and a *patasha*—the dry prasad of his village gurudwara. He never seemed to run out of supplies. Arjan Singh would notice his fingers—the way they would move rhythmically. His fingers were not the shape and complexion of the peasants—they looked fine and dexterous. And in those moments, he would feel a serene confidence filling his body at this brush with homeliness. He would then return to his tent, somewhat reassured. In those days of their encampment in Burma, Arjan became hugely dependent on Joginder, who thought it was his bounden duty to keep the morale of the troops high. Added to that was the kinship he felt for the young lad when he would confess his helplessness.

The British had gradually begun allowing soldiers to enter the echelons of officership and this became an established practice before Independence. Arjan Singh became a beneficiary of this new policy and stormed out of the ranks to join the academy at Dehradun and claim his place in officerhood. He climbed the rungs and got married. The newly wed, Arjan Singh, had to face the travails of Partition soon after marriage. Beeji was all of eighteen and belonged to a landed family from the village Okara in district Montgomery. They had a winter wedding, and just months later had to relocate to India. While Arjan Singh crossed over into Amritsar leading a convoy of Army Leyland Retriever Trucks at the crack of dawn one day in early August, Beeji, two-months pregnant, was visiting her parental family in her village Okara. It was then that the horror struck.

৪৩

II

Winter of Our Discontent

Sardar Gurbaaz Singh, Beeji's father, stood in his paddy fields. The business of the day was done, and he often surveyed his fields at the end of the day. He took in his surroundings with a degree of satisfaction, looking at the bumper crop in the current season. Rains had been adequate and timely and the sun had fallen with just the right slant, filling the pods with fleshy grains that would be ready by September–early October. In farming, it is very rare for all the benevolent forces to converge in one season. Something or the other invariably slackens. Not this year. Just the sight of the standing crop in the field was enough to put a lump in his throat. At such moments, he would feel the overwhelming benediction of *kudrat* (nature). As thanksgiving, he would ask the gurudwara bhaiji to add his share of lentils to the langar. As he stood there, he heard a vague tumult in the distance. He silenced the sounds in his head and concentrated hard in order to listen, over the lapping sound of water from the trickling stream that cut through his fields. He initially dismissed the sounds as coming from the temple in the nearby village. But, again, he heard the discordant sounds. This time it was unmistakable, and it seemed to be moving closer. It was a group of people, that was clear. As he stood there, straining his ears, Aslam, his neighbour, came charging on a horse and swooped down on him. He was totally taken aback and before he knew it, had been perched on the horse.

'*Aslam bai, aah ki kartab si?*—Aslam brother, what stunt was that?'

'*Vekhin…haddi pasli theek hai?*—I hope you haven't broken a bone.

Bhraa, khatra—brother, danger!'

Gurbaaz Singh's face suddenly paled—he had put two and two together.

'You don't mean the mob, do you?'

'Let's not waste another moment Gurbaaz *bhraa*…just get going… *Bharjai* and *Beebaji* are alone.'

The import of this warning suddenly dawned on Gurbaaz Singh. Aslam dropped him off and he thundered into his haveli, by which time the twilight was ominous, deeply stained purple. It was a very stuffy evening. Not a leaf moved.

His mind stopped working. A dread was taking hold of him, with his cheeks flushed and his hand shaking. What to do if they come hunting now? The easiest way out was to hide in the fodder room. The *toodi* room, located at the far end of the haveli, was a storage space for the hay meant for the buffaloes. Its walls were kutcha, with a coating of mud. There were two ventilators, which were positioned too high to afford any view. It was not meant for human habitation, after all. No one would really look for them there. He knew that it would be a brief 'encounter', if at all, after which, it would be safe for the women to come out. Since Beeji became pregnant, her water consumption had increased manifold. It had got worse on account of the humid weather in the past month. So Gurbaaz took an earthen pitcher to the fodder room, where they could be expected to spend a couple hours.

As the women settled themselves in, a din was heard in the alley outside.

'The dogs are here,' Gurbaaz spewed venom.

He had heard of the recent incident in the adjoining village, where a Sikh family of five had been slaughtered at daytime.

'Here, lock it well, and shhh…quiet… You'll be safe,' exhorted Gurbaaz. Before the women could reply, he was moving towards the front of the courtyard.

It was pitch dark. In hindsight, the one candle that they had put in the alcove appeared to be a stupid decision. If the beams, no matter how dim, were seen from the outside, they could be found out. No sooner were the women on their own, than they began to suspect everything. A new dread. Every movement startled them.

From inside the fodder room the women listened intently, with their hearts thumping inside their breasts. A fine dust hung in the darkness. Beeji's eyes felt gritty. Both women trained their ears on the wall, trying to hear the sounds outside. There was a furious jangling of chains striking against the metal knobs of the haveli gate. They heard strident voices, collectively demanding to be let into the house. The gate eventually seemed to give way to the obstinate mob, which now seemed to have forcibly filled the courtyard. The fear at this time was of another kind—it had invaded the intimate space of their home and hearth. Fear of the strange and unknown belonged outside, not inside your own house. Who were these people? The women had receded to the crevices of their own house to escape assault. They listened more intently.

'Now…now, shhh…some disagreement. Your *Daarji* is not relenting.'

The dissonance of a fracas. Gurbaaz was in no mood to

give in. Now the one dominant voice that was negotiating became many decibels louder. Gurbaaz's voice could not match up. Louder. More voices joined him. Then more. And more.

'Then let's just enter the damn house and get it for ourselves—bloody idiots, they ask for the death of dogs. Even if you want to be good to them.'

'Don't spare him.'

'Bloody Sikh…go to Hindustan.'

'Listen, *Bhraa*…we used to meet every day, look at me, what has changed overnight? Why, we studied together with Maulvi Khuda Bakshji, you forgot?'

'Yes, forgot, ever since your people killed Abbu, Ammi— you know they have been murdered?' The voice rose, loud and hysterical.

'Ajmal…*bhraa*…'

'No, no, no…no time for this *sanjhi vaarta*…this nonsense talk of togetherness…bakwaas—crap. I don't even spit on it.' And he spat.

Beeji waded through the pile of hay to stand next to the kutcha wall. Her throat was parched and she was beginning to feel suffocated. She could feel the pressure of the embryo on her uterus, and an involuntary trickle of urine wet her salwar. The possibility of an imminent assault. They heard footsteps immediately outside. Beeji held her breath and swallowed hard.

'Can you hear your *daarji*? Try and listen. Can you?'

They expected a lone voice of dissent. Somebody to stop the mob from advancing. But they were now entering the rooms regardless. A shuffling of steps…and then, suddenly, all movement abated. It became quiet. Too sudden. The silence was ominous.

They heard hasty, shuffling footsteps, exiting through the

back entrance of the haveli. Some vanished into the night sky by the terrace.

Sardar Gurbaaz Singh had been murdered.

৯৩

It was past 3 a.m. in the morning when Maanji and Beeji finally emerged from the fodder room and saw Gurbaaz lying in a heap in the verandah. Blood had gushed out in torrents from his stomach where they had jabbed him with a butcher's knife. His green voile turban lay at some distance, stiff with blotches of caked blood. His face was cold and mouth twisted with frozen horror. Death had been wholly unexpected. Beeji broke down and fell on the body. Maanji felt something hardening within, her insides getting jammed. Like when somebody switches off a bulky, noisy machine, and it grinds to a halt. She ambled around the courtyard, intermittently asking the daughter to '*bas kar hun...bas kar*—Stop it now...stop it.' Beeji was bent over Gurbaaz's corpse and crying copiously. But something had snapped inside Maanji. She had to look beyond this horror to escape it. Her mind raced. *The mobs must still be in the vicinity of the village. In these times, you could get away with anything. Last night there were shrieks from Harbans Singh's house also. For all you know, they have pillaged and knifed the whole village. They would not know. Cremation, yes, my husband has to be given a decent cremation...can't run with his body rotting here.*

She did that day what she had not done since she was a teenager in her parental house in Gujranwalla. She rode a horse buggy. She had learnt to ride a horse but never one tied to a buggy as she did that day. Maanji performed an *ardas* and her daughter stood there with her eyes closed. They then swathed the body in a white sheet and loaded it on to the buggy. Beeji, in her eighteen years, had never seen a corpse. She sat guard while her mother took the reigns. Her father's final journey. *Ab hum chali thakur pae haar*—Now I depart exhausted, to my Lord and Master.

The mother rode on, clumsily at first, but then the horse picked up a rhythm. She knew they would make it. There was a pond on the outskirts of the village with full-grown kikkars. Mother and daughter took care to pull out the dry branches. This, together with the dry branches of the cotton plants, *chhatiyan*, that were always stacked in the house for fuel, made for an adequate pyre. They then lifted the corpse and rested it on the bed of dry twigs. On it, Maanji poured desi ghee from her kitchen. She then prompted her daughter to light it. She nudged her forward, holding her shaky hands. The fire sputtered and fizzled at first, and her mother was worried if they had got the right wood. But then flames fed on flames and a huge blaze grew. Gurbaaz had been duly cremated.

There was no time to mourn. They postponed their grief. Gurbaaz's murder had wrenched them free of the illusion they had nursed for a while now. No, they could not stay back in Okara—that was amply clear. No, they would not be harvesting the paddy in October this year. No, they would not be celebrating the grandchild's arrival in this house—that was also clear. For now, they would do everything in their power to save their own lives. Everyone else was moving to the safer side. So would they.

Beeji's mother fetched two big cloth bags from the storeroom. What were they to pack? Where were they headed? For how long? Where was Arjan Singh presently? With all these imperatives shrouded in mystery, they were at a loss. So the mother used her good old common sense. She threw in the essentials: some clothes—three bosky salwars, her regular *shaneel* and *mulmul* shirts, her special green *kheenkhaab* suit, a minimal supply of essential toiletries and undergarments, some sarson oil for the daily massage, anar seeds, which the daughter had been consuming to boost her blood count, her ivory comb, because it was precious and photographs of her now deceased husband. As an afterthought, she kept a copper thali that had 'Sardar Gurbaaz Singh 1932' engraved on the back. They had got it done at the Peer Daata mela last year.

It then struck her like lightning. They would be coming back, but who knew when? So she took a small earthen pitcher and emptied the contents of her wood chest into it. There was a gold *pech* kara—an ornate bangle with a screw hidden in the peacock motifs, a three-tiered Patiala necklace sprayed with *tukdis*—motifs in gold adjusted at various levels, her wedding kundan danglers with *saharas*—pearly extensions, and a *jadau* neckpiece with *navratan*—encrusted with nine stones. She could always sell these for money if the need arose. She then picked some dry grass from the fodder room and stuffed it in the pot. This she shoved inside the cloth bag. Beeji's head was spinning. She saw her mother securing cherished keepsakes as well as the ingredients of her prosaic existence in one go, bundling it all into a bag and pulling the drawstring. There was an unbelievable earnestness in her mother's actions. There was a horror that she seemed to be skirting around, presently giving her attention solely to the essentials. Gleaning her survival from the monument of this loss. She could not afford to think. They must flee.

The women affixed a bulky padlock on the outer gate of the haveli. The monsoon sky looked overcast and threw the refracted beams of the imminent dawn on the Nanakshahi bricks of the haveli. The women began walking, the haveli receding further and further. The village gurudwara had stirred with the morning hymn and a flock of sparrows alighted from its parapet. The old mazar, with buntings of red threads that the faithful had tied to the branches of the old peepal, stood there, touched by a new day. Though the older woman believed she would come back to reclaim her haveli, Beeji somehow knew in her gut that she was looking at it for the last time. Okara. She took in the view as intently as possible. The hows and whys she did not know. She did not have the courage to say it to her mother, but she knew. Otherwise, there was nothing momentous about the earth beneath their feet just moving one fine morning.

After a day-long, circuitous route from Lahore, where they had arrived by train from Okara, mother and daughter eventually landed in Amritsar. They saw hordes of people—caravans of bullock carts, horse buggies and on-foot people crossing over or crossing in. Nobody owned them. No panchayats, no sarkar. No word from anywhere. They were face to face with the unknown.

᳀

Wait, what was that? It was a samagam—a celebration of Indian Independence. What pageantry it was! What pomp! Horses had troughs full of green chanas to eat and there were motorcades of fine European cars. For a while they were tempted to join the audience, but they simply did not have the time. Some hungry people were squatting there in hope of getting sweets at the end of whatever function it was. It was an efficient way to distract the wailing toddlers. Or for the homeless, to catch their breath.

Or for the sick, to listen to some music. At least music if not food. Something. A young girl with a dirty phulkari dupatta was singing aloud. And, being overdressed for the occasion, she looked out of place, as if she was separated from a wedding party. Singled out. She sang unusually loud, as if to ward off something. Or maybe in the hope that someone in the melee would recognize her song.

Others were resting, putting down the loads they had been carrying on their heads for what seemed like a very long way. On the far end there was another pageant. Impressive, really! Good show! Well-fed men in starched dhotis looking very important. Fresh shave and oiled hair. A good bath. A good bath would feel like heaven today. But it was highly unlikely. What's more, these men had marigold garlands around their necks. They were in no hurry to get anywhere. And they just did not seem to look in our direction. Their eyes, as if trained by invisible blinkers, like the kind they have on horses, looked ahead in just one direction—the direction of the middle-of-the-night speech. Who was speaking so much? And why, pray, in the middle of the night? Unearthly hour. And by God, so talkative! Gallan joge. Nikamme. Worth only words. Nonsense. It did not look like they had lost anything. In good condition, all. And they talk so much sense. Here we are having problems even listening to such profundities. We are sleepy, tired. But impressive. Really good. The speech appropriately bombastic on such an important day. The world is watching. But so much poise? When the streets have become rivers of blood. Dog eat dog. It's madness out there. Free for all. People dying like flies. You could be trudging to the other side. This side, that side. And the next moment, the ground beneath your feet could be your grave. Or you could be with your own people and the ground beneath your feet could be a mass grave. Why, on the way we saw an old man sit down for a moment to catch his breath, and the poor man just collapsed and died. Just like that.

There was a woman with a neyana, an infant, on her breast—no more than a few days old, with faeces on his shriveled hips and streaks of vomit on his protruding body. His hair was a tangled, rusty knot. He was throwing up milk, but the mother continued feeding him; there was no time to rest, so it was all on the go. Whether it was her milk that kept the kid alive, or the kid that kept the emaciated mother from falling, no one knew. They held on to each other. Her husband sat there on his haunches, catching his breath. Waheguru jaanda. Khawre pahunche ke nahi (The Lord only knows, whether they made it. No idea if they made it). Many many such tabbars. Saw them on the way to this side. Most people had just lost their homes and hearths and their fields and their standing crop; many thousands, their kith and kin. Overnight. Just like that. One fine day, they had woken up to find them all gone. How absurd! Nirra pagalpan (Sheer madness). Hard to believe even if somebody said it to you like a bad joke! Others had lost people—in the melee, people's husbands, wives, parents or children had gone missing. Some had lost their lovers. They, however, could not even say it aloud. They mourned silently. Others beat their breasts and moved on, but some did not have the time for even that.

Some had stayed back when they were supposed to move. They had a sense of humour. They thought it was all just a joke. Laughable. Dimag tan theek hai tera—Are you mad? I am staying put. I'll take care of the house. Tussi ghum aayo —you all go take a walk on the other side and come back. Thus some were left behind. They could not cross over once the government decided they had allowed an optimum number to cross. It was like the government had decided to punish them for their laxity. Where were you when we had opened the gates? No no no no... now you can't. They put a ban. The poor folks had nowhere to go, so they stayed back. The lucky ones got killed—and misery ended for them. But not for others. Hain? (What?) How can, they said, the house you live in cease to exist in your country overnight? How can your country just cease to be? It's like a game. OK, now let's imagine that the country has vanished. The village exists, but country? Pfft. Gone. Mulk udd gaya. Gayab—the country just vanished. Gone! Just imagine. How will you reach the new country? Let's just board this train. No, not this, this one has blood splattered on the seats. And the dead bodies at the feet would be inconvenient. The other one. Where are we going? Let's see where the train is headed. OK, Jodhpur, sounds good, Let's go to Jodhpur. Then we'll see. For now, let's get out of here. Maximum points for the one who reaches first. On the way you could be bitten by serpents or waylaid by thugs. Snakes and Ladders. If you feel hungry or thirsty, you get a penalty. How will you reach? Nobody knows. But tell me... Are you sure, Bhraaji (Big Brother)? Are you sure, Bharjai (Sister-in-law)? Are you sure, Maanji (Mother)? Pitaji (Father)? How can you be expected to just lock your houses and move, never to return? Listen carefully, come here, shh... not so loud...walls have ears...put your head close to mine. I have buried all my jewellery in the backyard of the haveli. We'll find it secure when we are back—hafta das din—in a week or ten days. Should not take more. Listen, this will not go on. Trust me. Where else will we live but here, in our house, in our village? How are you supposed to just move? Eiven kiven? How on earth? We have never done it before, we have never even

heard of it in the fantastic qissas our dadis and nanis told us,
they who were given to exaggerating facts with namak, mirch
and masala. Fact? Fiction? Story? Dream? Collective madness?
What was this? Now, even these doubts are a luxury. A doubt
could cost you your life. You want to survive this? Vadda raula
(The big riot). Just move, don't think...just move.

ଔ

Mother and daughter were shown into a tent in Sardar
Dhamala Singh Refugee Camp near Lawrence Road. Both
collapsed on the military holdall. And then the two cried—
they had finally come face to face with their reality. There was
no getting away now. So they held on to each other's tired,
limp bodies and wailed themselves sore.

Captain Arjan Singh came the following day. He had been
able to trace them quite efficiently with military help. He had
been moved to Jalandhar Cantonment and promptly allotted
military accommodation. Upon alighting from his jeep, they
found a modest, low-roofed colonial bungalow surrounded
by a garden. They learnt their way around the many army
instructions passed down to them by Arjan Singh. For months
on end, Maanji behaved like a guest. She continued to believe
that she would be dropped off to her Okara village when
the *gormint* allowed it. Every evening at 5.45, when they
relayed news on the radio, she would switch on the bulky
Murphy set in the living room. The radio, like much of the
furniture in the house, was MES (Military Engineer Services)
property. However, within a few days of the women moving
in, its starkness had been appropriately covered with a piece
of white cambric cloth. Maanji had asked for a needle and
hemmed its rough edges and, on all four corners, made little

motifs of sindhi stitch embroidery. The older woman would religiously troop to the living room, sit cross-legged on the low diwan next to the window and tune in. Each day she expected the *gormint* to make an announcement. Now the overwhelming disquiet was nagging her from inside. Apart from the understandable urge to return, she also felt like something of an intruder in her married daughter's home. She had definitely overstayed. Under no circumstance would this kind of arrangement be deemed respectable. However, she could hardly express what she felt. Her appetite slackened and she was perennially preoccupied with the compelling need to return. But in the formal relationship she had with her son-in-law Arjan, she maintained the tedium of being overtly alright while increasingly feeling perturbed from the inside.

The one thing she felt terrible about was her inability to conduct the *antim ardas* (final prayers) for her husband and the reading of Guru Granth Sahib, a practice that was customary on death. She had thought to herself she would go back to Okara and have it arranged. Have the Guru Granth Sahib installed in the verandah and get the *granthi ji* to read it continuously, end to end. But the possibility seemed increasingly remote. So she confided in Beeji about this. In no time, Arjan Singh made arrangements for the Akhand Path to be conducted at home. A *granthi ji* came from the Singh Sabha Gurudwara in Jalandhar city and read the Granth. Between him and a younger apprentice, handing over the reading to each other like a baton in a relay race, they completed the reading in three days. They marked the customary half-reading and final reading of the Granth by distributing *karah parsad*—pudding made with flour and ghee, distributed as divine offerings. It had a calming effect on Maanji. At once, a quick vision of Okara, the pond, her husband, his pyre and the red brick haveli passed before her eyes in a whirl. She accepted it all like the *parsad. Bhana mann leya.* She accepted it all that instant as God's will. They held an *ardas* to mark the completion and prayed for peace for the departed soul. She was satisfied for now.

But the urge to return was still lurking. And the fact that there was no news made her restless. She started feeling suffocated at night. Days on end, Maanji would wake up with a start at 2 a.m., feeling she was trapped inside the fodder room, only to realize that her fears were unwarranted. And then thoughts of Okara and the haveli would flood her. She could see it very clearly. The long passage running around her bedroom and Beeji's room followed by the storage areas—one for grains and the other for trunks. Her mind would have crystal clear visions of the inside of the haveli. Many jobs were left unfinished. *What will happen to the paddy?* In some days her husband would have harvested it. Their earthen pots would have overflowed with grain. Their coffers would be jangling once again, and she would have got herself and her daughter new clothes made. Like she did on each of Beeji's visits. Take her to the *bajaj* in the adjoining town and order him to show her only the finest materials—silk from China, *kheenkhaab, bosky* and *mulmuls* and *jamawar.* The *bajaj* would be seated there, propped against a white bolster, sitting cross-legged on the white sheets lining the length of the shop's platform. The women too would remove their jutties and join him there. He would first offer them Rooh Afza sherbet and then start the exhibition. They were the big sardars, so the finest materials only.

'For whom?' he would ask as a point of departure. Mother would point to the daughter, who would have flushed cheeks at becoming the centre of attention, even if for half a second. The *bajaj* would size her up in one look and then start the exhibition. 'Bright colours for her,' he would say as an affirmation to himself and as a prescription to them. His exhortation to the ladies would be conclusive. The clothes would be wound on spools and spread in front, one after another, opened with brisk movements. Here, *bhenji* (sister)... he would unroll spool after spool...chikan, cotton, silk... *Mundeya* (boy)...show the special ones too here...ah yes...*aah vekho* (look here)...*kheenkhaab, bosky*. He had a lot of variety on offer, and even if the women did not feel the urge to pick up stuff, he would betray no sign whatsoever of disappointment. By the end, however, the women would have invariably picked a motley assortment. He would then pull out a red clothbound ledger, place it on his low desk and record the details of the purchases. He would write with a lot of effort, and each time he would throw his head down at an angle, two frown lines deepening on his forehead and his tongue jutting out like it was an extra hand, helping him negotiate the scribbles on the page. This done, the shop assistant would walk them to the tonga for their journey back to Okara. The *bajaj* would get paid for the sold stuff months after the actual sale. He would have to wait till Baisakhi, for then they would have the cash to spare. So after Baisakhi he would come pedalling down to Okara, to Sardar Gurbaaz Singh's haveli, claiming his payment. He would be offered a meal. At times, it would get dark and he would be offered bedding for the night. Okara, *bajaj*, red ledgers—it played in her head on a loop.

She needed to get back home now. An urgency gripped her. How long could one be a guest in one's married daughter's house?

One particular night, Maanji unlocked her room and walked out. She pulled a cot out into the verandah, perfunctorily spread a double bed sheet and slept. At least some semblance of her earlier life. In Okara they always slept in the open courtyard, looking up at the night sky. She and Gurbaaz on cots side by side, spread out on white sheets. Each night as she would lay there, her gaze would travel skywards. Gurbaaz would tell her the day's account and she would be engrossed in observing the starry sky. What *bhet*! Mysteries! A Prussian blue velvet canopy hanging from the heavens, like the one they have over the Guru Granth in Darbar Sahib, with a silver bauble here and there, sometimes getting lost in the expanse and sometimes emerging from behind a cloud, luminous points of light, billions and billions of miles away. *Paatala pataal...lakh agasaan, agaas*—netherworld after netherworld, a million skies. Where are these other worlds? Are they real? Why were we cast into this one, to look from afar, to look with longing? She would let her imagination run unbridled for a while and the shapes of strange creatures would leap at her. Clouds, constellations.

Gagan main thaal rav chand deepak bane.

(The sky a big tray, the sun and the moon are but earthen lamps.)

This sky, with its enormous orbs, is an act of prayer; where is the need to stand in temples with the symbols of prayer, the *thaali* and the diya? Just an acknowledgment of this cosmic magnificence is enough.

And then she would forget they were stars, and a million silvery *bootis* motifs seemed embroidered on a Prussian blue phulkari. The heat and dust of a summer day would give way to gentle cool winds at this hour. Aching bones from a day of hard labour would find succour like none other in these nightly hours. Then, turning her attention towards the child Beeji, she would throw her some riddles, a favourite nightly pastime.

'*Hun dass*, now, listen carefully and guess.

Nikki jehi kudi
Lai paranda turi.'

(A pretty little maid
How she saunters with her braid.)

Then some more:

'*Hari si mann bhari si*
Naal motiyan jadi si
Raja ji de baag vich
Dushala odhe khadi si.'

(Green and glowing she was
Studded with pearls and standing tall
In the king's fields
She stood by herself, wrapped in a shawl.)

Thus would hours roll. That was then.

The next morning, as Beeji came out, she was shocked to find Maanji lying there, in her *mulmul* shirt, in the morning light. Beeji was horrified to see her lying spread-eagled on the charpoy in the outer verandah. It seemed when the wattage went out last night, she had felt suffocated in the room and walked out. It seemed she had just hurriedly thrown a sheet on the cot before lying down. The prickly coir of the charpoy could be very uncomfortable, but she lay there, completely unmindful, the knot of her silvery hair falling in tangles over her shoulders, her dark nipples prominent under the gauzy shirt, and her bare spindly legs jutting through the salwar. There was something deeply unnerving to see her lying there. Beeji could not have imagined her like this a couple of years ago, considering how 'proper' she always had been, and to the now memsahib Beeji, the sight somehow looked unseemly, with the orderlies about to report for duty. Beeji gently cajoled her mother to catch up with the rest of her sleep in her bedroom. But she could not sleep after the interruption. So both sat up for an early morning cuppa.

∾

Arjan Singh suggested that Beeji listen to Gurbani *shabads* every morning. That would be a distraction, and would also give her some succour. The phonograph was duly moved to the deep niche in her mother's room. Every single evening, come what may, strains of Gurbani flowed from her room ever since.

Each time she heard it on the radio, the image of Guru Gobind Singh resting under a tree in the Machhiwara forest would emerge in her mind. The Guru, having lost his sons in the battle, was in exile. He lay on a bed of twigs and leaves, with the regalia of his clothing—the silks and the pearly string, the jewelled plume on his turban, all signs of kingship—looking out of place. The grief must have been immense, but presently a fiercer, worldly battle lay ahead of him:

> *Mittar pyare nu haal mureedan da kehna*
> *Tudh bin rog rajayian da oden, naag nivasa de rehna*
> *Sul surahi, khanjar pyala, bing kasayian da sehna*
> *Yaarde da sanu sathar changa, path khereya de rehna.*
> (Go tell the wise, loving one, of his young devotee's travails
> Without you, the snug quilts have become diseased,
> This house lies teeming with serpents,
> Our water pitchers have become containers of death

Our cups, deadly daggers
I suffer like animals at the hands of the butcher
My beloved's straw bed is more pleasing than burning
in these furnace-like mansions.)

At this time she felt an acute affinity with the exiled condition
of the Guru. When she had earlier heard these accounts, she
had accepted it all unthinkingly, given that the Guru was a
man of superhuman powers. But lately she had developed an
empathy she had not known before. The Guru was a man after
all, a father after all, with his share of fatherly grief.

One day she asked for the new railways map guide from
Arjan Singh, who brought it from his office in the afternoon.
For hours, she began to pore over the detailed maps of Punjab
to locate Okara. She had a good mind to find out the closest
station that would take her there. For all you know, there is a
connection from Jalandhar Cantonment to Okara. She made
up her mind to find out and just silently leave. She had some
money of her own that she had set aside. Why, she could try
pawning off a jewellery piece somewhere for money. If she
could trudge over to this side, she could also always go back.

She was a girl, all of sixteen, when she had had arrived
at the Okara station as a young bride. She had been seen off
by her parents in Gujranwalla and the marriage party had
taken the train to bring the new bride home. It was a sleepy,
nondescript station—a pale-yellow building with a big peepal
at the entrance. In the evenings it would fill up with thousands
of roosting sparrows on the parapets and the twilight would
be noisy deaf with their raucous cacophony. She so wanted
to go home. She had begun to compulsively knot up one end
of her voil dupatta whenever this urge rose within her. She

would not sit still. And could hardly eat till this wave subsided. Again, about time. She tried in vain for two days, and when she could not find it on the map, she sought Arjan Singh's help. She wanted him to approach the *gormint* and apprise them of her urgent need to go back, as there were many matters pending. Arjan Singh would never say no. With his hands on her frail shoulders, he would sit her down and ask her to be patient. *Sabr rakho, Maanji* (Be patient, Mother). As months passed, her fond hope of return began to crack.

In March, Beeji gave birth to a daughter. Maanji's help became vital in those initial months. With the help of an orderly to run the house, she and Beeji reared the child comfortably between them. She gradually noticed how Arjan and Beeji began to avoid the topic of Okara all together. They looked so self-absorbed in this new existence. Arjan Singh was gradually climbing the rungs of service. Beeji was glowing in her new life. The infant became the centre of their world. Maanji felt utterly powerless. To be not allowed to go back to one's own home was beyond her comprehension, even now. She had never heard of an absurd thing like that. '*Kise da ki jaanda*—How would that possibly hurt anybody?' She would mutter to herself.

For many months she resisted her daughter's advice to get new clothes stitched from the tailor. To her, getting new clothes would be an acceptance of the fact of no return. She continued to use the two bosky salwars and *mulmul* shirts she had hastily got from home. Now they were getting discoloured and frayed at the ends. As the prospect of her return dimmed, one day she reluctantly agreed to accompany Beeji to pick fabric from Paltan Bazaar, and then to the tailor-master for stitching. She stood there, expressionless, and Beeji had to answer most queries. She would just nod absent-mindedly. She was inordinately glum that evening. She kept repeating that they don't make them like the *bajaj* back home. She complained about the cheap quality and poor finish on the fabrics. She claimed that this side was not cultured enough. Then she fell silent. Her worst fears were coming true. It looked like she had to stay.

ತಿ

She complained about the heat in June. She said she had never known such heat. In the evenings, she would lock herself in the bathroom for a good half an hour. Beeji would hear a constant splashing about from the outside, which would get really loud at times, and she would knock on the door to check with her. Beeji would then get her room washed—upon her insistence, the orderly would throw buckets of water in the corners and sweep till she was satisfied. He would then switch on the pedestal fan and the room would be filled with cool air. The khus *chiks* affixed on the arches around the length of the bungalow's outer corridor would create a heady fragrance in the evenings. It would rise like a wave, particularly when a draught of summer breeze unexpectedly blew in. Maanji was, however, persistent in her litany of complaints: 'But I have never felt such heat,' she would keep repeating to herself, all the while shaking her head. 'But never...' she would reiterate, furiously airing herself with a hand fan. Maanji, who had never stepped out of her room without a dupatta, started to roam the house in a thin muslin shirt. She did not want to wear her bra and complained to Beeji that it dug into her skin. Beeji then stitched her new shirts and undershirts of *mulmul*. Her appetite drastically dropped. From her usual diet of three chapattis, Maanji came down to one. She would instead keep drinking water from the surahi, because she was convinced that the water from the new bulky white contraption—the fridge—was adulterated. She would screw up her nose in silent denunciation of the gadget, buzzing non-stop, sometimes letting out a sudden series of loud clicks owing to the frequent electricity fluctuation, which would throw Maanji off balance. She was convinced it had something against her. Why, it mostly happened when she was alone. To alleviate her discomfort was futile. She would not be listening, just complaining.

August 1948 also came and went. With the year coming full circle, she had hoped to return. Like this was an expiry date of sorts. This is betrayal—when you leave in the fond hope of return but are not allowed to. When you leave it is your village, and the following day it becomes a foreign country. More foreign than foreign. You can travel to any country you like but not this one. You cannot go back. They will kill you. You cannot go back now. The gormint will kill you. The house stands there, the village Okara too, but the country has changed. Now new people will inhabit this village. They have also lost their houses. They will enter this house to see blood caked on the verandah. By now dry crust. Where Sardar Gurbaaz Singh lay dead with his gut open and blood pooling under his body. This is his blood. The women of the house will have to give the floor a thorough scrub. Blood stains are not easy to remove. Yes, and they will enter the rooms and see my bedding. Perhaps a young girl will fit into my daughter's clothes. Or it'll all be a waste because they too lost a young daughter in the Vadda Raula. These clothes will haunt them. They will want to go back. How crazy! I don't want to be here and they don't want to be there. They can't be here and I can't be there. How absurd! It is like someone just did it in jest. What value does my life have? Nothing. Has nobody thought of this? They live with my nightmares, I live with theirs. And then learn to ignore these sounds I hear from the crevices of the new house. Each night I plug my ears and shut my eyes. A new story over my story. The slate has been wiped clean. With blood.

Her life got split in two parts: then and now—Okara and Jalandhar.

She gradually came to accept the fact that she would have to stay put, but it was hard on her. While trying to be a gracious mother-in-law to Arjan, she wrestled within.

Gradually Beeji got very busy with her toddler and her duties as an army wife—the welfare activities kept her preoccupied. Maanji, on the other hand, became increasingly reclusive, nursing a huge grudge against Beeji for not wanting to return to Okara. Not wanting it badly enough. Her one resentment was that Beeji could accept the loss of their house so 'unproblematically'. That she could dress up for parties without feeling a pang. She felt exhausted: her energy first spent wanting so sorely to return, and then accepting the loss as final. As her old life in Okara was fast becoming just a story to be told, she too was becoming irrelevant, like an out-of-use currency or an old train route, defunct. Her body became slightly bent over and the folds of her skin began to hang loose, like they had lost interest in life. And all like a misunderstanding, like someone your own, someone very close, had tricked you, had surreptitiously moved the very roof from over your head.

❦

It started with her memory lapsing occasionally and her gradual withdrawal. She retreated into a shell of her own making. In time the loquacious Maanji embraced silence. She would sit in her room all day and stare out of the window. She looked at the plants in the garden. These reminded her of their paddy in Okara. Poor cousins. Yet. 'Listen, that has to be harvested.' 'Who will do it'? Earlier she would talk to the malis to give them some tips, but gradually she stopped doing it. Silence was growing fast and covering her room like insidious ivy. Every night it increased by a few imperceptible inches. Slowly it was covering up everything that fell in its way. Occasionally, the cloak of silence was torn at night by her sudden, shrill cry. It used to create panic in the neighbourhood, but then everyone understood. People generally understand. At times she would start laughing hysterically. Mostly when the tune of *Sare Jahan Se Achha* was played by the regiment pipe band.

What is this Hindustan?

And she would let out a peal of raucous laughter, which would continue unabated for many minutes.

'Achha tell me, I didn't hear the latest…*gall viche reh gayi*— you never really answered… *Azaadi mil gayi?*—did we finally get freedom?' She would put her head close to Arjan Singh and wait for an answer.

Arjan Singh would reply in the affirmative. She would then involuntarily curl her hand in a question, her lips would turn downwards and the two furrows on her forehead would deepen.

She gradually lost recognition—of her daughter and then her granddaughter. She would only recall Arjan Singh, her way of clinging on to the genteel respect for the son-in-law. The last thing she said, lying there dying, was, 'Arjan Singh, *leh pahunch gaye Okara teshan*—see, we have arrived at Okara station.'

Meanwhile, a few months ago, somewhere in Okara—or no,

wait, Jalandhar, actually—does it really matter where? Come to think of it, it could have happened on this side or that:

Marasi[2] 1: You are not running? Everybody is on the run.

Marasi 2: That is the whole point. I am here because everybody has run away. I stayed on. Saadi majh sooyi si—our buffalo was expecting. But things changed overnight. The town has gone empty. Now, it's free for all. At least till the new janta comes. Lutt kassutt. Big Loot!

Marasi 1 (slaps him with a leather strap): 'Lutt Kassutt!' (mimics him.) You clever rascal! But really, tell me are you not worried about your life?

Marasi 2: Life? Yesterday they set a big gurudwara on fire with people trapped inside. They tried to escape when the blaze got big. A mob sat right opposite the burning building. Each time the poor people came running to the exit, they were shot dead. They had to die either way. They could choose how. Either get roasted in fire or get shot. Basically you could choose your suffering.

Marasi 1: Die this way or that—tell me how. And now that you say it, it's strange the same episode happened in a mosque. Why, Ali down the lane told me all about it.

Marasi 2: If I run, there is a good chance I'll meet a mob that will hack me to pieces in minutes. If not, I could die of exhaustion and hunger. And the very thought of walking so many miles tires me. Just the thought. And even if I make it, God willing, I will

---

[2]Marasis are traditional, tramp-like figures in Punjabi performing theatre. They indulge in dialogue and entertaining repartee to inject humour, irony and satire in conversations about events and matters of significance for the community at large.

die of heartache, for if I will not have lost my life, I certainly will have lost my home, some or all family members, my pind, my zameen—my village, my lands. So I will anyway be half-dead. So I don't see much point. And besides, once this place is empty, I'll go from one empty haveli to the other, picking what I like. Presently there are some stubborn oldies, some lunatics, hijras, nomads, babies and the crippled, who did not flee or had to be abandoned or mai keha, I dare say, could not tell the difference. Chance of a lifetime! To be honest.

Marasi 1: Chance of a lifetime! Tikhha bada hai saala—the bugger is a clever fox!

Marasi 2: Got to fend for yourself when the sarkar is sleeping. I am sure they have no idea what they have done.

Marasi 1: Whose sarkar rules us now?

Marasi 2: Of these matters I know not, Marasia. They say angrez sarkar has left. I don't believe it. Why would our own sarkar do this to us?

Marasi 1: But then this kind of carnage did not happen when the angrez ruled.

Marasi 2: That is true...this kind of carnage did not happen when the angrez ruled... I did not think about that.

Marasi 1: I think there is no sarkar now. The sarkar is running for its life.

Marasi 2 (slaps him with a letter strap): Go try your luck there also, in this free-for-all, who knows kamineya (you rascal), you may end up becoming sarkar. Shakal teri vi madhi nahi—why! You have a decent face!

III

Such as We Are

Subedar Joginder Singh, Nanaji's connection to his boyhood years in the army, now lived in Mohali. Post retirement, in the 1960s, he had moved into this house—procured after selling a portion of his ancestral land. Joginder Singh never married. His one love since childhood had been embroidery. As a child he would sit with his mother, a skilled embroiderer, and watch her work on her craft for hours on end. She would snatch out little parcels of time from her arduous household schedule, put out a little low stool in the verandah, empty the contents of two cloth bags that contained coloured threads and needles, and begin to embroider. The lunch hour being over and his father being in the fields meant a couple of leisure hours before the drudgery of dinner preparation would have to resume. But, she would have to do it on the sly. Her ailing mother-in-law in the next room would have none of this and thought of it as utterly superfluous—the scheming daughter-in-law's antics to escape housework. She, nevertheless, persisted.

No sooner would the mother-in-law's screeching cough settle into a snoring rumble in the afternoon than she would gather her stuff and get started. She had reserved the best box for her threads—the inlay wooden box her father had got made at considerable expense through a cousin from Hoshiarpur and had given her as dowry. Joginder, all of seven, would squat next to her. For a child his age, he was patient and would not move his eyes from the piece of cloth. The shoving of the needle into an end below and its appearance at precisely the point where the last stitch had been, gave him an unusual thrill—nothing less than an adventure, to see figurines, animals, birds, streams and calligraphy emerge by and by on pieces of tapestry. At times, he would punctuate the utter silence of these hours with an involuntary gasp of exultation. He would effortlessly slip into the role of his mother's assistant: picking out from the box whatever thread she demanded. Like an able apprentice, he would rummage through the bunch of coloured yarn and extricate the two or three shades of whatever colour it was the mother wanted. She would then choose.

'Jogeya', she would call out affectionately, 'this one, this bright *sooha* red. Give me this. This bridal phulkari will not do with the jaded, *fikka* one.'

Or,

'Jogeya, no, not this dull mehndi green. For the parrots, take out the sharp *totiya* (bright) green.'

Joginder would promptly run her orders. The otherwise boisterous child became extremely pliant in these hours. While the yawning days at the small nondescript village were all the same, these were the moments that both of them looked forward to. In the long summer afternoons, with the lunch hour being over, the embers in the tandoor cooling down, the babies exhausted from day-long play, the women would put the padlocks on the clunky doors and sit down awhile to rest. The village in this hour, before the activities of the evening resumed, would be shrouded in eerie silence. The quiet dusty lanes, the village square resounding with the echoes of stillness, where in the morning it had seen a flurry of activity. Nobody came, nobody went.

The silence would sometimes be punctuated by a grunting buffalo, the cacophony of a flight of house sparrows, or the occasional cooing of pigeons in the ledge above the window. And on some days, it would be pierced by Lajjo's shriek. Lajjo, the homeless one. Lajjo, who had no one and called the gurudwara her home. It was a strange shriek that would start with a steady laughter, then grow into guffaws that would echo insidiously in the air, and then transform into sobs and culminate in unceasing crying that would morph into barely audible hiccups before merging with silence again. Lajjo's daily ritual from the outer ramparts of the gurudwara were, by now, part of the village soundscape. She was harmless like the pigeons. But sometimes Joginder noticed the strange effect Lajjo's cries had on his mother. It would begin with her lips trembling, and then she would struggle hard to contain sighs, which would progressively threaten to become louder. She would try and repress them and discreetly take the end of her dupatta to quickly wipe a stray tear on her cheek. Joginder would not move his eyes away from her. He would be perplexed, but somehow never had the guts to question her. *Something gets her*, he would think. But he never asked her. She never told him either.

Mother and son sat on the floor, their heads joined, poring over the fabric. For the mother, it was a flight of fancy, her imagination and discipline at her bidding, like two dependable minions, producing colourful phulkaris, cloth drawstring bags with two parrots facing each other with a decorative vine of flowers cutting through the centre, cloth fans with geometrical patterns and frills attached at the edges and suits embroidered with the famous sindhi stitch. When engrossed in producing the stitches, mother, with son in tow, would wander about in fantasy lands of their own making, tucked away in the folds of fabric and hidden inside acres of running stitches. All this in the span of an afternoon.

They were making a new phulkari. This was more elaborate than the ones gone before. Mother decided on two colours: red and gold. She began to embroider the staple phulkari motif, a geometrical flower, alternately in red and gold. In its intricacy, it began to resemble a bagh, as she laid the motifs close enough so as to ensure not a centimetre was unembroidered. The labour was intensive—they worked for weeks on end. But one day they ran out of threads while at least half of the cloth remained to be embroidered. Mother then left a request with the village grocer to procure the threads for her the next time he went to the town for supplies. This was the only way for them. This meant they had to wait for a fortnight or more.

Joginder was beginning to get impatient at the prospect. His mother came up with a solution. She took out the bunch of old leftover threads and created a profusion of multicoloured animals and birds on the margins, where traditionally the flower motif sat. A variety of animals meant that she could use up the supplies of all the other colours she had in her box. So an elephant here and a horse there, parrots perched on a half-visible branch here, partridges and quails there. On the other end, she innovated even more and inserted figurines of two Nihangs in cobalt tunics, their oversized turbans studded with jangling nickel badges, carrying gleaming swords, astride white horses. She had heard accounts of rare, precious Arabian horses as a girl. She had never seen one, but she tried to make them look like the handsome steeds that the prized creatures were meant to be.

Then she scrawled a floral motif that Joginder thought was only a flower. Later, when he began to read the Punjabi alphabet at the Maulvi ji's, he realized that it was actually a word. It could be read. It said, 'Kirpal.' He stayed with this knowledge for a long time. It was many years later, only by fluke, that he would learn of Kirpal. Kirpal, who lived in his mother's village. Kirpal, whom she had wanted to marry. Kirpal, who owned no lands and was not accepted by her family. Kirpal, whom she began to forget by and by. Kirpal, whom she did not think of when she began to collect her trousseau and when they bought her the gold jhumkis. She did not think of him when she settled in her husband's home. For some days she did not think of him. But thenceforth, he was the Kirpal she could not forget. So she hid him here and there. She had not gone to school but had taught herself to scrawl his name by reading from the Sukhmani Sahib Gutka. She was not sure if it was the right spelling, but could not ask anybody, and it gave her a thrill, the kind of thrill you get from working with a foreign language—especially when it helps you with some secrets, when you can have your own codes.

When she had the patience, she would begin work on bed sheets and covers for trunks. Whereas people's storerooms were dumping yards, her store room had stacks of neatly arranged boxes and trunks. Cavernous petis contained the family bedding—the quilts and the bulky cotton-filled mattresses, which were always extra. You never knew when you would need them—in the eventuality of unexpected guests, or a village wedding, in which case utter strangers comprising the marriage party could end up as your guests. It would be a travesty for a self-respecting family to not have clean bedding to offer them. On the petis were mounted trunks of various sizes, going from the big to the small in pyramids that would virtually touch the beamed roof of the dark room. Each of these trunks was swathed in white embroidered covers made by his mother. She was inordinately proud of this little kingdom of hers and would ensure it was always meticulously kept.

Joginder was all of seventeen when he was recruited in the British army as a sepoy. At the eve of World War II, a recruitment team had visited his village and he was one of the two boys they picked up. The theatre of war made some arduous demands on the young village boy. His existence thereon burst open. He spent a good two and a half decades as a soldier and got far-flung postings during his stint—he started his service in Burma and then got posted in Jorhat and subsequently in Cannanore. His parents had died one after the other in quick succession—while he could perform his father's last rites, he could not visit his village from Jorhat in the eastern sector upon his mother's sudden death. There had been an unusual spate of flooding for days. This one fact always troubled him. Like a sharp, quick sensation, it would come back as a reminder in the most unexpected ways. And he would immerse himself in a new piece of embroidery to numb the feeling. What began as a distraction became an antidote and then a consuming interest. The needle pierced the little bubbles of guilt that insidiously popped around him. The embroidery hour became the comforting sanctuary he sought. Even during his toughest postings, he would eke out time for this. When he was manning the post in NEFA (North-East Frontier Agency), which was more of an ice cave, he ordered a particularly thick needle, like the ones used to sew quilts, so that he could do it without taking off his gloves. In Jaipur, while the other jawans visited the local bazaars on their off days and outings, Joginder would quickly grab his green cloth bag, spread a sheet outside his quarter and begin from where he had left off. Since he never married, he had none of the obligations that the other jawans had, who would spend their holidays buying trinkets for their wives and toys for their children. Joginder would be left all alone on these days and be joyfully embroidering for those two hours. This thrill, few could understand.

Nanaji and Nanaki came to visit Joginder Singh one Sunday morning. He was bent over a row of chrysanthemum saplings in the outer garden. He wore a kurta pyjama and stray hair from his ivory beard fell here and there. His long hair, usually tucked under a turban, was held back in a loose ponytail. His amber eyes shone with the sharp glint of midday sunlight. There was a relaxed pace about him that subsumed the tightrope of destiny and many decades of work.

'*Langh aao, langh aao*—walk right in.' He showed them into the modest drawing room. The wartime equation Joginder had shared with Nanaji had always remained despite the reversal of their rank equation, and they addressed each other as 'Sa'ab.' Joginder Singh was rather voluble and was soon recounting many stories. Nanaki noticed his gleaming hands and supple fingers. His Hindi was heavily accented with a marked Doabi Punjabi cadence, but he insisted on speaking it. While it would make perfect sense for him to speak in Punjabi with grandfather, this switch to Hindi, no matter how broken, was an old, ingrained habit from his army days that he could not rid himself of. So he laboured on:

'*Sa'ab ji, kya laeyenge aap*—what will you have?'

He made some tea and offered them glucose biscuits and dry fruits. As Nanaki took a bite of the biscuit, it just collapsed limp, caught between her teeth—it had gone terribly soggy. The almonds that he served smelt like he had preserved them in his dank kitchen cupboard for many weeks. They had variously absorbed the fumes and flavours of curry and spices.

Joginder Singh was still athletic. He offered to show them his gallery—when he had got this house constructed after retirement, he had modified the garage space into the gallery. With a jerk, he parted the heavy curtains and sunlight flooded the room, lined with embroidered panels on both the walls. These panels, framed taut in walnut wood, were expansive embroideries, some covering the width of the room—roof to floor. Nanaki gasped. She had been told about his skill by Nanaji, but nothing had prepared her for this.

The one that immediately caught her eye was a large floor-to-ceiling sized piece depicting an orange orchard with birds on an ivory silk panel. The fruits, embroidered in hues varying from burnt sienna to deep red, hung from trees with elongated sap green leaves. The calm of the orchard was punctuated by the hullabaloo of pheasants. A particularly striking one sat on a central branch, spreading out its regalia of vibrant plumage. One was caught in the moment of alighting on a branch. One baby pheasant, with eyes a tad bigger than the adults, exuded tacit inexperience. There were other frames with birds—in their detailing they were much like colonial botanical drawings, but surpassed them in their liveliness. Nanaki was besotted and her belief was strengthened that only the technical part of art could be taught, that education was no guarantee that it would produce a good artist, that, conversely, it could happen to unschooled people in the most unlikely circumstances and in the most obscure of places—

while at other times, the conventions of a standard education could completely be rewritten.

'How long did you take to finish the pheasants?'

'That took me seven months of continuous work, Beeba ji, and this was some five years ago. *Din raat ik kar ditta si—* I burnt the midnight oil. I wonder if I can muster the strength now. My eyesight is also failing. After the cataract operation, my eyes have not been the same. *O gall nahi rahi—*It's not the same,' he said with no hint of regret or bitterness.

What pulsated with an urgency now within Nanaki was the imperative need to somehow document and preserve Joginder Singh's work.

Just after Independence, Joginder Singh was attached to one Col. Harwant Singh 'Hardy', an officer of the Poona Horse. His wife, Meera, had fine taste and had put together an impressive personal collection of artefacts and memorabilia. It included Chinese carvings on lacquer boards, encrusted with jade and coral, Meissen porcelain, Spode Chinaware and exquisite folk embroideries. Some of these were framed and hung in their drawing room and Joginder Singh would just stand and observe them for hours on end. Memsa'ab was initially perplexed, but when Joginder gifted her a bird embroidery, she got to know of his talent, her hesitation melted and she allowed him free access to observe. It was in her collection that he saw the Japanese silk scroll that captured his imagination. It was an ink-black silk panel, upon which were embroidered cranes and lilies. In the backdrop loomed Mount Fujiyama. The cream-silken threads of the cranes shone against the midnight blue of the backdrop, to foreground the birds with a finesse he had scarce witnessed before. The peculiar scarlet of the flowers gave a lively energy to the composition. Meera stood there observing, and then told him that an art professor at her university had once told her how cranes in the Japanese embroidery symbolically stood for longevity—that they were said to live for a thousand years. There was no immediate connection, but while he lingered, the composition made Joginder think of his village pond and the hoards of migratory cranes that descended there in the winters. Their cacophony on the otherwise still waters of the pond captivated him as a child. Once, upon his insistence, his mother had embroidered a pair of cranes on his school bag. Other children had parrots and sparrows but little Joginder had cranes. He decided at that instance that he would make a crane embroidery someday.

Once Joginder accompanied a despatch rider to the Colonel's bungalow to deliver important dak. It was the rarest of rare occasions—the colonel and his batman were out on a fishing trip and the cook had retired for the remainder of the afternoon. After waiting for the cook to answer the door bell for what seemed like an eternity, Meera pulled herself together in her gown and looked out of the window. Joginder stood there in his winter Angora uniform, his face framed in a starched olive turban and his beard dressed in a fine mesh. She opened the door and, despite informing him of Saab's absence, extended him the rare courtesy of looking at one more embroidery panel that had just been delivered the previous day. Joginder walked in with a trepidation he was not used to. He was not known to display the excessive servility that some did to their superiors. As a young man, he had quite a staid mannerism; his excessive volubility came late in life. He looked closely at the threadwork, running his tanned finger over the fabric to feel the texture, unmindful of all else. Meera stole a glance at him. He was handsome in an earthy way. His simplicity stood out as a foil to the excessive cordiality and propriety—sometimes hypocrisy—of the officer class. She felt for him a strange wave of sympathy that completely overwhelmed the irritability she had felt at being inconvenienced at this ungodly hour, considering that nothing was more precious to her than to draw the curtains, diminishing the sharp daylight post lunch and take a nap, and if not that then just to lie down for an hour. These couple of hours she could be just herself, away from the trappings of the official identity of the memsa'ab she had to maintain for the most part. She would not trade this luxury for anything in the world. But here she was, not complaining that her time had been unceremoniously usurped.

He looked up at her to take leave and found himself observing her porcelain neck dipping into the plunging blue neckline, silhouetting her taut breasts. The door of her bedroom was half open and he could see a diffused glow from the farther end of the room, owing to the heater. The gauzy net screens of her poster bed flapping to reveal a dark walnut headrest against the ivory sheets fresh from Ali Laundry in Paltan Bazaar.

He knew because clothes laundered there always gave off a peculiarly citric odour.

∞

Later, while serving under Nanaji in Srinagar, he had the occasion to observe the artisans of Kashmir, whose considerable clientele came from army wives. The needle embroideries on the pashminas hanging from the windows of emporia in Lal Chowk were vital lessons to an eager pupil like Joginder. He would stand on the cement platform outside the State Emporia window, observing the pieces—they always happened to display the best there. On Sundays, he would take a shikara ride down the Dal Lake and often visit the houseboat of the old kashidagar, Naeem Khan, who was known to produce inordinately exquisite pieces.

The armed forces were also big patrons of the Malerkotla artisans, who were known for their skill at working with metallic thread, *tilla*. The crests and insignia of various regiments, formations, anniversaries and jubilees, to be embroidered on uniforms, blazers, caps, berets, banners, flags and other regalia, had all been done by the artisans of Malerkotla for generations. Joginder would never lose an opportunity to volunteer for recces conducted for these jobs, and later to get the jobs executed with precision and patience. He would camp in the JCOs' (Junior Commissioned Officers') Mess at the Malerkotla cantonment for weeks and spend hours in the workshops looking at their craft closely. He became friends with Gulfam, who was an artisan with Zeeshan Embroideries in Vaidan Street. After the initial trepidation that other artisans felt with the odd fauji's presence in the workshop, they were gradually taken in by his unobtrusive nature and in no time he was one of them. He would sit with them on the durrie spread out on the floor, listening to the radio and observing them at their craft. This is how he schooled himself in the art, picking up nuances from wherever he could and combining it with an extraordinary inner fervour.

❧

Nanaki's studio was located on the second floor. It was a sparse brick structure with tall glass windows fixed in teak frames. There was ample light around the year and with a clear view of the sky, the elements were a *real* presence here. Summers could get searing hot and one could feel the *Loo* slapping against the glass panes in the afternoons. From a distance, the hot wind looked like it was moving in waves, creating thermal illusions on the terrace, like a hot tandoor. Monsoons were a relief, drowning the oppressive spiral of heat and dust in little gushing riverines running on the edges of the terrace and spiralling down the drain pipe making loud gushing sounds. On winter mornings, the windows would be hazy with fog outside. She could see the auras of two helium lamps on the neighbour's balcony. Nanaki liked this proximity to the elements, and she ensured that this time was an uninterrupted flow, away from the intrusions of social media. She would not carry her iPad and phone here.

One wall of the studio was completely book-lined, and her collection included books from her school days. There were tons of Russian books, which could be bought cheap from Punjab Book Centre in Sector 22 back then. At one time, it was a hang-out for the commies, artists and writers in the city. It still existed like a relic of the era when the erstwhile USSR invested heavily in literature. There were Russian folktales with such masterly illustrations that they could have come from the stables of the most accomplished painters. There was one particular storybook about a Russian family that goes for a picnic to the sea side. A common enough story about common enough folks. But what ethereal pencil drawings! Nanaki was particularly struck by some of the fine anatomical studies of the characters. Teenage Russian boys stripped to their underwears, ready to leap off a yacht. Their flaxen hair and blue eyes. Their mothers dressed in country shirts with heads secure in scarves. Russia looked like a fun place. People there looked strong and happy. One day she would want to visit this fabled land. She once had to narrate something in the school assembly. Beeji made her learn a condensed version of a story about a boy called Alexei, who did not eat his meals properly. A litany of the many everyday adventures he experienced on this account—big and small—ultimately being chastised by his nurse. Before long, he learns his lesson.

There were coffee-table books about art collections in the Museum of Petersburg, Museum of Moscow, their awe-inspiring still lifes, particularly the ones with rich tapestries, luscious burgundy plums and silver samovars, their onion-domed buildings, their neoclassical palaces with gilded pillars and walls, their public squares, stately with stone sculptures of Lenin and Marx. And of course the bound up old issues of the fortnightly *Misha* and *Sputnik*, the children's magazines that duly arrived from Moscow every month with clockwork regularity.

Then there was her personal collection of literature books— her influences had been diverse and eclectic—from Punjabi authors to Shakespeare to very contemporary Canadian and Australian writing. She was a compulsive hoarder. And now with online shopping becoming so convenient, she was ordering rather too frequently. Beeji had lately complained of the scores of Amazon delivery boxes strewn across the house. 'At this rate they will actually have to cut down the Amazon forest.'

On the wall opposite the tall windows stood her easel. Presently she was working on an abstract oil 'fog'. Broad ashen strokes of grey rose from the ground in a gradient of monochromatic brush work, merging into a screen of fine white dots at the top. Through the thick curtain of fog one could see little blobs of greenery—imperceptible dots of faded green, which could easily be missed. She was less than happy with the way it looked right now. The strokes at the bottom seemed a tad thicker than desirable, the strokes that she had added a week ago had solidified into an opaque crustiness—

this had taken away the diffused transience of the fog as she had hoped to capture it. The good thing about oils is that you can always rework them. Next to it stood her colour cupboard. This was an old console with a dozen drawers. Nanaji had got it custom-made for her colours and brushes at the old engineers' workshop in the cantonment. There were small cuboid drawers with sorters inside where she stored her colour tubes; there were long shallow ones where she stocked a variety of round and flat sable hair brushes. There were little bottles of linseed oil—half-empty and still unopened, and each time one entered the little space, its heady whiff hit the senses. To Nanaki, it was an indication, each time and always, of moving into a world that was her own, of her own choosing. A world she was building, one step at a time. A world with its own aura, its own peculiar smell.

∞

In the lobby of their Chandigarh house, they had always had a corner with an old gramophone and a little library of LPs, which were gradually replaced with CDs. Somewhere down the line, Nanaji had acquired a new Philips music system with amplifiers and had it been installed there without discarding the old system. So the old and the new brushed shoulders. The collection of music—old and young, from here and there, Indian and Western—grew like a honeycomb. From ghazal maestros like Mehdi Hassan, Begum Akhtar and Nayyara Noor to old Hindi film music, to a complete collection of S.D. Burman's music, to vintage Punjabi folk, Pathane Khan to Surinder Kaur, to a Rabindra Sangeet collection built during their Calcutta posting, to Western classical—Bach, Weber—to Prince, Joni Mitchell and U2—their collection was eclectic to say the least, and still growing.

This was also how they had grown. Having suffered the dislocation of Partition and having lived in different parts of India owing to their postings, they had come to acquire a diverse collection of art, artefacts, mementoes, shields and handicrafts and their house throbbed with the remnants of these experiences. Each time a new experience came along, it wriggled and made space for itself, like a school kid who gets into a crowded bus and upon finding all seats filled, adjusts himself next to a welcoming older passenger. Everyone finds space. Nanaji, while on his posting in Nagaland, had been gifted two tribal shell horns, which Beeji had carefully got mounted on the two sides of the big console. Two enamelled brass pots with lush ferns were placed on either side. But there was something very army-like in this symmetrical placement, which was, at times, disconcerting to Nanaki. Buildings with manicured lawns and gleaming glasses, plants arranged in pots of the same kind, whitewashed tree trunks, white numbers in black circles, labels, placards, seating arrangements, who-is-who, berets, badges, regiments, formations, appointments, commands, hierarchies, flags, flagstaff cars, lapels, lapels with ranks, brass on the chest, shoulder loops, collar dogs, ribbons in order, when was when, salute each time, salute anything that moves—a place for everything and everything in its place. This order gave them a semblance of sanity. Classify. Classify. Classify what life throws at you.

She would often see Nanaji leaning over the console, examining his collection. He would be rearranging the LPs or poring over the contents. In the collection, Faiz had an enviable place. Some evenings they would play Faiz. Beeji and Nanaji would then take a drink each—Nanaji, a peg of scotch and Beeji, her brandy in warm water. The two sitting there cut quite a picture. There they would be, languid, first on the armchairs and then gradually slipping on to the carpet—flushed with memories, losses, desire, fulfilled and unfulfilled longings, somehow intensified in those phantom hours.

'Hum jinhe soz-e-mohobbat ke siva
Koi but koi khuda yaad nahi'
(We, so suffused in the ardour of love,
Recall no idol, no God.)

Nanaki would fetch some bite-sized snacks—Afghani kebab or chicken tikka. Gradually, their banter would die down and the snack dish would be left with a couple of bites with no takers. A hush would then descend on the room and the ghazals would so fill the room that every syllable would be perceptible. This, by some strange stroke of association—or maybe it was the turn of phrase—would remind Beeji of the fodder room and the cloth bag, of her walk with Maanji this side of the border. As time had passed, it had all begun to appear more and more absurd to her. *How could a nation do this to its own people? We were naive, but what about them? Who did it to us? Nobody asked them why they did it?* Like your very hearth was suddenly heaving, contracting; it could contain you no more, sinking and rising, sinking and rising, threatening to suck you in if you did not flee. And the fodder room. The silence and the suffocation. The suspended husk making her eyes gritty. The leak in her salwar and then the hush. At this, she would try to stop her racing mind. Always, it used to be this precise point. Even then the errant mind would insidiously steal on her and she would be involuntarily imagining the fatal blow. Like a celluloid grab on a loop, running repeatedly in her mind. The lusty killer overpowering her father. The terror on his frozen face. How he must have resisted. How he must have asked to be spared. And his pallid face when the two found him dead. A gush of blood seeping into the green voile turban. The house, turning into his grave. She would give a start.

Faiz spoke to them in these moments. The Urdu was obscure for Nanaki and the words would be lost on her, yet his ghazals reminded her of a lost world, of Yadwinder. She could not think of anything but him. The show-and-tell, the reluctance and the revelation enthralled her, and in these moments she would be seized with an indescribable longing to see him. And just like the ghazal is a great vehicle of subterfuge, she was adept at hiding her feelings. The raspy voice of Madam Noorjehan would echo—wait, why did they call her madam? Only her? No idea. Why was she more madam than the rest? No idea. Anyway, '*Teri aankhon ke siva duniya mein rakha kya hai?*'

(What really remains in this world for me, but your eyes?)

In that moment of pregnant silence, when everybody listened in, Nanaki's eyes would be dilated and her cheeks flushed; she would have a vision of Yadwinder, so evocative it was like she could touch him and he could take her hand and then, just like that afternoon, give her a long, unhurried, languorous kiss. Here, then, she would want to linger awhile. A tremor would travel down her body like wave. She would close her eyes and, invariably, Nanaji would interrupt her reverie with a remark about some word or turn of phrase. At times he would give her a snap Urdu vocabulary check. And then the two would keep rattling off the meanings of words as Nanaki would make an effort to understand. She had even tried to learn the alphabet from an old *qaida*, Nanaji's primer from his school days. But she could not go beyond a few pages, and Nanaji suggested she would do better to just carefully hear out the words in these ghazals.

These were the rare evenings on which the otherwise clockwork meals of the household were disrupted. They would just have dinner picked up from a nearby eatery in Sector 8. Nanaki would then slump on the carpet and negotiate with Nanaji to play her new U2 CD also, to which he would reluctantly agree.

ॐ

While visiting home for the Dussehra break, the Gills had invited the grandparents for a Sukhmani Sahib path followed by langar the following Sunday. When Navneet came to formally invite them, she declared that there was no specific occasion—it was just for 'general happiness'. She mentioned, however, that the family of her husband's elder brother was also visiting and therefore it would be even more festive. Navneet sat there on a cot, soaking the sun, in the backyard with Beeji, having a late morning cuppa and biting into the special *alsi pinni* (flaxseed sweetmeat). In the forenoon, rays of winter sun filtered through the big jamun tree in the backyard. It threw quivering dappled coins of light and shadows on the floor. Overripe jamuns fell by the dozen in the season, which Beeji tried to retrieve every morning with her unbelievable reserves of enthusiasm. Some, however, were too squished to be any good and left splashy blobs of inky stains in the backyard. A little green patch next to the wall had been made into furrows where Beeji grew seasonal vegetables. Brinjals, tomatoes, cauliflower in winters and okra, ghiya, in summers. Creepers of karela festooned the hedge with fragile yellow flowers. Vines of seasonal sweet peas were trellised on a screen of bamboo stalks skirting the outer length of the lawn. Some parts of the lawn were eternally bare: grass refused to take root as these patches were forever shrouded in the shadow of the big trees.

The morning laundry was still dripping wet on the clothes line. Two of Nanaji's turbans, had been washed and spread out, these taking the most space. Navneet took small bites of the *pinni*, each one preceded and rounded off by a refrain as to how disastrous this single one could be, given that she was getting no exercise. Her gym membership had expired last month, not that she was anyway regular with it. All the same, her bites continued with the same gusto. Beeji, by the way of consolation and prompting her to go on, added that this *nikka jehi pinni*—(chit of a sweet) would do her no harm. Why, what difference does it make to consume it once a while, in fact it is desirable and kept one 'strong.' Beeji had her own definition of strong and healthy and had never given in to the diet plans she had heard discussed in the mahjong group at the Golf Club, or read in the scores of articles they had lately begun to carry in *The Tribune* weekends supplements. She had a deep-rooted suspicion of new fangled ideas that could outwardly get you in shape but always at the cost of something. She was all for a diet that had a bit of everything, even fat. 'Anyway, this might be desi ghee but actually the flaxseed more than makes up for any harm it could do.' She said, '*Alsi* is excellent for joints'—at this, Navneet's mouth fell because it reminded her of the looming fear of developing arthritic knees because of her bulk. She was at that precise moment a confused woman—who could not decide whether she should be eating the *pinni* or not. Whether it was doing her good or harm and whether Beeji meant well or was taking a dig at her.

Whether it was a compliment or a piece of consolation for the harm already done, she would never know. At this moment, Navneet involuntarily cast a glance at her ample thighs swathed in the rani-coloured salwar, she could see the contours of her dimpled skin gleaming through the sheer material. Her heavy breasts sized up in the contraption of an expensive push-up bra, nevertheless, seemed to sag, over the bulge of her stomach. When she looked further down, the stomach looked like a mound of freshly kneaded dough gleaming through the organza shirt. Despite the pleasant weather, she could feel beads of perspiration lining the length and folds of her body owing to the layers of dress materials. As far as her sartorial choices went, she always and each time chose vanity over utility.

Beeji, on the other hand, was a study in contrast. Her frugal eating habits and her clockwork walk schedule were visible in her naturally toned body. She eschewed experimentation and settled for simple, mostly hand-stitched clothes. In summers, it was pastel colours and fine floral prints in cottons and *mulmul*. In winters, it was spun or pashmina. Her salwars were mostly in Patiala style, in her favourite colours, beige and cream. She liked a little detailing with delicate laces—sometimes picking them from Sianco or Stitchcraft and sometimes tatting it herself. If she was feeling indulgent, she would bring out her old tin of anchor threads and embroider motifs on the cuffs or yoke. Her dupattas were always the standard chiffons or voils. And she would pair the outfits with jutties of all kinds. From the plain black leather ones with just an embroidered gold 'vine' running along the upper part to really ornate ones richly embroidered and studded with pearls, she had quite a collection. Nanaki would borrow from her at times. The meticulous Beeji would be careful to rid the used pair of any dust or moisture before storing it back. She had told Nanaki as to how one could use the juttis interchangeably on the feet; in fact it was advisable because that is how leather keeps its shape. Unlike any other kind, these shoes were neutral that way, as they could take on the shape of either feet with use. 'This is an egalitarian piece of footwear if ever there was one,' Nanaki would declare, speaking into a folded magazine, faking a mike.

On special occasions she indulged in her old printed silk sarees from their army days, or her *tanchois, jamavars* and pashminas that would, for the most part be stored in the old sanction army box. On these occasions she would touch up her strong aquiline features with just a hint of blush and knot her wavy salt-and-pepper hair in a bun that rested on her nape and slip on just a solitary piece of jeweller. She would look every inch an exquisite woman.

Coming back to Navneet's stomach, it seemed bigger today, bulging out in little portions all along the seam running across her sides. 'I need to start exercising, Beeji. And tell me some secrets. You have really maintained. How do you do it at your age?'

Beeji took it as a compliment even though what exactly she was referring to, vis-a-vis 'maintenance' was not clear. But before she could clarify, Navneet abruptly got up to leave. 'You must bring Nanaki along to the pathh. Now we hardly see her. By the way, what is she studying?'

And upon being told that she was studying Fine Arts BFA at The Delhi College of Art, she said, 'Why? But she is very *layak*—(bright). Not like our kakaji. We broke into a bhangra the day he passed 12th. But Nanaki, the intelligent one, should have tried Medical. There are good placements.' She had a tendency to throw in current words she had picked up. 'And why send her to Delhi—could have done it here. Should have made her understand. Anyway, kids do what they have to these days.' She prattled on. She was clearly not asking questions to get answers. She really liked listening to her own voice.

As Nanaki entered the backyard, she saw them sitting real close, heads almost touching, talking in whispers, however, the cadence and echoes drawing more attention than a regular chat would. Nanaki caught snatches of whispers 'ultrasound—abortion-girl child—years ago', which immediately stopped as soon as they saw her. Nanaki was disgusted with what she heard. What were they discussing on the sly? Why was Beeji giving her a hearing? As Nanaki stumbled in, a sudden hush descended. Trying hard to retain her composure, Navneet cleared her throat and opened the golden clasp of her patent leather Prada handbag and fished out a mini pellet dispenser. A charms bracelet tinkled on her wrist. Her manicured nails were painted a bright red. To Nanaki, they looked like talons. Navneet tapped the dispenser on her palm and pushed a pellet in her mouth. With an extended arm, she offered a mint to Nanaki, who promptly declined. In the shiny surface of the patent leather bag, Nanaki saw a reflection of Navneet's face—while she nervously smiled and offered her the mint, trapped in the sheen of the patent leather was a phizog of grotesqueness—painted eyes and a mouth sickly red with a lipper that seemed to be bleeding. Navneet extended the invitation to Nanaki, 'You have to come on Sunday, no excuses.' Nanaki, noticed that there were bags under her eyes and despite the grease paint and highlights in her coloured coiffure, she looked old and tired.

ॐ

IV

Grief Fills Up the Room of My Absent Child

It was 1989. That evening Beeji and Nanaji were at the Silver Fern Hospital to look up Mrs Harinder, who had been operated upon for hysterectomy. As they were climbing down the womens' ward, they heard loud wailing sounds from the lobby filling the air. There was something deeply disturbing about the relentless howl echoing through the corridors. 'Looks like somebody has died,' said Beeji. The prospect of encountering a stark dead body was very unnerving and she subconsciously quickened her pace. Nanaji patted her forearm.

As they stepped on the landing of the staircase, they came face to face with Navneet. Beeji had never quite seen her like this. She wore a magenta nightgown, her ample breasts hanging down beneath it. There were indistinct blotches on the yoke of her gown. Her hair was in disarray and while she screamed, two nerves visibly throbbed on her neck. Her eyes looked mildly dilated. The minute she saw Beeji, she fell into her arms, a heap of exhaustion. Her body looked visibly tired heaving with sweat and palpitation. Beeji was not prepared to receive her like this and here, of all the places.

Navneet insisted on going along with them. Beeji was taken aback. There was something going on and her heart raced.

Why would she want to go home with them in the presence of her mother-in-law? The senior Mrs Gill stood witnessing the goings-on at the door, her rather oversized diamond nose pin gleaming in the dank corridor. She just looked through the old couple and kept pressing her lips with her teeth.

'*Sabr rakh*, hold yourself,' said Beeji.

Beeji wanted to know what the matter was. However Navneet didn't look like she was in any position to recount. Mrs Gill looked almost hostile.

Beeji shot a look at Nanaji, who nodded. '*Ki gall ho gayi*— what is the matter, Mrs Gill?' he addressed the older woman in a tone he reserved for official matters.

'Came for routine check-up. Second month. But it looks like the pregnancy could not be sustained. And she got hysterical. Son is away, so we have a lot of responsibility...' the mother-in-law fumbled as she explained. Her unusually black hair framed a face that betrayed not a shred of emotion. Her lips were narrow and held in a frozen social smile. An oversized gold pendant in a heavy gold chain sat on her cleavage jutting out of a tight-fitting kameez. She came close to Navneet and held her by the arm.

'Take me home, Beeji,' Navneet pleaded cutting the old woman short.

'So we will take her,' said Beeji to Mrs Gill. Not asking, just informing. She felt responsible for the young woman and almost compelled to take her. Although it was her own people, Beeji could sense something very foul. Navneet was begging to be taken along. She slept at Beeji's place that night.

Navneet got up early the next morning. When she came into the living room, Beeji and Nanaji sat there. She walked very slowly and sat down. Beeji poured her a cup of tea.

Navneet raised the cup to her lips but could not bring herself to drink the tea, so she just sat there holding it in her hand.

Nanaki, who was all of six then, walked into the living room in her pyjamas, dragging a rag doll.

Nanaji received her with a bear hug like every morning. Beeji conversed with her in baby language:

'*Aa gayi meri guddi*—My little girl is here?'

'*Hanji*—yes', Nanaki said rubbing her eyes and yawning.

'*Theek sutti*—Did you sleep OK?'

'*Hanji*—yes', said the child.

'Cornflakes or Bournvita?'

'Bournvita.' Alert by now, she chirped and leapt out of her nanaji's lap, excited to show her doll to the guest.

Navneet sniffed and before they could gather, she had burst out crying.

Beeji rubbed her back.

'*Bas kar, bas kar, Beeba*—restrain yourself, child.'

'*Nire kasai*—they are butchers, Beeji. They killed my daughter.'

The mother-in-law had taken her to the doctor on the pretext of a routine examination and upon finding that it was a girl, had asked for the pregnancy to be terminated. She had been made to wait in the adjoining room while the old couple conferred with the doctor. She will never know what passed between them. The next thing she knew was she was made to lie down on a narrow bed next to a green curtain screen.

'*Examination karenge*—I will examine,' the doctor said as he closed down on her with a mask.

She lost consciousness after that and when she got up, it was like a lifetime had elapsed. A nurse was pottering around when she opened her eyes.

Theek ho gaya—Went fine. You will recover fast. And give me a good tip, you are big people, I'll pray you don't have to get it flushed the next time. It will be a son.

For a minute Navneet thought it was a case of mistaken identity or she had got it wrong but a moment later, it all began to make sense.

She leapt from the bed and went screaming into the corridor. The staff tried to calm her, after all, it wasn't the best thing, even for the reputation of the hospital. Then is when Beeji and Nanaji had heard her.

'So what do you feel now?' asked Beeji. You are most welcome to stay put here for as long as you want to Beeba. This is your house.

Navneet broke down once again.

'My own house,' she repeated. '*Aaho*! Where is that? I am made to commit murder in this one and my parents now dead, the Ludhiana house, the house of my childhood is gone. My brothers are in the US. Busy with their lives. My own house,' she sneered. 'Maybe if my husband was here, he would have prevented it. Maybe. Who knows?' She clutched on to the edge of her nightgown and repeatedly curled and uncurled it. She sat cross-legged and shook her feet constantly. 'I will have to stay put here Beeji, but I will need you. You have become my *ma pe*—my parents.'

As she picked up her wallet and moved towards the door, Beeji reminded her of the magenta nightgown.

'No, Beeji, I don't want it.'

'OK if you don't want to take it now—I'll get it washed and ironed and sent through the dhobi.'

'No…no…just throw it in trash.'

So she entered the threshold of her husband's house

once again. Since she had to stay, she became increasingly recalcitrant, and the victories in battles in the kitchen and backyard of the house became for her, her way of getting back at them. Setting up the boutique really clinched it for her and she felt in control like never before. Years of repressed grief and anger were sublimated at the altar of vanity: laces, fabrics, dyes, embroideries—one could fuss endlessly over these things without feeling threatened.

๛

Since 4 a.m. the following Sunday, the strains of Gurbani wafted through the air. Nanaki looked out from the window of her studio and could see an elaborate peach-and white-tent come up in the Gill mansion. A gate of fresh gladiolas and gerberas framed the entrance. Strings of rajnigandha dropped in straight lines from the pergola beams of the porch. Either side of the road was lined with cars, many bearing red beacons and accompanied by guards. The house was decked up. *Rather over decked*, Nanaki thought to herself. *What's the point? Such a waste.*

In preparation for installing the Guru Granth Sahib in the drawing room, they had moved the bulky furniture of the house to the backyard. Against the wall-sized windows of the drawing room, the Granth was installed in a canopied wooden 'bed'. The Granth is believed by the Sikhs to be the Guru incarnate after the tenth Guru, and therefore treated like a real personage. An appropriately comfortable mattress complete with mini pillows makes for the Guru's bedding. This is swathed in rich fabrics that are supposedly the Guru's clothing—*vastra*. Navneet had left no stone unturned in ensuring the beautification of these clothes—the *rumala sahib*. Starting weeks in advance, she had spent several hours getting patchwork done on maroon silk, finished with velvet. A matching velvet canopy was stretched on the inside of the 'roof'. She got little gold baubles to hang down from inside the canopy.

Around the Granth Sahib, mattresses were spread in the hall. These were covered with fresh white sheets from end to end. Flower arrangements were set at different points in the house, which exuded a festive air. Little children boisterously ran in and out of the hall and were constantly minded by the parents to behave themselves. Nanaki and Beeji were one of the first guests to arrive. They took seats close to the Granth Sahib. Nanaki sat there, her back next to a wall and legs crossed. She covered her head with a turquoise printed silk dupatta. Beeji thought Nanaki's face and kohled eyes framed with the dupatta, made her look very striking. Her white chikan kurta was intricately embroidered in the good old needle stitch and she wore very minute turquoise studs. It was cheerful to just sit there and observe people coming into offer obeisance and then setting down settle to partake the kirtan. A toddler gingerly trooped behind his mother. He held on to her trailing dupatta and walked behind her, watching his mother at each step and tentatively repeating the drill.

Soon the hall was filled to capacity. Apart from relatives, the MLA from their village district was also in attendance. A melee ensued as soon as he entered and the music of the *shabad kirtan* got lost with the shuffling feet inconsiderately moving in and out. Their leader made no effort to engage with the proceedings and after a brief obeisance installed himself on a chair in the garden outside. His brigade of young boys in dazzling white kurta pyjamas, now milled around him. His enormous paunch could not be missed and with his indigo turban, he towered above all. The focus of the function had shifted and a little crowd milled around him.

Nanaki and Beeji listened in. As she looked around, her gaze travelled outside through the window and was arrested by the sight of Yadwinder. Was it him? She thought it could be a case of skewed perception on account of her expecting him. She looked again. Indeed...there he stood in the lawn, talking to Karanveer. Next to them stood a tall lady leaning on him tad too close. Nanaki's first instinct was to just flee. How many hours had she spent missing him, thinking about him and how many days had she felt befuddled at his silence. How sorely she had wanted to see him and all that she had encountered was a wall—a blank wall. And there he was today—suddenly, without warning. Seven years is a long time and she could see his transition from an awkward teenager to a man. Some inches certainly added and his lean teenage body filled out, giving him a well-built frame. A pale-yellow turban and his abundant beard rolled around a strong jaw gave him a handsome profile, a white shirt and blue jeans casually rolled till his shins, his feet bare. There was an air of assurance about him. Now they were having a hearty laugh on what was perhaps a joke. The lady threw her head back and then very briefly brushed it against his shoulder.

The *bhaiji* circulated within the sangat, distributing *parsad*. Nanaki shut her eyes, trying to compose herself. Beeji nudged her when the *bhaiji* stood there, waiting with a blob of *parsad*. Nanaki started and quickly advanced her cupped hands to receive her share.

With the ceremony over, people got up and stood in small groups, catching up. Some women got up and walked to the backyard of the house where the langar was served. The sombre air of the religious ceremony transformed into a celebratory one. Some outstation guests made an early exit to be able to reach their destinations in good time. A buffet in silver stoves was catered by Ambrosia. Liveried waiters manned the counters where the customary langar food was laid. Nanaki could barely swallow a bite. Leaving Beeji with her plate, she made a rushed exit. As she cut through the backyard and crossed the lobby area, she suddenly came face to face with Yadwinder. The lady in a bright-pink suit was with him. Almost as tall as him. On her wrist a clunky watch shone. Her painted toes were visible through her patent leather peep toes.

'Hiii… Nanaki…isn't that you?' There was an effortless informality in Yadwinder's greeting.

Nanaki already felt easy even though her cheeks were flushed.

'How have you been…such a looong time,' he drawled on with a new twang that revealed an American stint.

They stood there for some time, catching-up.

'You were always the arty type, Nanaki. I am so glad you are doing what you really wanted to.'

Yadwinder had a lot to tell. His university in Pennsylvania, his Computer Science programme and his part-time job at a motorbike store. He was here for his annual visit and was due to return in a fortnight. Nanaki could not bring herself to say much. The lady betrayed some curiousity and looked keen to catch every snatch of conversation that passed between them. She hid her eyes behind oversized luxury shades. Peroxide bangs fell on her forehead; her bleached cheeks were gleaming in the afternoon sun. With a quick wave and a promise to catch-up, Nanaki shot through the gate towards her house.

She raced to her room and bolted the door. It was a terribly sultry day. By now she felt suffocated in her starched kurta and it seemed to bite into her skin. She pulled it out from over her head and threw it along with her undershirt and dupatta in a heap on the floor. She then collapsed on the bed, naked and burst into tears.

What was that? Is that it? You prepare for love for a lifetime and when you come face to face with it, you are as unschooled as a child. Nanaki just felt like a fool. For years, she had meditated about him, thought about him so long, so much that he was a familiar longing. In fact the way she had carried this expectation in her heart, she had barred any other feeling from taking root. For this? Something was amiss. What was it? His cool certainty. Yeah, though that had initially made her feel easy, now it tormented her. Why was he so confident? He talked so well. So well about the banal, the goings-on. Too well. The way he had called her the 'arty type.' In an impersonal way. Like you say it for someone distant. Casual acquaintances. People you don't know too well. As if he had nothing much to do with her. Like she existed somewhere on the margins. And like it was a nice thing to say. There was not a hint of vulnerability. But then, it was all her own doing. It was she who had given it more than its share. But then love does make perception skewed. Blights your ability to be judicious. You can never take things for what they are. So here she was. She had held on to a litany of questions for him, but they all became irrelevant in a stroke. They were the little records of her accrued angst and it was no longer relevant. She was in it alone and had been alone, so those questions were no longer meant for him. Is this all there was to it? The brutality of being jolted into this stark disillusionment. Is it how it always ends? This was it?

And then she thought to herself that if it was a cruel insight, it was also a moment of revelation. She no longer felt her life hostage to that unseen power she had allowed over herself for so long. She was alright at this moment for having seen it with so much clarity. Like an ancient misunderstanding had been cleared. A sediment added to her life.

𝕊𝕆

It was October. The spirit, harried by the monotony of long summers came alive. The cool air became progressively animated by the evenings when it carried assorted sounds of the several Ram Leelas sprung all over the city. The nine sacred days of ritualistic fasting, Navaratra, rounded off with a theatrical performance at night had its own magic. Not that Nanaki was into fasting, but the spirit of this festivity almost always caught her. The countdown to the biggest and grandest festival of them all, Diwali had begun. On days like these, she often thought about how important festivals were. While they ushered in an urge to ring in the new, they were remarkable in that they also were vastly reassuring. She thought that one understands this as one grows old and has left many such trails behind, but festivals were a great time to think of regeneration, renewal, change and initiative. Days were beginning to get short and by the time she would return home, the day would practically be over.

The Chandigarh Arts College was set up post Partition to fill the gap created by the Arts College, now in Lahore. The stone slab at the entrance of the college attested to that. It was one of those scores of institutions which needed to be set up this side after Partition. Chandigarh itself was established because the original capital of erstwhile United Punjab went to Pakistan. Chandigarh was made to order, a new entity to fill the loss of the old Lahore. It was perhaps the disenchantment with the old order, the mindset that had caused the devastation of Partition that was responsible for the contempt that was felt for tradition at that time that possibly led to commissioning of the design of a new capital. After all, they could have settled for Amritsar, which made for a good case. Lahore's twin, *sifti da ghar*, its unequivocal importance as a centre of pilgrimage, its wonderful food culture, its bustling commerce—it had a lot to recommend itself. Or for the more business oriented, it could have been Ludhiana—Manchester of the East, Industrial hub and fertile soil—a great choice. But after the holocaust—like emptiness, Punjab perhaps needed to start afresh—it needed a city without memory. Perhaps what was needed was a place without the curse of debasement that had become palpable in every street, every gali and koocha of Punjab. There was a dire need to escape the reminders of the past.

An alphabet of brutal violence let loose in the streets that had created twins: victims and perpetrators. Now one, now the other. One becoming the other. One blaming the other. The other blaming the one. The real perpetrator: Who will decide? OK, these lines will decide. These lines drawn on the negotiation table. Red here. Blue there. Ah! Looks neat! OK...decided. Get me a pastry knife. Will do the honours. OK. Heads joined over a map of the subcontinent. Overhead lamp throwing light. Tongues jutting out. Scratching heads. Call the experts. Cartographer: Cartographers to the Royal Queen. Since 1852. Shipped in. He usually prefers Staedtler brand drafting pencils, usually light to medium grade, 2B, HB, 4B, they are easily erased even though they use ink. Other supplies: ruler, T-square, compass, stencils

for drafting and design, two nos. masking tape, pen knife/
razor, soft brush, lint free cloth, erasing shield, drawing boards
and thumb tacks. Cartographer, Geographer, Political scientist:
Listen to them, they are experts, they make sense. Then there
are politicians. Everybody quiet, listen to them. Draw as they
say. It's all already in their heads. Just use a Staedtler. Now. Bit
of an inconvenience. Now move. Ummm…waters are messy. This
doesn't cut as clean. Inconvenience regretted. Party in capital
to continue. Bash on regardless. Retinue. Movement. Lots of
movement amidst celebration. Little upheavals expected. Along
the way. Small price. Paltry. Nothing in front of nation. C'mon.
Small price to pay. Miniscule. Fair enough. Nation calls for
sacrifice. Blood. It's not easy. It's never easy.

And then what was needed was a fresh start, a place without
history. More maps, more blueprints. A place that would not
keep throwing up reminders of violence that seeped into the
crevices of the old towns of Punjab, a place that would be far
removed from the galis and koochas, away from retribution,
loss, a place that could be made afresh. A new capital, without
any memory of bloodshed, whose recognition would not be
tinged with betrayal but would be drawn to the last detail on
a drawing board in the sanitized confines of a studio. What
solace—to take a piece of land onto a drawing board and cut
it into neat little pockets, all accomplished in an aloof space,
what they had left behind was the division drawn in blood.
And when the humungous project of institution building was
getting more and more nationalized in the nascent independent
India, here was Le Corbusier, a Swiss French architect flown
in to design the capital of New Punjab. It was easier to accept
alien designs on your existence than deal with old pain over

and over again. The scabs looked crusty but would take a while to heal deep down. They still oozed blood if touched.

ॐ

There were days Nanaki liked to visit the tea place located near the rear parking of the college. It was really a wild, neglected patch that wasn't in any reckoning, neither the malis nor the safai karamcharis spent any time here. Buttressed against the wall of the institution that overlooked the main road was the thatched tea shack that the students referred to as Karmo's canteen. Karmo was, by now, part of the college architecture. The students could not imagine the college without her. There was another fancier outlet selling coffee, sandwiches and other knick-knacks and it was all well, but there were times when all one needed was Karmo's tea and nothing else. Especially if one had had a gruelling day. Like today, when Nanaki spent the better part of the morning putting together a presentation for an upcoming meeting where they would be deliberating upon details of the new artists for the art gallery.

Karmo had collected discarded RCC slabs from a nearby construction site and joined them to make two 'benches.' She covered these with an old vinyl poster that had hung for months on the auditorium wall during the college students union's elections last month. They were about to dump it when she had carried it here. These made for cool counters—comfortable to sit, to work on and also at times to lie down for a siesta. They were easy to clean too. No fuss. The stall had 'walls' of old gunny sacks, upon which she sprinkled water in the summer months, so a cool draught circulated inside. On the far end was a glossy poster of a middle-aged man, her Guru, in a blingy sleeveless costume, his hand and smile in a pose of frozen benediction, seated on an elaborate chair flanked by a plaster-of-Paris peacock. While this picture occupied pride of place, it was flanked by small pictures of Hindu deities cut from old calendars, a glass-mounted golden image of Guru Nanak with a string of miniscule neon lights on the frame. These were kept in a wooden frame that hung on the wall. A half-burnt incense stick had steadily accumulated into a tiny ashen mountain at the base of the frame. A garland of plastic flowers festooned her chosen pantheon. An expansive canopy of an old gulmohar shaded her little shack—in the blazing summer months when the students proceeded to their homes. The tree would be ablaze with bunches of scarlet blossoms, compensating for the dreariness of the season. Nanaki settled on one of the several smooth rocks that dotted the area. She took out her iPad from her leather satchel and had barely begun when Karmo came and stood next to her.

As usual, she was dressed in a bright synthetic suit, with her hair oiled and tied in a bun. She always kept her dupatta knotted at the back, which invariably made Nanaki think of her as emerging out of a combat situation. She would use liberal doses of talc that would be prominent on her dark neck. By evening little tributaries of sweat criss-crossed the white talc all over the valleys and peaks of her body. Her face would look patchy, owing to the liberal dabs of cheap foundation and her lips mostly painted a deep maroon. Two front teeth prominently jutting out, perennially digging into her lower lip. Her eyebrows slightly arched at the centre of her forehead, made two prominent frown lines. She would perpetually be in white Rexine sneakers.

'*Chaa pilawan* Nanaki ji—Tea for you?'

Nanaki nodded.

She always found this tea business distracting. She would compulsively begin to notice Karmo's movements. Karmo pulled out a well-scrubbed tea pan from under the heap of freshly washed utensils stacked in a corner. She put it on the stove and as the water bubbled, plucked two leaves of tulsi from a little plant at the entrance. With deft movements, she then tossed in tea leaves from an old plastic container that had become scratchy and opaque with use. And then while simultaneously having a conversation with Nanaki, with a ladle, she would take some milk from the big patila and swirl it into the by now boiling water. Despite repeated remonstrations from Nanaki to go easy on the milk, she would not be satisfied till the tea was of a certain milky consistency. The malaise had something to do with the malai culture of Punjab.

More milk=more love, as simple as that.

Karmo also had a special talent with singing. Her harmonium wrapped in an old bed sheet was carefully kept on one platform in the far end of the canteen. She had learnt to play from the *bhaiji* of her village gurudwara. She had learnt two *shabads* to begin with 'Mithh bolna ji' and 'Lal rang tis ko laga'. The harmonium was the first of her articles loaded in the cart that was to take her other bridal stuff to her new address. It was a companion that somewhat assuaged her newly married angst. Whenever she would miss home, she would pull out the instrument, play with her hennaed hands and feel better. Life was not the same now. She had carried it to her tenement in Manimajra. It had also grown old with her and seemed to hold out an assurance. So on days when she was inordinately happy or sad, she would take out her harmonium and play. She had added quite a few folk songs to her repertoire and the young, in-love students would ask her for a repeat over and over again.

∾

On occasions Karmo liked to observe the goings-on of the painting classes from the tall windows facing the rear end of the college. The view through the grimy windows was indistinct and sometimes totally blocked off by old student election stickers still stuck on them. Even if they were removed, they left stubborn glutinous marks. If she got done with her work for a while and had some time before getting another order for tea, she would peer inside the studio. Once when Neil Sengupta stood facing the class making a point about graphite pencils, he suddenly noticed two eyes fixed on the window, peering in from the outside. He was disconcerted for a bit but soon realized it was Karmo. Next time he went out to have tea, he asked her if she would be interested in modelling for the class.

The college was perennially broke on the account of paying for these peripherals, so there was always a need for ad hoc arrangements. The *mali* had done it for donkey's years but since his retirement last year, they needed a replacement. So Karmo took it on. She would be asked to climb a low wooden platform in the hall and hold an expression for a class. Students would shuffle their gaze quickly, back and forth from her to their easels to get the details. She felt hugely self-conscious to begin with, with two dozen eager eyes gazing at her, taking in her every detail, warts and all, her cheeks flushed and her folded leg trembling involuntarily. She would make an extra effort to cover her front teeth by pulling the lower lip over them. This and her self-consciousness would tire her. But a few sessions down and she became used to the attention. And then, also she had never known such leisure. This sitting idle had its benefits. She realized she would find solution to many a pending question. She would make little budgeting of her savings in her head. Her mind would move from matters of the canteen to Pali's problem. At times, she would be so overcome with wretchedness that she would have to deliberately snap out of her thoughts and begin to inaudibly recite the *mool mantar*.[3] However, all in all, she began to look forward to this. Like zero hour. At the end of what was a fortnight or twenty days of sitting, she was overwhelmed, looking at a studio full of her portraits.

§

Nanaki dug into her iPad. She was going over an extensive report listing the credentials of artists who were in the reckoning for space in the art gallery. She was part of a committee constituted to finalize the names of the two artists. Other members were the Director of the college—Dr Iqbal Chaudhuri, a representative of the Panjab University, a representative of the administration, she and Neil Sengupta from the college. She had been made to understand through feelers from various quarters that she and Sengupta were mere stamps, the real decision eventually rested with the other three senior members. They had had their first meeting in the morning and the Director had emailed them a detailed description of the works of two shortlisted artists. After

---

[3]The opening twelve words of the Guru Granth Sahib. A composition by Guru Nanak, it succinctly sums up the core ideas of the Granth.

ploughing through what was extensive officialese, she was able to extract the details. Bureaucracy was particularly adept at the art of obfuscating information, she thought: with what skill the two grains were hidden in a mound of chaff. One could just give up midway. Most people did.

Nanaki was curious to see what had worked for these two, she was familiar with Mazhar Khan, of course everybody knew Mazhar Khan, but she was at a complete loss about the other name. The panel had to finalize two artists. Mazhar Khan, was the fairly well-known one, whose works had recently been auctioned through a firm in Zurich. He had been the critics' darling: his *Tree of Life* series had opened to stupendous reception few months ago. He had exhibited in most prominent art capitals including New York and Paris. Though for Nanaki these facts were not and never enough to clinch the worth of an artist, but her view of Mazhar Khan's work was more or less favourable. Combining tradition and experimentation in a good measure, he had both the stature and the oeuvre to make it into the portals of the gallery. The other name was that of an artist called Gurkanwal Kaur. Now here Nanaki drew a blank. She could not place her. She googled the name and the engine threw up a few links. Piecing together the information she found that Gurkanwal was a Chandigarh-based artist who had exhibited her works in the recent past, a couple of times in quick succession at the Government Art Gallery. That event seemingly got considerable media attention and pictures of the inaugural lamp-lighting ceremony were splashed about in various local dailies. In attendance were prominent politicos and bureaucrats. The revenue minister was prominent in his trademark saffron turban and the Chief Minister had himself inaugurated two of her exhibitions. Nanaki sat up and began fiddling with the cuboid amethyst in her gold chain. Surely one had to know more about her work. Another random link to a fortnight glossy and she discovered her to be the wife of the Chief Secretary, Punjab. Here they were, in a vanity shoot, decked up in finery and posing in a heavily draped Victorian drawing room. Two dachshunds, shampooed and combed took position on the floor, reflecting the gleaming conceit of the masters in full measure. The outline of a well-stocked bar was zoomed out at the far end in the background. Why were they posing like that? There was a surfeit of images like that in half a dozen lifestyle magazines that were celebrating the rich and the powerful, just for being that, rich and powerful. Brown sahibs. They did have a capacity to be so conceited and indifferent, especially when, for some of them, new structures of power combined with old feudal privilege yielded an obnoxious sense of entitlement.

The next meeting was a month from then and they would be calling both artists for a presentation before the panel. She better read up on their credentials while there was time. Other than that, before leaving for a meeting with the VC, Prof. Iqbal Chaudhuri had requested Nanaki to see in his lieu, one Himmat Singh Kaleka, an architect from Mumbai, who was expected in the afternoon.

It was already late. Quarter past five. The office and teaching staff had either left or were leaving the premises. There was still no sign of this Kaleka. She was mildly irritated for having been held up for an inane reason like that. Being preoccupied with the agenda of the meeting, she had paid little attention to the Director's mention of the visitor and had not even bothered to ask for his mobile number. Now she felt she should have asked. There was no way she could bother the Director at this point. He must be in the middle of the VC meeting. Anyway, she decided to stick around Karmo's canteen and watch out.

It was getting breezy and she felt a raindrop on her cheek. At first she brushed it aside, but then another one on her forehead and then another on her head landed in quick succession. It had started raining. She moved for shelter in the corridor of the, by now, deserted college. When she looked through the brick jali lining the entrance wall, she realized how dark it had become all of a sudden with thick clouds completely eclipsing whatever trace of faint sun there was in the sky. The grove of eucalyptus trees around Karmo's canteen let out a spiky odour that merged with the wet earth. The farther end of the ground with discarded remains of the sculpture class: a half-made bust of granite, discarded stone animals, debris of chipped sandstone were inundated in a gushing stream in no time. Thick raindrops were spattering on the lotus pond. Rain had now begun to fall in torrents, washing the dust off the red brick building as it swooshed down the walls in little riverines. It had suddenly become dark. As she looked out, a strong beam of a sodium headlamp glistened through the rain into the college gate. Who was this? Must be one of the several youngsters who flock the *geri* route in the evenings—the stretch of road linking the poshest pockets of the city. This was a popular pastime with young people taking a ride down the avenue with no defined purpose but to soak in the atmosphere. Some also ventured out to parade their locomotives: luxury bikes and open jeeps, pimped-up rides fitted with the total wherewithal for playing high-decibel Punjabi music. Some were out stalking and some desperate to hook up. At its best it was a mating ritual, at worst, a harassment ploy. Nanaki would often imagine the youngsters like dandy peacocks, desperate to display their plumage for attention. Boys from smaller towns here for college got instant makeovers that included hairstyle of the latest fashion, branded clothes from one of the half-a-dozen bargain stores and designer sunglasses, like new-age totems they could not imagine life without. All this had no truck whatsoever with the conditions back home, their travails as marginal farmers, their caste-ridden daily struggles, the patriarchal limits on the daily existence of the women. But, really, if you scratched the surface, the colleges were little sanctuaries mirroring the larger social politics, their student politics as ossified and as parochial as the regional politics. Somehow when it came to that, things seem to settle into the old patriarchal, feudal structures with capitalistic flourishes only outwardly changing appearances. In fact, all the more misleading—with modernity just limited to a seductive idea of affluence.

However, the bike stopped, the headlights were first put on low beam and then completely switched off. Through the rain she could see a silhouette of a tall, turbaned figure of a solitary rider alighting from the bike. He walked in quick strides towards the college entrance. He tentatively entered the foyer and there came face to face with Nanaki, waiting for him. He was slightly surprised to be met with a 'guide' when he was expecting to see a locked building owing to his inordinate delay.

'Could I know the way to the Director's office? Would he, by any chance be available at this time?'

'That is straight and then to your right, but he's not there. Mr Kaleka?'

'Yes. Oh thought so too.'

She extended her hand. 'Nanaki Singh. I teach here, I was expecting you, but it started pouring and I kind of understood that you must be held up.'

'Oh... I am sorry for keeping you waiting in this terrible weather. I am riding down from Patiala and my bike got a snag short of Rajpura. It was tough to get it going.' Despite the obvious hassle it must have been, he betrayed little irritation.

'That's alright, I can actually collect the documents you were meant to hand over to Prof. Chaudhuri,' Nanaki half listened to his explanation.

He set his leather satchel on a wooden bench, and rummaging his way through the documents, took out a wad of papers, transferred them into a clear bag and handed it over to Nanaki. She found his dexterous hands moving with a rhythm very absorbing, his earnest eyes looking for the right papers from amongst a thick sheaf.

'Here, let me mark it.'

He peeled off a blank white sticker from a sheet and with a thick marker inscribed: Prof. Iqbal Chaudhuri.

His handwriting came off forthright and bold.

He wore a biker jacket and olive cargoes. His navy turban appeared patchy with rain water. His beard was streaked with a few grey strands. Given his extraordinarily tall frame, there was a slight stoop in his upper body. His eyes, glinting from under particularly thick eyebrows, set in a tanned face, were very clear under the rimless glasses.

'So I'll take your leave.'

'Would you like a cup of tea? We have a canteen here—I can ask,' said Nanaki, extending a common college courtesy.

'Actually tea is a welcome thought. It has been such a tiresome journey and a hot cuppa would be just the thing before heading back home on another long ride. In this weather Patiala would easily take one and a half hours,' he said.

Karmo was inordinately quick, perhaps because she was almost closing shop when Nanaki detained her with the unexpected request. Mostly she ran out of milk by the end of the day but today, on the contrary, she had surplus. She quickly brought the tea and hastily asked Nanaki to be excused. She needed to catch the 5.45 bus, the last of the day to Manimajra, otherwise she would have to shell out a bomb for an auto. Upon Nanaki's nod, she clutched a polythene bag with her possessions and made a dash for the bus stop outside.

The two were left sitting under the little thatch extension of Karmo's canteen, sipping the hot ginger tea. Nanaki was suddenly struck by the fact that the college was totally empty by now.

Himmat Singh Kaleka belonged to Patiala and was a product of the Sir JJ College of Architecture in Mumbai. He now worked for a firm where he had risen to become a partner and had got in touch with Prof. Chaudhuri about leads for original artwork from Punjab, to be used for an upcoming project, a birding resort in Kasauli. He was staying put in Patiala for a few months to ensure the smooth completion of the project. He spoke slowly as if linking words in his mind, as if wrenching his conscious speech from other preoccupations. He was nothing like the glib professionals she was used to meeting, smooth talking their way through presentations, using statistics for effective marketing. If architecture was a discipline that called for a blend of art and science in equal measure, it looked like he leaned more towards art.

The rain had by now, inundated the kutcha path around the canteen. It gushed down the edges of the college elevation, noisy like a waterfall. The black stone sculptures dotting the outer lawns of the college looked like stoic men standing there unaffected, unflinching in the rain. The lotus pond had clearly overflown by now. From far the two silhouettes were visible, deepening their acquaintance. Nanaki did not feel he was sizing her up in ways you feel when meeting someone for the first time. They just sat there, and more time than they realized, had elapsed. The evening had not been ostensibly remarkable in any way and yet Nanaki found herself dwelling on the contents later.

As she lay in her bed she searched for 'Himmat Singh Kaleka' on FB, and in an instant his profile loaded. There he was with a group of people, slightly stooped, not very comfortable looking into the camera. He was tagged in the picture. Clearly, he wasn't much of a social-networking person. His status had been last updated three months ago.

As she was slipping under the razai, she could not suppress an urge to look at the envelope with his handwriting. Innocuous. Still.

ஃ

The following Sunday, Subedar Joginder Singh landed early in the morning. He had cycled all the way from Mohali. His complexion was flushed with the exercise and he was slightly out of breath as he entered. He handed over a cloth bag to Beeji, who with her usual efficiency emptied the contents on the kitchen counter. Out tumbled a generous share of vegetables—fresh ladyfingers with soft down visible on them, gourds, tomatoes, still not ripe. There was an old Coke bottle filled with home-made lassi. Produce from his kitchen garden. Transferring the vegetables into a wicker basket, Beeji filled the cloth bag with two packets of their farm rice and kept it on the lobby table for the subedar to carry home. When they sat down on the chairs set out in the sunny back verandah, he took out a white cloth roll from the carrier of his cycle. He set it on the centre table and patted it flat, running his wrinkled hands to even out the creases. He gingerly took out a cardboard folio.

'Been meaning to show these to you for almost a month now Beebaji. A *banda,* when done with such a job needs to see it through another's eyes.' Joginder addressed Nanaki.

He gingerly spread out a roll of black silk. Two cranes embroidered with cream silk threads, their elongated necks traced with a deft flourish. The village pond loomed in the backdrop and the composition was intricately filled with bunches of mustard yellow blossoms. He had improvised the classic Japanese stitch he had closely observed over the years and blended it with his mother's pet phulkari darn to create a composition with a novel appeal. Nanaki's heart skipped a beat. In a flash of insight she understood the value of what she was looking at. Just because art is sometimes served to us in quotidian surroundings by people who are unschooled, and just because they lack that astuteness that we have come to associate with art, does not take away from their genius. It was clear to her now. She had been struggling with the daunting task of picking a good name for the gallery list—Joginder Singh gloriously fitted the bill. She had not seen such felicity in local art for a while now.

ɛɔ

It being an extended Dusshera weekend, she decided to put it to good use. The same evening she was at Joginder Singh's house. When he opened the door in his discoloured kurta pyjama,

Nanaki felt the man had aged many years since morning, his silver hair tied in a loose ponytail.

'Beebaji, *langh aao*—walk right in.'

Nanaki adjusted her bulky DSLR and asked Joginder if she could photograph the embroideries right away. He offered to make her tea before that. He pottered around in the kitchen and emerged with two cups of tea. It looked weak and hardly the kind Nanaki would care for but, she took a sip, the rough grains of the chipped cup digging into her lips. It seemed like the stale flavours of army ration stored in the dank formica cupboard of his kitchen leeched into every item lying there. Just like the last time. His hands were unsteady and with some effort he ripped open a new packet of glucose biscuits—these likewise had a spicy soapy flavour. It seemed Joginder had got used to it and hardly noticed it. They proceeded to the gallery. In between was Joginder's bedroom and Nanaki could not help stealing a glance. The room was in disarray and as she crossed it, she could see a pile of unwashed clothes lying on the floor. There were old newspapers and unwashed dishes accumulated in a corner. A pair of dentures was visible, dipped in a glass of water on the side table.

Loneliness is an address and if you are also old, it comes with a curious smell.

She followed him into the gallery. He switched on the bulb and the dark space lit up. Details of the silk embroideries leapt at her as she observed them up close once again. She did not have a shred of doubt about their innate value at this moment. She was filled with a singular conviction: She had to document Joginder's art and ensure it found space in the art gallery. By the end of her visit she had countless good shots of the embroideries. She had put the non-professional lighting and home setting to good use in capturing the images. She had her task cut out for her and a surge of energy told her she was ready to take it on. She was certain the Director would see her point.

ℰꝋ

Nanaki had promised Nanaji she would drive them to Chandimandir Cantonment for a party in the evening at the Chief of Staff General Venkatesh's house. If not for Nanaki's help, the octogenarian couple would not be able to make it. Chandimandir was a good thirteen kms and Nanaji had lately become unsure of his night driving, so her help was reassuring. Nanaki had a different problem. She could never plan her wardrobe in advance. She would pull out whatever she was in the mood for, on the given day, and then accessorize it spontaneously. Today, she settled for her green kalamkari silk kurta and salwar. She paired it with the dressy jade earrings that her father had gifted her mother. He had picked them from Yangon when he went there once for The International Mathematics Society Congress. She slipped on her gold thread jutties and let her hair loose. On special days she would hold back a fringe of hair with her little gold comb. Beeji, too, looked resplendent in her Kashmiri silk saree—its deep maroon offset by fine-needled paisleys running the entire length of the border. She teamed the saree with a garnet string and studs and her grey hair tied in a neat bun. Even little effort at dressing up showed up on her. Nanaji, however, looked tired today: the folds of his teal turban looked somewhat loose. He had had a long day and then stubbornly had also gone for a game of 9 holes. Nanaki suddenly saw them in a different light. They looked old now. Older than they had ever looked.

Nanaki pulled up the Thar in the earmarked parking outside the appointment house 'The Abbot.' A soldier from military police stood there with a lighted baton, directing cars into the parking area. The skill with which Nanaki pulled the vehicle into the designated spot suddenly reminded Beeji of her own mother riding the tonga that fateful morning when they left Okara for good. Nanaki often reminded Beeji of her mother; there would be instant flashes of recognition through some synchronicity.

The entrance of the dimly lit bungalow was lined with earthen lamps that flickered in the evening breeze. Gen. and Mrs Venkatesh received them and the conversation at the entrance went on for quite some time. The general had served under Nanaji way back in the early '80s when he was on his last leg appointment at the Badami Bagh cantonment in Srinagar. Mrs Venkatesh had, at that time, been a young bride who looked upto Beeji for guidance. Before long they were recounting a funny, old incident about a young Major Nanaji getting drunk at one of the parties, dancing with the CO's wife, mistaking her for Beeji. Could have led him into huge trouble, but he was tipped off just in time by a brother officer. At first Nanaji would not believe it because he recognized that saree but then cantonments were small places and often times the wives ended up with identical sarees from the AWWA outlet. All doubt was laid to rest when his friend presented Beeji right there on the dancing floor as proof.

℘

The bar was flowing and a regimental band was in attendance. Beeji was instantly at home and found two old acquaintances and before long was deep in conversation with them. Liveried waiters circulated snacks in the familiar drill: by now it was all a part of the landscape.

Just then a little commotion was heard at the entrance. Gen. and Mrs Venkatesh moved to the entrance once again. Apparently there was an 'important' guest. But the prime suspect, the army commander was already in attendance. There was a little circle perpetually milling around him—like a swarm of bees. Nanaji looked at the scene with contempt—'it's supposed to be courtesy, not sycophancy.' *Look at the Chief Engineer himself grovelling, what can be said about the rest?* Nanaji shook his head. But looking towards the gate again—who could this be? A gleaming white Ambassador with a red beacon pulled up right upto the door of the house. A burly, turbaned bodyguard in civvies promptly emerged from the front seat of the car and held the door for the couple. Power was written all over them. The man, in a grey suit and blue turban, and the woman, in a green crepe salwar kameez, greeted the General and mingled with the crowd. The woman carried a rather oversized bag and wore oversized diamonds that gleamed on her hands and ears. Col. Dutta pointed out 'The Chief Secretary, Punjab, Mr Adeshpratap Singh Dhillon and Mrs.'

Nanaki went and occupied a seat close to Beeji. Mrs Baljeet and Mrs Gurdarshan went on and on about this cloth shop and that, about their children and children's children, about this cake recipe and that chicken masala. Nanaki felt she had no contribution to make to their fairly advanced and informed dialogue. That is when Mrs Dhillon, the fashionably late, sparkling Mrs Dhillon sought permission to take a seat in their group. Beeji smilingly encouraged her to join them— 'Come, come.'

Gurkanwal Dhillon, said 'hi' with an awkwardness of having to introduce herself. Such occasions were very rare in the civil side.

By and by the ice melted and soon, the ladies had included her in the gup-shup, and she seemed to be doing pretty well. Before long she had discovered two ladies who had gone to her school—Tara Hall, Simla. So the kinship got thicker. She was soon emerging as that well-informed 'civilian' who knew of all the happening cafes, restaurants and boutiques of the city, someone who could tip off the cantonment bound army wives—where to get a stylish suit tailored, where to get the authentic jutti, where to pick up exotic varieties of palms for the mess complex. Gurkanwal had the tips. She knew the useful bits. All the hacks.

'Like this tussar kurta she is wearing,' she pointed to Nanaki, 'from Fabindia—three grand.'

Nanaki cringed.

The topic turned to embroidery on suits. She rattled off the names of two masterjis who did very fine work.

'If you want more regular and cheaper varieties, there is a chap in Pallika Bazaar in Sector 19 who will replicate any design you give him at half the cost. Why I had to get some work done when my kaarigar suddenly fell sick and this guy did a fantastic job of filling up the incomplete patches. I just throw my odds and ends with him and he delivers.'

A collective gasp went out from the ladies' end. They all wanted his address.

She was clearly enjoying the attention when a waiter tripped over somebody's big leather bag and fell on the bare ground with a tall mojito flying briefly in the air before landing precariously on Gurkanwal's crepe salwar. All hell broke loose.

She directed a volley of insults at the poor, apologetic man. He just kept saying 'Sorry, sir' even though he was addressing madam. That was the authority she exuded. The officer concerned explained he was from the hills and new at the job. But she would have none of it.

'I don't care. You should have taken care. At least train them properly before getting them in a party...' she kept repeating, underlining how upset she was and that she would not be talked out of taking offence.

'No...no...no,' she kept repeating.

Something about her was familiar, thought Nanaki. Something. Something she could not immediately pin point.

Then it struck her like lightning.

Gurkanwal—embroidery. Boy oh boy, no, no no no!

Was it her? The candidate for the gallery space. Maybe it is a mistake. No, not a mistake. Yes of course, Chief Secretary's wife, Gurkanwal and her 'knowledge' of embroidery. Could it be, could it be that the substandard stuff she had 'curated' overnight for two exhibitions in quick succession were not even her work? Could very well be. Nanaki drove back from the cantonment that evening feeling sick in the gut.

ॐ

The following evening Nanaki drifted into the neighbourhood gurudwara. She was in her tees and lowers, taking a walk when on an impulse she took a detour into the gurudwara lane. Not many people here on a cold winter weekday evening. This is how she liked it best: not very crowded and when she had the luxury of time to sit and listen to Gurbani. There was no hurry. It wasn't very late. She pulled out a scarf to cover her head from amongst a pile in the basket kept at the entrance.

The effect of the exercise was still palpable in her flushed cheeks. Her heaving chest settled into regular breathing rhythm in some time. She sat there witnessing the proceedings. Her favourite part of the ritual of a gurudwara visit was definitely Gurbani music followed by the *karah parshad*. She closed her eyes, sitting there in the hall, and the strains of the gurbani enveloped her like a wave, lapping about gently and dislodging an obstructing pebble here, pushing forth a fibrous driftwood there, inundating the troughs and the whirlpools with one decisive calming wave. Sitting there, she would think of many issues. She would find solutions to long-standing matters that had plagued her for days. It was like her personal zero hour when her mind was in a state of no excitation, when one strand here and one strand there would emerge, solutions that had eluded her would materialize.

It was getting late and after *ardas*, the granthi began to prepare for the Granth Sahib to be transported to the little curtained room on the first floor of the gurudwara. From the hall, one could see the curtained glass walls of the Granth Sahib's resting place. Since the Holy Granth is deemed guru— the courtesies due to a living guru are extended to the holy book. Swathed in silks and propped up with pillows, a small procession of *sangat* bids a nightly farewell, accompanying the book in a little train to its resting abode. The chief priest hoists it on his head and as he makes his way to the room, the congregation bows to the book at each step.

It was late evening and as she came out to wear her sneakers, she was met by not a very charitable glance of another *bhaiji*. He always sat there, at the entrance, as a kind of watchman. He commented on Nanaki's scarf and advised her to come properly clad in a dupatta. She walked out in a

huff, heckles raised. Who was this man? Who was he to tell
her how she ought to be dressed? Whose rules were these?
In all honesty, Nanaki's visit to the gurudwara was her own
personal matter. It was more or less an aesthetic experience,
feeding a very personal need for which she felt she owed no
one an explanation. It was between her and the guru.

೭೧

It was on her mind all night. She had to find a way to stop
Gurkanwal's access to the ramparts of the gallery. It would
be nothing short of sacrilege to see her monstrosities rub
shoulders with the others. A woman making it to the gallery
on the basis of her husband's 'importance' was abominable
enough, but what she found even more detestable was the sheer
arrogance with which she assumed entitlement. This nepotism,
this promoting kith and kin was a culture that flowed from
top to bottom. Once they make it into the corridors of power,
they take it like a responsibility to scan their surroundings for
any relative, no matter how far flung, who needs bolstering.
The unemployed find employment, the underemployed find
better employment and the merely aesthetic hanger-ones get
prettier ways to hang-on. Like the wife in the present case. The
husband and wife have everything going for them in terms of
power and pelf, but now they want their share of glory too.
That will distinguish them. Good taste—that will catapult them
from the category of rich and powerful to rich and cultured.
They will matter more. Out to prove their civilizational mettle
to the world now. That will surely put them in a league above
the rest. Now how to buy that? The means they use to buy
themselves this distinction is as lowly as the means they use
when they come to enter the other frays. Till now art was

immune to the likes of these. But now, now they want a piece of the pie here as well—to set forth the same dynamics here as everywhere—in the colleges, universities, academies. It is one thing to be ideologically driven but quite another to be subject to the machinations of the political class to the extent that they take on the role of arbiters of taste and in the process destroy art. Nanaki would have to take it on. The Director was apparently unaware.

Next morning, she reached the college half an hour before her scheduled lecture on Indian Textiles with the Final Year students. She had decided to first see the Director and apprise him of the matter. Prof. Chaudhuri was busy dictating to his secretary when Nanaki walked in. He motioned to her with his hand to take a seat.

'Nanaki, if you don't mind, just two minutes.'

The man inspired trust. There was something about him. He wrapped his task before Nanaki had expected and turned his attention to her.

'Yes, tell me, Nanaki.'

'Two things, sir. First, here are the papers for you Mr Kaleka left with me on Saturday.' She handed over the brown envelope to him.

'Oh yes. So he met you. Got an email from his end about the same. Now the man is an architect and has a birding resort coming up in Kasauli for which he needs to source art. Nanaki, why don't you take this on? Just give him some recommendations. We don't plan to get involved in the financial aspect, all he expects is some consultancy from our end for which his firm is bearing a fee. I have no doubt you will do a good job.'

Nanaki was not prepared for this in the least. But she felt

there was no harm taking it on, after all she had been wanting
to have some art-consultancy experience.

'So this done. Nanaki, you are good for the financial health
of this college—talking of health, would you like some green
tea?'

'I don't mind, Sir.'

He rang a brass gong lying on his table. It was an exquisite
little Buddhist art piece with enamel insides and inscriptions
on the wooden handle. Nanaki's eyes then drifted to the
two gigantic *thangkas* on the wooden backdrop of Prof.
Chaudhuri's immense office. These were additions made in his
tenure and could be traced to his more-than-cursory interest
in Buddhism. His doctorate was on the philosophical basis of
Buddhist Art. His table, procured from Bhutan, was a piece
in teak with a detachable frontpiece with engraved Buddhist
motifs. It was a well-done-up space—befitting the office of the
Director of an arts college. The modernist mix of RCC slabs
and wood was appealing and somehow in harmony with the
Buddhist art pieces procured by Chaudhuri. On one wall, there
were portraits of all the preceding Director Principals since
1886. The first four were British and the rest Indian. It was
heartening to see a lone woman holding office in the years
1974–78. Mrs Resham Seth. There she was, in a handloom
saree, bespectacled and hair tied in a bun. There was something
austere but exceedingly striking about her. Nanaki always felt
a connection with this woman. Never met her, yet she felt
that her present achievements were possible only because
of the struggles Mrs Seth must have undertaken as a young
woman. Far removed in time, but a connection nevertheless.
She almost always found herself gazing at Mrs Seth's face and
receiving a surge of inspiration. Her gaze was arrested by a

muddy meandering trail on the wall. A procession of termites had struck. They seemed to be oozing out of the far end of the wall and could very well be mistaken for a streak of dirt.

Green tea duly arrived.

'Now that taken care of Sir, I have an important matter to discuss. For which I came.'

'Nanaki, listen, can you hold on till afternoon?' He suddenly got up. 'A meeting is lined up today with the Chief Secretary, Punjab and I am already running late. I should be leaving the premises now. I want to hear you out well.'

'Right, sir,' said Nanaki getting up with a start at the aborted meeting. 'I shall talk with you in the afternoon. Is post lunch three o'clock fine?'

'Suits me perfectly well, I shall see you,' he said with an amiable nod.

Nanaki delivered her lecture but something kept rankling at the back of her mind. Was it too much of a coincidence that Prof. Chaudhuri had a meeting slated with the Chief Secretary, Punjab.

She needed one of Karmo's cuppas. She sat herself down and it all started playing in her head. The very fact that Gurkanwal was in the reckoning proved that some quarters had been satisfied with her case. How involved had the Director been in giving her the push, she wondered? Whatever the case she would have to talk to him about it. In the larger picture, it was a case of dilution of aesthetic standards, the choice was indefensible and no one but they would be responsible for the damage to the reputation of the art gallery. Was this not of any concern to the Director, she wondered, either he was being naive or he was trying to help the Gurkanwal case—both scenarios were equally deplorable.

'*Ki haal hai*—How are you, Karmo?' Nanaki noticed that she was not her usual buoyant self. With a stoop, she was collecting the discarded teacups left here and there by the students. She then sat down on her haunches to scrub them at the cemented platform under a tap. She rubbed her sweaty face with the sleeve of her suit. When she turned to face her, Nanaki saw bloodshot eyes and dark circles under her sunken eyes. The usual foundation and bright lipstick were missing today. Her face looked wet and flushed as if she had just had a bout of crying.

'Nanaki madam, I was running a fever', she offered a weak explanation, trying to pooh-pooh the matter.

'*Eithe aa*—come here. Sit next to me. Are you sure you are alright—pakka?' Nanaki probed.

Karmo broke down. '*Tuhade to ki parda*—What can I hide from you)? Pali is not doing fine in the centre. They called up yesterday. Might have to take him out from there—but what do I do now? I visited the dargah of the Dahda peer for a good twenty-one Thursdays continuously. I would sit there praying hard for a solution. Some village women warned me that I had begun to look like a *kamli*, a woman possessed. But all that failed, then I did what Dera Babaji told me. You know very well I shut shop for a full two months to do seva at the dera. What more can a woman do? This *chandri lat,* cursed addiction, will take my son's life. The centre was my last hope. You are a witness to my plight. He was a happy healthy boy in the village—naturally fit and I took extra care of his diet. Did well in studies too. Why his masterji had often complimented me. He said he was no less than the jatt boys. And then he started seeing that *chandra,* good for nothing, fellow Gurjant, the jutti-maker's son. I don't know what *jadu-toona* he did, my son was never the same again. He would be restless, looking for every opportunity to take money from me. I was fed up. Saw his health declining and even my good diet of milk and eggs daily was doing him no good. Like it was all going down a dark empty well. My poor husband, may Waheguru rest him in peace, even cut from his own stomach to get him a rich diet of chicken daily. Every day on his way back from the farm, he would stop by at Lalli kasai's shop and get payia (quarter kilo) chicken or mutton. Every day for Pali. But the boy just got listless and distracted. He stopped listening to us. He would refuse to take a bath. His hair became matted and his body began to stink. His neck became grimy. It became embarrassing. People began to ask questions. It was like a spirit had begun to possess his mind and body. He would stare out of the window and refuse to move. And then he stopped going to school. One fine day, he just stopped. Days passed. I argued with him, shouted and threatened him, but it made no difference. He became a stone. He didn't even argue back. At times, he was too weak to retort. At other times, he just wasn't listening. It was scary.

'And then the army recruitment rally came to our adjoining town. My husband thought this was his chance. Probably the discipline of army will do him good. All they wanted was eighth pass. For regular combatant role, you needed tenth but for trades like cook and tailoring, eighth was acceptable. With much reluctance he got ready. Father and son set out early on the bus that day. Took the Class VIII report along with their Dalit caste certificate attested by the naib-tahsildar. Paperwork took a long time. They spent the whole day at the rally. I stood at the door all evening. They came back downcast. One big army sahib had told them what we had feared all along. He said we should worry about his life, not employment. He had failed in most physical tests and the doctor detected a sure-shot case of drug addiction—*munde nu ta lat si*. My husband just could not tolerate this. He was a peasant and worked for the Bajwas—the big sardars. Overnight he lost all interest in labour. Like the soul-numbing labour day-in-day out in the killing heat had no use. Why? Why has my son become like this? In fact, soon he could not bring himself to do any work. He just gave up, without even trying.

'I had no choice in the matter then, Nanaki madam. I thought I would do labour and run my house. But people made my life hell. As if what I was dealing within my house was not bad enough, they started talking behind my back, holding me responsible, even my own jaat biradri started shunning me in the fear that their children might end up like Pali. The bhaiyas, the migrant labourers were the only ones who talked to us then. Not that it wasn't happening to children of good families, but they had the resources and power to deal with it. Also to hush it up. And then one fine day, Pali's father did not get up from the bed. Passed away in his sleep. From there it was me and my son. I decided to leave Jaito mandi. My village, my *saura* village—where I came as a bride but left as a widow and a troubled mother. The women in our gali lined up when the *rehra* took me with all the stuff laden on it. They looked at us, hanging at their doors, some eyes looking at us, mother and son, furtively, from behind their baaris (windows), but they did not come to say bye. These people who had been in my dukh-sukh, I had given them fat shagans on births and weddings, now they shunned me like a stranger. They wanted to have nothing to do with me. That day and today—Waheguru knows I never felt like going back.

'I found out about this rehabilitation centre in Ludhiana and without wasting anytime went to a jeweller and sold my only gold possession—my valis that my father had got made from Pritam suniyar for my wedding. But this was more important—my son's life—if they could somehow help him kick the habit. What were these jewels? I left him there and moved to Chandigarh. I had a cousin working in the college here and he asked me to become a helper at the college tea shop. That is how I landed here, Nanaki madam—a *pendu* villager woman who had not stepped out of Jaito. But I worked hard and the next thing I knew was that the canteen contractor was leaving. So I jumped in and thought of getting the contract. I collected all my resources, the money I had earned, my leftover from the gold I had sold and a small loan from the kind Professor Gurdial Singh Sa'ab. I did not look back and felt he would be fine and I would bring him here. He would then run the canteen. He was alright and they discharged him once and he even gave me good company and then is when I got the Manimajra tenement. But there was a relapse. And he was out and now a relapse again. What am I to do now, Nanaki madam?

'Achha, you are *padhe-likhe log*, Nanaki madam, they show a lot of news on drugs on Punjabi channels these days. They show the police is cracking down on lot of them red-handed coming from the other side of the border. But somebody at the dera told me that actually it is the good-looking, well-dressed sidekick of the big minister himself who is doing all this? Is it true? And the news also belongs to them because the channel belongs to them. They are running videos of the entire khaandan doing charity. Why the poor Cablewala Sharma, he was beaten black and blue the other day for showing a rival news channel.'

'*Khyal rakhi, Karmo*—take care', said Nanaki. 'Let Pali continue with the treatment. These are temporary setbacks. He will come out of it.' Nanaki felt somewhat shallow saying it to her.

There was a little crowd of college students nearby. Karmo looked at them and thought of Pali. Their able, muscular bodies, primed for the purpose of their lives—what a blessing! And her poor son getting wasted by the day. His healthy body now shrivelled like a *chuhara*—a dry date. She could not bear to look at the young people.

෴

Marasi 1: You are here now. Meeting you after a long time. I think the last time was in 1947.

Marasi 2: You forgot, bai, after Lehnda Punjab we met here in 1984 also.

Marasi 1: Oh yes...now I remember. It was horrible then. We'll talk about it another day. How are things with you?

Marasi 2: There are some opportunities here now. In this era of globalijation and liberalijation, we can also eat some laddoos.

Marasi 1 (slaps him with a leather strap): Hain....ki keha— what did you say? Kamina, rascal...always speaking difficult English! Show off—fukra!

Marasi 2: If the sadr—the Chief Minister himself—does it, I am just a nacheez—a small fry. And is it not true that people follow their beloved leaders in all matters of importance? Foremost in these times is making profits. Ki mai jhoot boleya—tell me, do I lie?

Marasi 1 (completes the folk song): Koi na...bai, koi na. (Both do a little jig) Not at all. Come to think of it, what you are saying is indeed right. I hear the sand of Punjab was mined in a matter of months and now sits as silver in the coffers of the mighty. First they divided the rivers, so that Punjab of five rivers became a misnomer, kahda Punj-aab—what land of five waters? Ok, we tolerated that, but now their greed pushes them to rob the very sand of the leftover river beds. Thing is, they don't spare anything worth exploiting. Anything. Hospital, school, college, Panchayats—eat their funds too. Milk them for own benefit. Whatever can be exploited. Loot it, mutilate it.

Marasi 2: Yes, but don't get carried away. Kamle ni baneeda. Baa'hla ni sochida—don't be a fool! Don't think too much! Think about yourself. As I was saying we can get some laddoos too. After all, we also have our rights.

Marasi 1: Here everything is getting plundered and you are thinking of laddoos. Sharm kar sharm kar—have some shame! (Slaps him.)

Marasi 2: Bai, these laddoos come from the Rajasthan border and are sold at the chemist shops. I hear putting up a chemist hatti is the most thriving business in Punjab today.

Marasi 1: How come?

Marasi 2: The Gormint is extremely helpful. They do not ever raid your shop and then refer the nashedi boys, the druggies, to get their de-addiction medicines from you too. They have these centres running all over the place. There are not even proper doctors running those hell holes. They will just keep prescribing sleeping pills. Sutte raho—keep sleeping. While your house burns. Till the cramps return. Suits them fine. Win-win situation. To whom it may concern. I beg to state. Yours sincerely. Gormint and Chemist.

Marasi 1: But the Gormint is helpful.

Marasi 2: Very. To all.

Marasi 1: To all, especially to their shareeq (kin).

Marasi 2: Like this woman. Nooh rani. Daughter-in-law. Face of their party. They helped her rise. Woman power. She reached the corridors of power, all the way till Delhi. She is very efficient. You give her a party mistake and she will speak so well and hold her own so well that she will turn it around. Rectify it. Agli tip-top hai. Always immaculate! Any mistake, no problem. She will set it right.

Marasi 1: And they are helpful. Especially in their tabbar (family).

Masrasi 2: They all help each other. They are very clear on this. Even when the rival party comes to power. They help each other. In this they are all the same. Why do you think things never change no matter who sits on the chair? They help.

Marasi 1: A lot.

Marasi 2: They are helpful. They are good. Kind to each other. From the outside, they might bicker, but they are very helpful in reality. Bahut changey—very good.

Marasi 2: I heard their leader was very upset in the central command at Delhi. Kept asking them not to fight. You have to be disciplined if you want power. You are supposed to fight outside, not inside. Slight misunderstanding. I mean they were fighting each other. Otherwise very noble people.

Marasi 1: Very. Palaces and riches they have seen. They could not help the common people too much because they were unable to understand.

Marasi 2: Unable to understand what?

Marasi 1: Common problems. Hor ki—what else? Not their fault. They have no idea what it feels like: to work on minimum wages in the fields, to see your young man die of drugs, to have villages wiped out by cancer, to have your farmer father commit suicide, to have your young bright son wait endlessly

*for a government job that is auctioned off on the sly. They
don't. Not their fault. They just can't feel it. Limitations of being
rich. Vade log, vadiyan gallan—big people, big concerns. But
yes, you should see them in the vote season. Their women go
around exchanging dupattas with the likes of us to get votes.
Why, the nooh rani went swapping it with Mathri down our
gali. (Guffaws) hahaha...who can imagine?*

*Marasi 2: You can say what you like but they are helpful; this
cuts across party lines. Yes.*

*Marasi 1: Yes I agree. Ok, bai. Tata, see you. This heavy talk
gets to me. Thinking of getting a funky hairstyle like Jazzy B—
spikes and gel. Bai kamal gaanda hai—Bro sings really well.
(Breaks into a Jazzy B number, 'Jinde sun jinde sun') I like his
Canadian accent (says it in Canadian accent).*

*Marasi 2: Kya baat hai! Kaim hai, bai! You rock! (Slaps him)
I hope you are not headed to Canada?*

*Marasi 1: Who knows? They say they will make Punjab into
California in the next five years. They have been saying it for
fifteen years now. This was during the last election. Now the next
one is due in two months. I guess it's better to just end up there.
All said and done, he can't convert the jattis into mems (white
women). Sexy mems. Makhan vargiyan—smooth, like butter.*

Marasi 2 (Slaps him with a leather strap): Chup kar, shatt up!

*Marasi 1: Hor vi koi gall kar—You have nothing better to say.
Shatt up, shatt up! (Mimics him.) OK. I keep quiet. Bas? OK?
Happy?*

V

Patch Grief with Proverbs

Look close, all these flaws within you.
These, these are the flaws in your art.

She entered the Director's office with some trepidation. She knew that he had been in a long meeting with the Chief Secretary in the morning and the cynics would deem it enough to presume a larger politics at play, she still decided to discuss the matter with him. The Director gave her an effusive welcome and asked her to take a seat. He was briefing a journalist who was doing an extensive story on the 120 years of the founding of the Arts College. The lady was wrapping up and asking him to give final remarks.

'I want to say,' he said gravely, 'that we have to find the lost connect between society and art. Art is nothing if it is not organic. Excessive intellectualization on the one hand and commercialization on the other is leading us to a situation where we are manufacturing rather than recognizing art. And now, it is coming to that odious entity: art management. We are getting obsessed with managing art, like other things. Art has to flow out of people's lived experiences: mimetic in its reflection and yet prophetic in its answers; and at the same time match up to those touchstones that help us distinguish art as a valued civilizational activity.'

The twenty-something journalist furiously took notes. Prof. Chaudhuri nodded at her with a look of satisfaction at having succinctly summed up his view of art. The journalist too was visibly exulted at the meaty interview she had been able to eke out despite the man's busy schedule. She profusely thanked him and as a parting request, asked him to pose for the cameraman who had been waiting patiently on the corner chair.

The Director readily obliged. He seemed an old hand at this. He positioned his chair in such a way as to get the backdrop of the coffee-table-book-lined Sri Lankan teak side board. He was very much the suave artist in his electric-blue kurta paired with jeans. With his salt- and- pepper mop, he was the distinguished, albeit unconventional, professor. As he posed, Nanaki too looked at him with new eyes. She knew he would agree to her very valid objection. The journalist duo took leave.

'Nanaki, I am sorry to put you through this. You schedule an appointment and it invariably ends up eating into another.'

'That's alright, Sir, I didn't mind it at all. It was fun actually… to watch this. In any case I was done for the day.'

'OK before I forget, we have to get down to the Kaleka job. I received another mail from their Mumbai office and it seems they are working with a tight timeline. So we have to take it on priority. If it's OK with you I will schedule a meeting between you and Kaleka on…say the 12th, suits you?'

'Umm…let's see…Nanaki scratched her head. 'Yes, I think it works.'

'12th, then 4 p.m. is fine? By that time you are done with the lectures and studio?'

'Yes, yes, perfect.'

'OK. So one thing taken care of. Now tell me, what do you have playing on your mind?'

'Sir,' she gathered herself. 'This is to do with our nominations to the Art Gallery. Last meeting, we were given two shortlisted candidates. With Mazhar Khan, there is no problem. But with the other name, Gurkanwal Kaur, I have serious reservations.'

'And what are those, may I ask?' asked Prof. Chaudhuri, completely unfazed.

Nanaki, too felt encouraged at this show of singular patience by him. At least that is what she construed. She continued, '...There are problems with her credentials, work everything.'

'As in?' he probed further with a curiosity that was disarming in its seeming naivety.

'As in she has zero artistic sensibility and her so-called exhibits are nothing more than ripp-offs, not even done by her but by darzis and poor karigars. And, what is worse, no credit is given to them.' Nanaki said it in an involuntary burst and her heart was pounding and she was embarrassed at the surge of hot blood on her cheeks.

Now she was beginning to be irritated. This man thought nothing of all this.

'Now, now,' when he spoke she could gather a subtle hint of acrimony in his words. 'Look here, Nanaki, how I look at it, these points that you have put up are very lame.' His initial show of openness was clearly replaced by a clearly offensive counterargument. 'What you say is plain conjecture. Just saying so does not prove a thing. I might say the opposite. So? And about her work being rip-offs, well, pop art is all about that. Look at what Andy Warhol did with Campbell's soup cans or for that matter, that the most convincing point in Cultural Studies today is the undeniable fact that all art is reproduction, all imagination borrowed.'

So the devil is quoting the scripture for his purpose, she thought. His eloquence was more pronounced than usual. He could just demolish you with words. Words that resounded in spaces of privilege from the ramparts of authority. Words that got more strident and sinewy in the face of threat. 'Sir, did you not just say to the journalist lady that we ought to value organic art as opposed to manufactured art? And even if for a minute I assume what you are saying about artistic production under Cultural Studies to be true, we have to look for that one distinguished addition to material that will transform it into art. That one thought that will put a spark. Otherwise it is just that: material production. And let us not also forget it all flows from a context.'

'What I said was in a very different context. And in any case I don't feel the need to explain myself to you,' he blurted.

So that indeed was the truth. As he said these words, Nanaki knew that the Director could not possibly discuss the issue further with her. And actually this 'open' discussion was all a sham. He had already made up his mind on the matter. His answers had issued forth as if they had been revised multiple times in front of his toilet mirror. Though he had lost his cool. That certainly did not look like it was planned. He had possibly never visualized himself ever being confronted by a junior colleague. He had convinced himself, listening to the echoes of his own argument over and over again. Plus his obliging advisors, who echoed his words. He was fond of his voice. There was no possibility of another voice entering from anywhere.

'I am not totally convinced. Sir, at this position,' Nanaki thought it had to be stated bluntly.

'Think about it at length,' he said regaining his composure.

'I have already,' she blurted and felt a stark gloom closing in on her.

'OK and 12th then for your meeting with Kaleka. Let's concentrate on your first consultancy job. Good luck,' he hollered. He had blurted a nicety at this awkward moment— he was clearly not used to such situations.

'Thank you,' she made a quick exit and closed the door behind her.

A mask had just fallen.

∞

Nanaki was tired. She entered her office and slumped on the chair. There were two hours to go for the last lecture of the day. She pulled out the book of essays by Subramanayan. And then something from the side window of her room suddenly caught her eye. A sudden flurry of activity. A white, red beacon Ambassador barged its way into the college compound, apparently without making the mandatory entry in the guard register. The old JCO, Sampooran Singh, was always fastidious with chasing down errant vehicles till he had his register signed. He gave the Ambassador a good chase while the driver drove on heedless. This had caused quite a commotion in the otherwise sedate college surroundings. Sampooran Singh banged on the car window and motioned to the driver to lower the window pane. They were embroiled in a heated argument. What was worse was he had disregarded instructions to park on the designated 'Guests Parking' and drove insolently right upto the foyer. The driver, a burly fellow, climbed out of the vehicle and stood facing the guard in total defiance. The college superintendent had, by now, joined the melee and taken over. He motioned to the guard to go back to the gate. At this the driver nodded and click-opened the boot of the car. The superintendent called for the peon who was busy dusting the corridor windows to lend a hand. He dropped the grimy duster right away and wiping his hands on his old uniform pants, stood there, ready to lend a hand. A dozen frames lay in the boot of the car wrapped in old newspapers. They seem to have been just thown into the car by a similar helper at the other end. Making lots of four each, Ram Parsad carted them inside. Gurkanwal's art pieces had been duly received by the college. With all the administrative support.

ಜಾ

Friday, the 12th, was here. Nanaki had had a long day, what with one tutorial and two studios. She had some reading to do as well for a paper she was writing on Pahari miniatures. There was still time before the Kaleka meeting and she thought it was a good idea to grab a coffee and spend some time in the library of the main museum building catching-up with work. She laid her hands on an encyclopaedic volume and was poring over an illustration, when she found Kamlesh, the college peon. She started. He whispered, a tad loud to her about a visitor asking for her. The heads buried in books on adjoining tables all looked up, visibly distracted.

'Kamlesh…shhh…shh…*hauli*…not so loud,' said Nanaki, visibly flustered. Despite his whispering, he was very loud.

So Kaleka had arrived sooner than expected today. Sooner or later, never on time, this Kaleka. 'Haanji…ok ji…' he started again, ostensibly whispering to avoid disturbing people, not realizing that the whooshing whispers were drawing more attention. He was now taking the instruction of the 'Silence Please' board very seriously.

'Kamlesh, do me a favour. *Ek kamm kar.* Send him here. And in ten minutes get me two cups of tea with Good Day. biscuits'

'*Theek hai,*' he whispered once again, bringing his head close to Nanaki. Eyes wide, he sounded like a secret agent now. Nanaki motioned with her hand for him to leave. '*Tu* normal *bol*—you speak normally.' But it was lost on the poor chap. He was not sure what exactly it was that he was not doing right. Just following instructions.

Nanaki settled in the Reading Room, watching out for Kaleka. It was a good place to observe the goings-on. Today, of course it was for a reason, but Nanaki often did this for no reason at all. She would pick a sandwich and a coffee and sit on one of the green benches near the Sector 17 plaza bird fountain and just watch people. Just watch. The bird fountain there, perhaps a modernist reading of the gargoyle. Wasn't grotesque though. Rather a gentle, homely bird, a chubby mama sparrow of concrete spouting three jets of clear water. She would take out her old Moleskine from the canvas bag and from time to time take notes. This was her 'ideas notebook.' The world a big mela. And what better than to step back from this give and take for a while and become an observer. To step back and observe. The goings and the comings, the comings and goings, this moment could enclose an eternity.

There were days, she would look at people's shoes, just shoes: sneakers and kohlapuris, juttis and wedges, stilettos, flats, moccasins, Oxford schoolgirl shoes, canvas PT shoes, pencil heels, chappals, and so on and so forth, and she would think about pace. How 'better' in the world of shoes had meant better pace for the most part. Vanity and comfort too, but largely the progress was for pace. *Why are we obsessing about pace?* The worth of the nation has come to be measured in its access to bandwidth, quantum of data streaming. And what are we going to do with all the data. That can go around the world twice in a jiffy. The next moment is a tide that comes gushing, uprooting one constantly from experience. With a promise of a better one ahead, and ahead, and ahead—a never-ending chimera. And yes, here is the never-ending stream of people with stories orbiting their bodies. Living fables.

Nanaki would be besotted for many hours. She would watch like a novice, like she was in a foreign country, with fresh eyes. Like starting all over again. Like wiping clean a film of experience from eyes and starting afresh, like a child. She would then do a very Chandigarh thing—buy herself a tub of buttered popcorn and continue observing. On days she would get so late that the blue of the sky would deepen into a flush of Prussian. Poor seller boys launched neon frisbees to attract little children taking a walk with parents. The sodium pole lamps would be lit and the water of the bird fountain would become a psychedelic pink. She would continue to observe—not in a way that would make people uncomfortable but in a detached, wholesome way, like she was part of the surroundings. This was also one of the early lessons by her favourite Prof. Ramanujan at DCA, who always said that observation was the key. Nature or culture.

There was no doubt that she felt an acute anticipation for Himmat. Why and how she did not really know. She hardly knew him and yet. She wanted to be easily spotted by him before they went into the conference room. From the overhanging balcony, she saw him. He entered through the mammoth wooden entrance door, his olive turban standing out. He looked around and then asked for 'Conference Room' from the lady at the reception. Nanaki could see him from the mezzanine floor and had a strange urge to observe him for a while before calling out to him. 'Female gaze,' she chuckled. She just sat back, observing. He then took the ramp going up to the mezzanine. On the big walls buffeting the ramp, were hung two massive Buddhist frescoes. His movement became tad slow as he crossed them, took a minute to take a closer look and then stood back two feet and observed from a distance for a minute before starting again. *Bodhisattva Padampani.* He prevaricated in appreciation, but his purposefulness was unmistakable. He wore loose cargoes and a looped linen shirt and carried that same earnest look that Nanaki had noticed on their first meeting. Soon he was face to face with Nanaki. After a cursory greeting, which in any case could not be loud in the library, Nanaki led him to the conference hall on the second floor.

The room was equipped with a conference table and chairs. It had a downlighter hanging in the middle, bathing the room in a subtle yellow glow. The walls were clad in veneer and two Mughal miniatures hung there prominently. They took seats across the table.

'Mr Kaleka, last time I met you, I had no idea I was going to be dealing with your project.'

'Yeah, sometimes we have no way of knowing.'

'So I am waiting to hear all about the requirements.'

'This is a project we took up two years back,' he began in earnest. 'This is actually an extension of the Old Birders Club at Kasauli, which you know is a heritage property that was built in 1893, I think. Around that time. The project is an initiative of the club management members, mostly old-time residents. Since birding is a popular interest there, they came up with the idea of adding some facilities on the 125th year of the club. They were able to rise substantial corporate funding. After several rounds, our firm was finally selected to draw up the plans. We executed the building three months ago and then started with the furnishing part. We plan to have at least four to five wall-size art pieces to use in this space. I need recommendations for that.'

'Any preferences?'

'I can tell you what I don't want. I don't want miniature—that has been done to death. I am open to more eclectic/contemporary styles. Even the medium at this point is not a restriction. Doesn't have to be a well-known artist.'

'And what is the time frame we are working with, Mr Kaleka?'

'I should say, not more than a month's time to finalize and buy. We have to hand over the project in two. What I have with me are the plans of the building. You can take a good look at these. I am leaving this booklet with the original drawings and photographs of the site with you. What we can do is, a tour of the site sometime next week at a mutually convenient time. In fact, I wanted to ask you how does 18th next week sit with you?' He met her gaze directly at this point. His face had a disarming sincerity. The amber light from the downlighter softened his features and added that extra glint in his eyes. Against what was fundamentally a handsome tan face, his beard was held under the chin in two knots, Patiala style. His involvement in the project was complete. And his total lack of self-consciousness was appealing to Nanaki. The casually rolled sleeves of his looped shirt revealed tanned forearms sporting an old chronograph watch. He casually slung a satchel backpack over his shoulders. True to the stationery snobbery of architects, and also the only sign of conceit she ever saw in him, the Waterman in his shirt pocket was unmistakable. Otherwise there was something a bit worn out, a bit world-weary about his manner.

'Umm… Can I confirm by tomorrow?'

'Yeah sure, not a problem.'

He pulled out a booklet from his satchel and handed it over to Nanaki.

'I shall look through this.'

'Thanks, ma'am.'

'Please call me Nanaki, I prefer that.'

'By the same token, call me Himmat. Mr Kaleka sounds like an old man from my village. It's not me, at any rate. Nobody calls me that,' he joked. Nanaki saw the smile—it was a true smile.

'Himmat, OK.' She nodded. 'Point taken, *babaji*,' she said, taking a jibe at the 'old man'.

'I'll walk you to the parking. Even I am on my way out,' she said. 'So how did you come down today?'

'Oh I use my Enfield, old boy mostly.'

'Headed back to Patiala?'

'Yeah, should be back in good time if I start now.'

'And you?'

'Oh I walk it. My house is like five minutes, in the same sector. I wouldn't trade this walk for anything.'

'Can I give you a ride?' said Himmat, getting on the bike.

Without thinking, and on impulse, Nanaki nodded. 'OK. That'll be fun. Haven't done one in a long time.'

It took some effort for her to balance herself. But once the bike took off, it was easy. While she soaked it in, she found herself noticing Himmat from an interesting vantage point. He had strong arms and hands that held the handles, biker's hands, somewhat calloused, she thought. His tall torso with the olive turban lent him a subtle grace. He was not muscular in the way gymmed bodies are, but in the way bodies of hardworking, adventure-loving men are. Nanaki suddenly shook herself.

Am I noticing too much? She mused.

'All Prof. Ramanujan's fault,' she said aloud.

'What fault?' he hollered over the din of the bike. 'Did I miss a turn?'

'No,' she chuckled. 'This *is* the way.'

ɬ

Saturday evening Nanaji got back from his game of golf, looking dazed. He went straight to his room and after a wash, slipped into a kurta pyjama. He looked utterly exhausted. On the dining table, Nanaki observed that he was not his alert self and his movements were somewhat clumsy. He dropped the spoon twice before finally picking it and while he served himself, a trickle of dal flew in the air before landing on the tablecloth in two small puddles. Beeji quickly pulled out two paper napkins from the holder and dabbed it. He confessed that while playing with Col. Datta in the morning he had had a blackout at the eighth hole.

'Just for a fraction of a second and before I knew it, I was at the game again. Datta took me to the course clinic and they took my BP and heartbeat after a while. That seemed to be OK. In fact, we came back and completed the eighteen holes.'

He made attempts at underplaying the episode.

'Yet,' said Nanaki, 'we need to show to the doctor.'

'Must be exhaustion. I think I need to sleep longer at my age. This staying up late, writing for *Indian Defence Strategy* is not done, I think.'

Next Saturday saw Nanaki and Nanaji at the Neurology Dept at Command Hospital in Chandimandir. The doctor, Col. Tushar Lahiri, MD devoted a good twenty minutes first to taking notes on his history and then to asking him specific questions about the blackout. After putting together results of the MRI scan he announced that what he had suffered on the golf course was indeed a mini stroke. They were to watch out for any changes in gait, movements and balance. He immediately put Nanaji on medication and advised a review in a fortnight.

This was somewhat hard on Nanaji. He had never complained of bodily pain or discomfort and had always thought that not mentioning it would make it go away. Talking about disease makes it familiar, like an old guest who becomes so comfortable in your home that you no longer want them to stay. Merely talking about it would validate its existence and make it further entrenched in your body. Beeji, on the other hand, looked at disease in a pragmatic way. You just take it for what it is and treat it for what it is. No more, no less.

Contrary to expectation, there was a spurt in Nanaji's energy levels in the following weeks. Where earlier he had been a playing golf once a week, he started doing it twice. He was also getting up early and helping out Beeji in sundry tasks. But as they were about to write off the episode as just a one-off instance, he had another blackout in the following fortnight while locking the main gate of the house one night.

There was no escaping now. The medication for the condition had to be started in right earnest.

Nanaki realized it then that her grandparents were not going to be around forever. It came to her like a flash that they were now old and it was her turn to take charge of a lot of practical matters, including finances.

ଛଠ

Nanaki gladly took over the vegetable shopping on Wednesdays, which saw the old park of the sector convert into a mammoth open market, the kisan mandi. As early as seven in the morning, tractor trollies overflowing with seasonal vegetables would begin lining up in the open park. Gradually they would set up their individual little 'shops'. In a clearing, they would spread their wet gunny sacks, a covering for the wares. Then they would empty their produce and sit in small groups to start the business of the day. Nanaki liked to visit the mandi. She would take it as an opportunity for portraiture. These faces were very interesting—unlike the urban ones that concealed age and marks of adversity, the faces of these folk carried experience like a badge. There were the worn-out old farmers with deep furrows lining their sagged faces; there were radiant ones, flushed with good health and shiny white beards. Some of them were fighting hard battles, poor produce and circles of debts, but there was something deeply empowering about their magnanimity and laughter. Like a deep joie de vivre that could only be acquired when you were in tune with the earth. They wore cotton kurtas with chequered lungis or pyjamas. By mid-morning some of the younger lot would be sitting in the empty trailers and having a hearty breakfast of chapattis and dal or missi roti. The langar was perennially on. Nanaki always felt there was something magnanimous about them: was it their casual carelessness with the produce that they dropped in big heaps on the ground or their spontaneous camaraderie or their hearty turn of phrase? They were not cut out to do business, this was clear. Some young ones showed the enthusiasm of being out for a picnic to the city and looked at city people with aspiration. Nanaki would turn her ears to catch their language—a direct and heartfelt idiom, a quality very distinct, that set it apart from the language of the city dwellers whose professions had taken them away from land and hammered out their instinctual expression to make it staid and 'cultured', more for hiding than expressing. When she heard the farmers speak, she felt a nostalgia which she found very puzzling. After all, she had never lived in a village, but it stirred something primeval within her, something of the land. She felt she belonged to these people. She could not have imagined herself as any other. It evoked a feeling in her—a twin feeling of silence and freedom, of riding a bicycle on a dirt track cutting through fields. She felt anchored, like she had come home after a long circuitous journey and now she could rest. She felt she was wired to feel these images of a collective folk experience that was somewhere locked in the recesses of her mind. This visit to the mandi was always invigorating in ways that were perplexing.

Beeji would go down on her haunches to select ladyfinger or gourd or cauliflower or whatever it was from a pile of farmer's produce and really fuss about the quality. Invariably she would abort the 'selection process' and abruptly get up, shaking her head 'it's no good—let's check further.' Nanaki would be flustered but having little choice in the matter, trudge on behind her. Beeji would walk really purposefully and then plonk herself and then again begin the enquiry about the rates. 'But, bhai, he was giving it for ten and you are saying twelve. Chal, chal, now give it for ten.' And the farmer, still a novice to the haggling machinations of marketplaces, would give in. Nanaki would be really annoyed with Beeji for doing this. But the frugal, economical Beeji, all her survival skills primed here—her self-proclaimed jurisdiction to practice bargaining was not to be deterred. Nanaki, on the other hand, felt that the farmers hardly got the returns on the hard work they put in. Labouring days on end in scorching heat and biting Punjab cold, for what? For this? She, on occasions would be so embarrassed with Beeji's stinginess that at the time of this exchange, she would take two steps forward or sideways, looking in the opposite direction—as if she had nothing to do with this middle-class haggling woman.

On the other end of the mandi was the part where the migrant labourers sold their vegetables. These were mostly garlic and ginger, chillies and lemons—vegetables that were mostly procured from cold storage and commercial markets. The difference between the two spaces was pretty marked. While the farmers got their produce in tractor trollies, the migrant labourers could only afford to get little purchases on their carts. Unlike the farmers whose produce was carelessly dropped on the ground in big heaps, these vendors would make tiny hills of lemons here, chillies there and sometimes decorating the edges with rows of the reddest tomatoes. While the farmers sat in little groups beside their produce, these men worked at creating little pretty shops. They would keep sprinkling water on their produce so that it remained 'fresh' for longer. The farmers would not bother with such rituals. It was enough for them to get some money immediately—the thrill was instantaneous as opposed to going through *ahrtiyas*—the middlemen who would keep them on credit for the longest time. Vegetables were little side crops that they grew to get fast cash, the grains had them waiting an entire season. Then there were fruit vendors and lastly on the edges of the sprawling vegetable fair were, little vendors selling wares of all kinds—from cheap cosmetics and toiletries to kitchen utility items like sieves and clothline clips to assorted plastic wares like buckets and mugs. Spread of glass bangles and spices. Nanaki would always go for the mandi a bit reluctantly but always and each time, by the end of it she would have been taken in by the sheer range of the bursting sensory stimulation. By twilight, these places would be buzzing, like little fairs. One constant was a vendor of home-made cottage cheese—paneer—a really obese turbaned man who would precariously perch himself on an upturned bucket—in front he would lay out slabs of fresh crumbly paneer covered with a wet white muslin cloth. On each visit, Nanaki would be tempted to buy the one with cumin in it, but Beeji would disapprove of buying such a thing from the mandi. Their paneer would only come from Gobind in 7—there were some things Beeji would never compromise on.

Monday morning Nanaki carried the photographs of Joginder's embroideries with her to college. She had got the best shots printed from Roshan's, and at his suggestion in a matte finish. The texture of Joginder's threads was almost tactile in the shots.

Prof. Neil Sengupta veered his Maruti WagonR into the parking lot just as Nanaki was entering the college. There was a screech and a honk, a standard ritual with Neil. Even without turning, Nanaki knew it was him. He waved to her and pointing to his watch hollered, 'I am late—will catch up after the lecture.' He adjusted his laptop backpack and pulled out a voluminous book from the rear seat. 'OK then,' Nanaki said,' I'll see you at Karmo's canteen. After the lecture. 11.15, OK?' 'OK,' he shot back. Not waiting for Nanaki, he rushed through the entrance. They were at a stage of friendship where it was alright to do away with courtesies such as these.

Dr Neil Sengupta, affectionately called Enn Ess—Nanaki joked that since in Punjab, the 'Ess' could be thought of as truncated 'Singh', the nickname was to his advantage. He had been selected through the UPSC and had been working here for the past eight years. When Nanaki joined later, he had shepherded her through the initial days. She also found in him an intellectual compatriot with whom she could discuss both academic as well as administrative issues of the college. They had picked up a joint INTACH project to document forts and palaces around Fatehgarh Sahib region.

'What I want to discuss with you has nothing to do with the INTACH thingy.'

'Really? What's the excitement about?'

'Did you see the handouts about the shortlisted artists for the gallery?'

'Actually to be honest, haven't really engaged with that. These are administrative decisions and one is really a rubber stamp, so to be honest did not really bother. About the Mazhar Khan fellow I know, but I haven't heard of the other name...*whatsit*? Some Gurpreet Kaur?'

'Gurkanwal Kaur.'

'Yeah. Yeah. All the same. Why are you guys so ingenious with names? Or is it about your egalitarianism? Men and women at par.'

'Jokes apart, Enn Ess, tell me.'

'To be honest, I haven't even heard of her. Secretly, I don't care.'

'And we are helping them out. Because they are quietly bringing her in through the back door.'

'Who is she?'

'Very good question. I'll show you.'

She showed him the links to her 'exhibitions', really various self-managed, self-promoting events.

'If you have power in this city of babus and are from the "right" school, in the right neighbourhood, which really boils down to a sector number, it is not difficult to promote yourself. Social media is your new ally where lazy media gets all its cues. People who matter largely move in the same circles, everybody knows everybody and there is such homogeneity of taste in most matters that if you have pulled the right strings and cut the figure, you get attention—and if your husband happens to be a top government official, all the better—if they will not come to keep up with the Joneses, they will come to massage you ego. And what is the big fuss really—no big risk in calling something pretty. What has been going on in the name of art here are some hastily put-together embroideries that Gurkanwal has neither conceived nor made herself. This extracurricular interest of a bored, albeit ambitious wife's attempts to keep herself fashionable is advertised as art and is on the verge of taking it to the ramparts of the gallery. And truth be told, Chaudhuri is with her. And let me tell you, his mind is pretty made up. About the university nominee and the administrative nominee, they are anyway more liable to be manipulated. I mean if they could manage to reign in Chaudhuri, others just fall in line and this is what they are presuming they will do to us.'

'Really? Chaudhuri is with them? And they were smart enough to not have anyone else in the reckoning. No trace of competition.'

'But I have a serious contender for this space.' She picked the *mulmul* bag and took out the large prints and spread them on the table.

'Just look at this.'

Prof. Sengupta let out a gasp. 'Whose is this? Haven't seen anything like this in a long time.'

'I'll tell you. For starters, I have mailed copies of these to all the members. I'm somehow hopeful.'

❧

Nanaki's day started on a note of anticipation. She had been, in a subtle, silent way, really looking forward to this. She pulled out her favourite khaki linen pants and white shirt. She paired it with her moccasins. She also packed her light jacket and a white semi-pashmina stole. She had a tendency to feel really cold on her feet, so she kept an extra pair of socks. She packed her DSLR and secured her old Moleskine in her backpack. Himmat rode down from Patiala, Nanaki having earlier WhatsApped her availability. They decided to start early from Chandigarh so as to visit the site and get back on time. When they met in the college compound at six, the pale moon was visible in the still inky sky.

'Yeah, started around 4.30. The earlier, the better, actually. And not to mention that I have to hit the road back to Patiala after we are done. Let's call your cab guy.'

Nanaki dialled and spoke: 'Yes, we are already here. Waiting. What? Not before nine? That's too late. I called you yesterday and you confirmed for seven. What is this, Gogi ji?

Not done. I'll just call you back if we need it. OK.'

'He says not before nine. The driver has to come from Zirakpur. That's way behind schedule,' she complained. She pursed her lips. 'Listen, how about I get my Willys? I am pretty OK taking it till Kasauli. I've done the highway before.'

'In that case, why not my old chappy here?' Himmat thumped the seat of his Enfield. I mean…if it's OK with you.' He added, lest he sounded too forward.

'Let's go', said Nanaki without a moment's hesitation.

The early morning air was crisp. Once they were on the highway the bike just seemed to glide. Nanaki had never done this before. A simple thing really—driving to the mountains on a bike—but no, not in her twenty-six years. Some of her biker friends vouched for it, but this was a first for her. The mountain air came in waves and hit her face, looking over his shoulder. His navy shirt flapping in the breeze, alternately trapping and releasing the mountain air. He wore a khaki turban and aviators and paired his corduroys with ankle-high riding shoes. Nanaki took a while getting her proximity to him right but beyond a point, there was no choice but to circle her arm around his waist. He stoically patted her hand in place. He looked ahead with an eagle's concentration and rode on. There was this stripped-down austerity in him. Nanaki was beginning to like him.

'So, since when have you been riding?' Nanaki hollered.

'Sorry?'

'Since when have you been riding?' she went decibels louder.

'Me? Started at 4.30.'

Nanaki realized it wasn't easy to have a conversation on a bike.

'Never mind.'

This was better. Why did she anyway want to know innocuous things like that? So she kept quiet, suddenly feeling OK with the silence. She looked around and began to look as far up over the passing hills as possible. The change in vegetation was palpable by now and the silhouettes of conifers with their needles against the deep azure of the sky went past them like a film. For a while she just looked at the clear sky and nebulous clouds. They passed a verdant patch with hundreds of deodars. The day's first sun rays had begun to filter through the trees making dappled patterns on the mossy terrain. She then saw the familiar rock tunnel scooped out of a mountain, a colonial structure. Despite the gay markings, it did not seem intrusive in the least. The use of cut rock on its facade was a clever way to merge architecture with the mountains. She suddenly saw a train chugging on a track cut on the mountains on the other side.

'Himmat, look!'

'Yeah? What's that?'

'Never mind. It's gone.'

Not that she had not seen these sights before. Today, however, there was an immediacy about it all. It probably had to do with the fact that she was on a motorcycle. The frame of a car window was gone. So liberating in a way. It was also probably owing to the fact that she was with Himmat. 'Maybe,' she mused, 'that is the reason I am noticing more.'

By ten they had entered the club premises. When Himmat took a sudden left turn into a lane lined with tall deodars on both sides, she did not realize that they had entered the precincts of the club. The winding lane was lined with lavender and white full-sized rhododendrons. A couple of kilometres down, the building swam into view. It was a stone-and-wood structure nestled in a slight depression in what resembled a valley. The doors and windows of the club were poster green, which together with a gay red postbox and clear blue sky lent a cheerful air.

'We'll use the resort entrance. Cutting across the club lobby is a waste of time. I am bound to run into someone or the other and forced to have a polite conversation. Waste of time. Many Patiala folks come up for a retreat. Let's avoid.'

And so he navigated a grassy patch to arrive at the quieter end of the club, the birding resort. His stride suddenly changed. He walked with the quiet familiarity of a man in his zone. He was the creator of this part—from conception to execution, he had had an intimate involvement with the most intricate of decisions. He had spent many hours here.

The building was done with the construction and paint job. Now the furnishers from Chandigarh had taken over the premises for their job. In a corridor, spools of fabrics and tapestries were stocked up in what resembled a temporary workshop. Two tailors were busy on their sewing machines, their heads bent over. A radio tuned to Vividh Bharti was belting out old Hindi numbers. They were all set to upholster the furniture. Himmat led Nanaki through the outer deck into what was the lobby. The still empty hall looked cavernous.

Himmat began to explain the rough plan of the building and pointed out the two front walls he was considering for the artwork. He led her further into the dining area. This had been partially furnished with an oak sideboard, where they planned to display a collection of white porcelain birds he was getting fabricated in Khurja. 'These would be all ivory,' he explained, 'and all as close to the real birds they are meant to depict. And mind you,' he said, 'the birds we have chosen to model these pieces on are all found in the vicinity. Birds of the Himalayas. Having spent long boyhood years in Sanawar also helped with this. Wasn't much to do in the holidays, with others gone to their homes or guardians, I spent many hours birdwatching. Sen sir had asked me to get the Grimmet book from the library and keep it handy. But obviously I was an amateur; I was just passing time then. In fact, why just birds, I had the luxury to look at the surroundings, the architecture, all packed in the long, languid hours I had at hand. And nowhere to go. And I am also getting two bespoke dining sets in porcelain with the same birds embossed in a circle on the edges of the plates. I am really excited about this one. It came like a flash one fine evening to me, but then I wasn't sure if I would find the right person to do it for me. It was simmering in my head and I kept it on low flame, thinking it through, till I swooped in at the right time and held it tight.'

Nanaki smiled. 'Yes, good one—hold on tight—to ideas. At times, since we are talking so much about birds and all things avian, these flighty things do have a tendency to spread their gossamer wings and take flight. At times, you don't even know how many of these frisky things you thought of instantly frolicked their way into some wonderland. There they remain latent. Sometimes for mere moments, sometimes days, sometimes months and years. And then in a flash. They come back without warning, at times stealthily, in our most unguarded moments: good for you if you hold them then and there, for if you think you will sit yourself down one day with the wrong end of the pen in your mouth, or the laptop loaded with the works, or the dream paints on the palette, to capture what you see in your mind's stratosphere—you just blink and find it's just an obdurate blankness you see, the thought has yet not entered your conscious mind—it's just hovering between the sleeping world and the conscious one, and eventually just falls off the edge. Never makes it. Yes, they are flighty things.' She rounded it with a peal of laughter, amused with the little story she had concocted.

Himmat listened intently. He smiled, the crow's feet around his eyes deepened.

'Anyway, Nanaki, what I was coming to, was that here and here', he pointed to the either sides of the sideboard, 'are where we require two artworks, or maybe we can make it four small.' Nanaki went to the other end of the room and observed the walls from there.

'Hmm.'

He then gave her a tour of the proposed library. 'Herein apart from the books, we plan a little performance space in an intimate setting and available for showing documentaries and films on weekends... And yes, birdsong, if we are lucky we'll get to hear today. I am hungry, why don't we grab a quick bite? Let's go to the club restaurant.'

'I have a better idea. Club food bores me to death. It's been donkey's years I took a walk down the Mall. Let's go down and have some bun-samosa. Sharma ji's legendary bun-samosa. What say?'

'Brilliant.'

∞

She stood for a while outside Kumar photographs gazing at the old black-and-white photographs of the many celebrities who visited the town at different points, mostly to mark anniversaries and founders of the Lawrence School and the celebrations of the brigade stationed there. The photographs were like personal memorabilia, while for the celebrities, they were no more than a dent in the whirlwind lives they led. But the locals have been holding on to these images for decades and decades as some form of self validation. Anyway, these made for beautiful prints, like a nugget of local history in the window dressing. Nanaki was absorbed and Himmat had to nudge her to hurry up. They crossed a provision store that sold local honey and umbrellas and further down the road were stalls of Tibetan refugees selling anoraks, stoles, wraparounds, t-shirts, skirts and floaters. These were punctuated by tiny kitchens selling momos. Actually what appeared like a shack market from the outside hid a whole village inside. These were displaced people and the shops doubled up as living quarters hidden at the rear. Tibetan women, men and children, young and old, sold their wares while knitting and gossiping, and they passed by one old woman minding a pomeranian at her feet. They crossed over into each other's stalls, like they would have into each other's courtyards, back in their village, discussing the day's business or what was for lunch and such quotidian details. These people were displaced, but they had created a snug village here. She often secretly desired to spend time living their kind of nomadic life. She could easily live off thukpa and chicken momos for sometime at least. She could try.

Finally they sat down on the ramshackle Rexine sofas of the Sharma sweet shop in Lower Mall to eat their bun-samosas. A greasy bottle of tomato ketchup was passed on to them, its contents falling out in clumps as they shook it. A toddler was getting a bottom thrashing from a severe Victorian headmaster. The tea was sweet and milky. Nanaki did not complain, she did not notice it today. A bad cup of tea usually ruined her evening. Not today. It was not a usual evening.

They went back to the club to pick up the bike. Through a clearing, they stepped into a wild grove at the back of the club deck. You could not suspect from the outside, what full forests those depths enclosed. He put a finger on his lips and with a movement of his hand, asked her to follow. One minute they were in a manicured garden, sipping tea and the next, discovering a cavernous fantasy. It was a wonderland. He cut through veined walls of thick creepers—innocuous barriers that could be knocked down with a swipe of a hand. He kept moving into the distance and cutting through the tangle till he came to a small clear patch, which nevertheless, was surrounded with barks and branches and glistening leaves, and whispered 'Now listen.'

She stood there expectantly, her ears primed. And then, it rose. Somewhere from inside the thicket emanated a chorus of chirping birds coming home to roost. The excitement was palpable. A raucous rush of cheeping and chirping, wee bit loud for those tiny frames, combined with a lusty flapping of sinewy wings, repeatedly hitting the breasts. A while elapsed before the winged family settled into the rhythm of their spare hours and let out an elaborate chorus. Now from behind that bush, now from the branch over there. Alternately loud and hushed.

Himmat faced the thicket, taut and alert, tuning in to the song with his mouth slightly open. When the song reached a crescendo, he looked at Nanaki, like you anticipate a reaction when you offered somebody the contents of your secret treasure chest. She looked at him wide-eyed, gasping.

∞

They had to start back soon. They were already way behind schedule. Sitting silently on the rear of his bike, she threw back her head, letting the wind run through her hair. It was twilight and she could see the mountains turn into dark, indistinct shapes, which together with the spark of lights from a distance, looked strangely mystical. She moved closer to Himmat at this point and instinctively put her arm around his waist. For an instant he released his hand from the bike to touch her arm and put it more firmly in place. She bent forward, resting her whole body on the curve of his back. She could feel his rising and falling breath. The dark of the twilight closed on to their gliding silhouettes.

ဢ

The next morning she got up to an overcast sky. Thoughts of Himmat had constantly hovered on her mind since last night. It was a vague delightful expectation, that hung there all day. Love was slowing her down. She was constantly distracted, her mind vacillating between the rainy evening at the deserted college, when they were strangers but a sense of common courtesy had ensured they held cups of sugary college tea and make polite conversation while watching the rain lash about them. It came down in swirls, inundating the college grounds. Then the sight of him framed in the art gallery that she had quietly spotted from a distance and observed for long. And how she had secretly observed him from the pillion. She had been undeniably pulled to him, and the realization had become singularly clear in the mountains. His ears keen to hear the birds and turning to her for a validation of his desire. There was a flash of recognition in their eyes—the two locked in their own private universe. In this space silence had sealed a bond. A definite acknowledgment had silently descended. Bit by bit. Like they were spun off into an alternate space and time. A new dimension. A story of love.

And when she found herself constantly thinking of Himmat, the world-weary look on his face, his lean frame, her heart would skip and somersault, traverse a neat circle, while simultaneously igniting a tremble. What was this? She could not pinpoint it except that she felt luminous, as if someone had placed a diya in the deepest alcove of her heart and it was now letting out beams she could hardly contain.

Her body was coming alive in unknown ways. It was like a sleeping spirit had been stirred. A spirit that had been under a long spell, just like in the fables. And someone had decreed its liberation only with the touch of such and such. She felt her body arched and alive, her breasts taut, seeking that touch; a constant longing seized her.

She climbed up to the terrace and found that it had rained while she was taking her afternoon nap. Everything was washed clean. It was still very windy. The fronds of the areca palms were swaying noisily. The leaves of the guava were glistening and like an offering, the tree had deposited a fruity harvest together with some stray twigs and dry leaves on the cast iron cover of the drainpipe. Nanaki pulled out a twig from the tree and swept it all aside to release the rainwater accumulated on the terrace. The water began to trickle and then moved in a sudden swirl, whooshing down the pipe like a deluge. Nanaki looked at the clear sky and wondered if it had rained in Patiala. She could see Himmat on his bike, riding by himself in the rain, not hassled one bit, willingly getting soaked to the bone, feeling the water running down his body. What if she was riding with him in the rain, her wet kurta clinging to her body and with squelching wetness, holding him from behind: her body close to him and resting her head on his back and letting the water wash down on them. Their bodies melting into each other, the whirl of rain making the two indistinct. And now he parks the bike under a tree. Rain trickles through the branches. She gets off from behind and gets on the bike from the front and now sits facing him. They sit face to face, their legs locked on the stationary machine. Water pours down on them. They kiss long, deep languorous kisses. He pulls her close. Now his hand travels up her wet shirt. Time ceases. But again.

When the moment of truth conveys to you the distance between your desire and the given, the untravelled land of possibilities, it is all at the same time—creation and destruction, all at the same time.

After such knowledge, what forgiveness?

ᘓ

The rain lasted all evening. The robustness of monsoons. It was pouring and she made a trip to Krishna in Sector 15 for some art material supplies. She needed to stock up on new oil pastels which were now either running out or caking, in mostly sucked-out tin tubes. She always bought this stuff in bulk. As she started back for home, the whiff from the new linseed oil bottle filled the car. This was a happy odour. It had the power to evoke a creative calm within her. She cut through the rainy day traffic by the university lights and made her way past a car with blaring music. What was this pomposity which you had to showcase on the road of all places? She put on her favourite Leonard Cohen CD and 'Did I really love you' played. What she liked best about the song was the mournful violin that filled up the bare space between stanzas. Was it sad? Was it the swinging perplexity of indecision? Was it longing? Longing for what you can create with another—what possibilities are hidden in that promise. It was a happy sad song, or a sad happy song—no answers, just a litany of possibilities. It was echoes of a song still unheard, like a thrill that erupted at the thought of that possibility, no matter how remote.

She would have reached back home in ten minutes straight but some vague impulse prompted her to drive on the other side—the side of the mountains. She kept at it and felt oddly exhilarated. It was an abandon of a different kind. She wanted to keep driving, feel the mountain air and be back home for dinner. Since Chandigarh lies at the foothills of the Shivaliks, reaching the Himalayas is doable in less than an hour. As she got on to Madhya Marg, she felt that the day had gone suddenly dark. Lights had come on vehicles and bulbs flickered through the buildings lining Madhya Marg. Rain was now falling in torrents on her windscreen. She switched on the wipers and found it increasingly hard to see through the traffic. As her car pulled up at the red light near the Press chowk, she saw a dust-coloured Enfield ahead of her. Through the rain she could make out the turbaned silhouette on the weather-beaten bike. Looked like Himmat. Was it him? Just yesterday she had ridden with him. Her heart raced. She looked harder through the rain. Before she could, the light turned green and the traffic snaked ahead. Nanaki could not tear her gaze and continued to look for the bike in the rush. She tailed it for a stretch, trying not to let it out of sight. She was not sure how this would help. It was very unlikely that she was going to haul him up for a hello. Or may be she would. What was so extraordinary about it? But there was something that propelled her forward. She was not even sure if it was him. She continued to follow him through the rush, all the time her gaze steadily on the bike. She followed him down Madhya Marg, feeling her heart thumping inside. She kept driving on and following him, taking a detour into a sector road inside. There was no reason in all of this. She kept going ahead nevertheless. She followed the dot of red light ahead—now she saw it, now she lost it behind other vehicles. So she could not see it for a minute and then again it came into view, a grainy dot of red through the screen of rain and the strains of Cohen's violin filling the car. She was revelling in this moment, her own little adventure.

Was it ever settled
Was it ever over
And is it still raining
Back in November

And then a bulky trailer truck seemed to appear from nowhere in front. It emerged like a wall and completely blocked off her view. By the time it cleared up, she had lost the bike. Her heart sank. It was inane really. This disappointment was hard to understand. She wasn't even sure if it was him, she wasn't even sure why she was doing this, she just gave in to an impulse that was now becoming overwhelming. The strains of Cohen's violin filling up the car.

The lemon trees blossom
The almond trees wither
Was I ever someone
Who could love you forever

❧

Karmo stood in the kitchen, lost in a cloud of asafoetida fumes. She thought Pali would like some porridge after her attempts to get him to eat roti with dal proved futile. 'Yes, he always had a sweet tooth,' she said to herself, 'must be one of those days, wanting something sweet.' Theirs was a one-room tenement in the heart of Manimajra town. Located on the first floor of a bustling bazaar, the entrance was through a dingy winding staircase that opened into a narrow verandah leading to the door of Karmo's portion. The walls of the sitting area were whitewashed with generous amounts of indigo. A big ceramic vase with peacock feathers stood in one corner of the room and there was a foggy Old Monk bottle with an overgrown money plant perched at some height, its multiple shoots meandering in all directions. One golden plastic pot was installed in what was a niche overlooking the street. It was a decorative fountain made with thin plastic fibres. When it was switched on, it changed colours alternately from green to magenta to yellow with the ends of the tubes lit up with miniscule sparkles like a permanent firework. A collection of cassettes was lying ramshackle and dust laden behind a three-tiered stereo system. The two speakers piled atop the player, were swathed in cloth covers. In the centre shelf, a framed poster of their 'guru' was installed. He was dressed, like always, in an elaborate costume, this time with real peacock feathers and a plumed turban and with a purple Ferrari lurking in the backdrop. He had an expression of practiced piety and had one palm open in a pose of benediction. Two incense sticks were installed before his picture, half burnt, dug in little piles of ashes. Skeletal remains.

She partly chose this place because of its proximity to the grocery shop, you just had to climb down the steps to buy your daily needs when you wanted. You didn't have to splurge on an auto.

'Mummy, mummy,' a screechy voice called out with urgency.

'*Haan, put...* Yes, son...coming,' she dropped the ladle and rushed out, the furrows on her forehead deepening.

Pali wanted to be rubbed on his abdomen. A sharp shooting pain had started all over again. Son and mother had been up most of last night because he could not sleep despite the pills. She kept an old bottle of mustard oil on his bedside and vigorously rubbed it in circular motions around his navel. His shrivelled body seemed to have shrunk in size. His skin looked loose for his years. He would clutch at his writhing middle and double up, letting out constant cries of 'hai' like merely articulating this would do something to dissipate it. If you heard these cries from a distance, they seemed very ominous. On other occasions, his head would go from side to side in jerky moves, causing a delirium that would keep his world in a constant spin. His head would feel heavy with an incessant throbbing and often felt like it would explode.

Karmo set up the pillow next to the wall and spread a towel on it. She then propped Pali's frame against it. Her gaze travelled to his legs, that had, by now become virtual bones sticking out sharply at some angles. His knees seemed uneven precisely because of this reason. His face had gone gaunt and two dark saucers looked out vacantly. His smile, though was still the smile of his childhood, thought Karmo. His smile had remained. Sometimes she would catch herself thinking: *What is this smile? Is it all that is left of the child? Or is it the will that pushes him on, despite the hell he goes through? Or is it the mocking laughter of the whole village that continued till they cringed with terror thinking of such a fate for their own children? Has it got stuck on my son's face?*

He had to be helped into clothes after his bath, which until now he had managed to do. In his shirtless state, he looked like a heap of bones. Karmo would be tormented thinking of him as a healthy village kid swimming in the pond, climbing the trees without as much as thinking, boisterously clambering from the terrace of their house, all the way to that of the sarpanch's house six lanes away, and he would do it like lightning. The boys chasing him down the alley and he always leading the pack. How it was difficult to contain him and how he would come into the kitchen breathlessly asking for lassi. Over and over again. Till Karmo would run out of milk and curd. *What has happened to him? God gave me a neyana, who I nursed on my breast and nurtured with all my heart, who grew into a beautiful boy but then the canker set in. Like it destroys the standing wheat in the fields. One day you have a lush field that you see and your heart swells with pride and the next day, it is still standing but when you look close, it's nothing but a field of stubs. The stalks are perforated; their life sap sucked out overnight by parasites. They stand there deceptively for a week or two and then begin cracking midway. They all drop one by one and there you have it—your field turned into a graveyard.*

'Why, son?'

ꙮ

When she would see the young boys and girls hanging around her college tea shack, she would be tormented with the thought of Pali. He was their age. *Look at their able bodies, their cheerful lives, their purposefulness. And my son, wasting away limb by limb into a living corpse. His childhood was another lifetime.*

And all I can do is watch, helplessly watch him getting consumed.
Apply balm here or there, press his listless legs, soothe this nerve
or that, and watch him turn into a shadow.

'Why, son?'

❧

Nanaki entered the college foyer with some trepidation. She
had somehow persuaded Joginder Singh to accompany her.
Her feet were heavy and she had to make an effort to navigate
through the corridor. The passage looked rather dingy today.
She noticed the dampness on the walls and at places the paint
had fallen off in crusts, exposing the bare concrete beneath.
Spores of fungus had taken root and stood on ends like
goosebumps on a hairy arm. Nanaki felt a weight inside of
her. They walked past the administrative block towards her
studio. Half-a-dozen clerks perched behind desks sat staring
at the blinking screens. Karmo was in the office, serving hard-
boiled, mid-morning tea. They reached out for it mechanically,
not even looking at her. Nanaki looked at the scene from
the edge of her eye. She really did not like this part of the
college. She quickened her pace towards the studio. A wisp
of an idea presented itself. *Why not just toe the Director's*
line? The thought itself was one of relief. She knew picking
issues with him would mean a protracted, lonely fight. And
also futile. More than anything else, it would eat into her
hours. What difference does it make, really? She could help
out Joginder all the same and find him another space. This
idea became stubborn. It was very tempting to succumb to
the wily mind and its arguments. But then she realigned her
thoughts: *Should not forget my purpose today: To introduce*
Joginder to the Director. For all you know, he'll be taken in by

the man's genuine talent.

She emerged from the class feeling lighter. It was paradoxical that here she was having expended an hour worth of energy, lecturing and demonstrating, and yet got rid of the tiredness she felt in the morning. Joginder had been waiting in her cabin. Chaudhuri's profile was visible through the half glass partition of his office entrance. There he was haranguing, with two colleagues in attendance. He always seemed to be talking important matters. How self-important he looked. How he pointed out people. She asked Joginder to wait till called out and walked first into his office. Without warning, she spread out three of his embroideries in front of the Director. Chaudhuri was not prepared to be confronted in this manner. He was initially overwhelmed and also curious to know who the artist was and yet rigid enough at the end of it in being totally non committal to Nanaki's proposal of Joginder's inclusion.

'Can I introduce him to you? He is right outside?'

'Not today. Pretty caught up.'

She came out downcast, rehearsing how she was going to break it to Joginder. This was very humiliating. As she looked up, he was not there. She saw him riding back on his cycle outside the college gate, his beard going haywire. It was an exceptionally windy day. He had put on a brand-new kurta for the occasion. There was no use calling out to him. He had ridden off by then.

Down the corridor in the room adjoining the library, she saw sudden frantic activity. More of Gurkanwal's panels had arrived. The college staff was busy ferrying them packaged in newspapers from the red beacon car in the foyer to this room. There were at least twenty of them. The peon had lined them up against the wall. The college administration had taken up this work, it seemed, like their own.

❧

Nanaki and Himmat rang the door bell outside Joginder Singh's house repeatedly. There was no response. His mobile phone too went unanswered. Just as they were about to give up, a shuffling sound was heard from inside followed by Joginder's staggering gait that reached up to answer the door. He apologized, explaining that he had dozed off.

'*Tabiyat nasaaz si*—was not too well.'

He looked at Himmat as he said it.

'*Sa'ab ji, ki tareef?*' he said, hoping to be introduced to Himmat.

'Oh sorry. I should have introduced. This is Himmat Singh Kaleka from Mumbai. He is an architect and would like to see some of your pieces.'

'Why?' Joginder shot back.

Nanaki had not anticipated this. Joginder's tone was almost belligerent. He stormed into the house and went straight into his bedroom, refusing to hear anything in the matter. Nanaki motioned to Himmat to stay in the drawing room while she followed him inside.

'Quite simply, Nanaki madam, I do not sell them to business people. I would have done it long ago if I was interested. Many people came. I accompanied you that day upon your insistence. I got my share of insult. I am not interested anymore.'

Nanaki was a bit hurt by the 'madam' bit. It reeked of a sudden distance that had come up between them. She had hitherto been *Beebaji* for him.

She stood in silence. The bedroom was a picture of neglect.

The curtains were discoloured with all the dirt. Silvery threads of spider webs glistened as the yellow light from two naked bulbs shone on them. The fan moved with a whirr, sounding very tired. There was a steel plate and dish lying in the corner with leftover yellow dal and a piece of mango pickle dried up into a crust. The discarded edges of a chapatti sat in the plate. In a flash Nanaki understood the man's loneliness and mortality. There wasn't much time really and he was getting it all wrong. She would try and make him see how for him the best prospect for his collection was to be preserved in a museum and some art could be bought by Himmat.

Joginder, however, would not hear any of it.

Himmat and Nanaki parked themselves in his drawing room. She even fetched two glasses of water from the kitchen. Joginder, who was an inordinately hospitable man, had not bothered with the tea today. At last he emerged from his room.

'*Sa'ab, ethe aao.* Come here…' Nanaki patted the sofa on which she was sitting. '*Suno…* Listen. Do you know I work for a sarkari College of Art?'

'*Haanji…*OK…' Joginder said. He belonged to a generation that venerated government institutions.

'It is a government-run college and it has an art gallery that displays paintings, textiles and other items. Now they sometimes, say, once in ten years or so, make additions to this gallery and this time they wanted someone whose work is on Punjab. My only aim is to take your work there—so that it reaches an audience where it will get its rightful place. Just that some high-ups do not agree with me.'

'You know, Beeba, to tell you the truth, I have been really worried with the question of what I am going to do with all this. You showed me some hope so I accompanied you. It is a *sirdard,* a real headache. Especially because it is not easy to part with. You know I have donated some pieces to the army, where they did take very good care, but it remained in the officer's messes. Who knows, a new memsa'ab will come along and get these removed to display what she fancies. And nobody would be able to argue with that. And then I shudder at the thought of selling these to private people. I am not able to put a price on these and one or two did turn up to offer me an amount, but I feel they will cheat me. Plus, I did not know where they would end up. So I just turned them away from the door. I did not even offer them water. I feel comfortable having the embroideries close to me, even though I know these will have to eventually go. And at my age, *ki pata, beeba,* who knows? I trust you, but this gentleman here, like your big sa'ab honestly, I feel he could be tricking you and me,' he said it well within Himmat's earshot.

Himmat stood there, unaffected and waited for Nanaki to clear the air.

'He is my colleague, we work together. Sa'ab is an architect and has built a club in Kasauli.'

The gleam in Joginder's eyes returned.

'I was posted in Kasauli once…must have been 1964–67. Yes, they did have the old club there at that point.' Joginder looked slightly upwards as if trying to imagine the building.

Nanaki then flicked open her iPad and showed him images of both her college and the birding resort. He recognized the old Kasauli club building and a flush of nostalgia flooded his face. There was a glint in his eyes which were still very clear for his age. He went into another winding description of his time at Kasauli; in fact, that is where he had picked up his rank of subedar. His quarter was a stone cottage and by far the best in service and he had managed to create quite a few embroideries there, getting his supplies from the *muniyari dukaan* in the lower bazaar. Why on his way back he would often sit at Sharma Halwai's and get his fix of bun-samosa. Something suddenly energized him. He then hobbled into his kitchen and made his trademark tea. By the end of it all, he got up to open the room for them to look at the embroidery panels.

Joginder Singh opened a roll of cream silk and adjusted it before his visitors. This was his latest. Two kingfishers frolicking amidst branches of a small fig tree. Fleshy petals with streaks of pale-yellow hiding a spread of fine black dots, embroidered in gradient with dark shades of saffron gradually giving way to yellow. Two birds alighting from the flower bush: one with its spindly beak, looking upwards—wings spread out, oversized head with a gay blue breast. The creature looked skywards, poised for a higher flight. The one below hovered over stalks of lilies. Its Prussian blue head highlighted with lighter shades of blue and its orange body tapering in a stubby tail. One more fig blossom seemingly at a distance from the main frame looked more of a spectral double of its full-bodied cousin, while a whole array of vegetation with stalky leaves seen two notches away as shadows embroidered in grey. The fabric was old and it was from a whole spool he had procured at Srinagar. He had paid a tidy sum for it at that point, but it had worked out for him. Saved him the bother of visiting Chandigarh shops. By the look of it also, the silk seemed finer than what the local shops generally stocked. He had been cutting out the required material from the spool as and when required. One could however tell it had aged. On closer inspection, there were indistinct, greasy marks—looked like oil or perhaps spoilt in transportation: for the twenty-five metre spool had travelled with him to all his postings before he settled in Mohali for good. Now, Joginder covered it with a length of white muslin cloth and had it standing in a corner of his sideboard. The drawers were used to stock up on threads: one for cotton and one for silk, apart from his needles and frames. By now Joginder seemed to have shed his recalcitrance and looked towards Nanaki to gauge her reaction. His grey hair tied in a little bun, his skin gleaming in the falling sunlight, which would flood the room precisely at this hour every day. His inquiring eyes revealed a vulnerability he always hid behind a defensive look, a look he reserved for his embroideries. He would not show them to all. He hid them, as if its layers would be ripped off with their very eyes. They, who would not understand it or merely look at the 'product' and not understand what went into their making, they, who would want to sell it, they, who would want to buy it. He could not tolerate that look. That was all there was to it.

ও

Himmat and Nanaki drove back from Mohali and landed at the college gate in fifteen minutes flat. Himmat's bike was parked there and he needed to start back for Patiala. As she got on the road next to Leisure Valley that led to the college, she began to unexpectedly speed further up. For a moment, Himmat thought she had missed the turn, but she only said 'Mr Patiala, let's do some sightseeing today.' Himmat laughed at this indiscretion and by now, the beams of the setting sun were turning an unusually brilliant-orange and flooding the SUV. Bathed in the beams, he seemed somewhat livelier than usual. The pallor that mostly stuck to his cheeks and that perennial hint of disenchantment that was dug into the furrows of his face, was getting dissembled, much to Nanaki's gratification.

'Mr Patiala, let me show you around the Rock Garden: the pride of Chandigarh—ding dong,' she said in falsetto, imitating the cheap radio jingles. Nanaki was averse to listening to the local FM channels. All day, the advertisements of realty businesses on the loop: a deluxe condo in Zirakpur and an apartment block in Derabassi, on airport road in Mohali and Greater Chandigarh and what have you. Killing the city from all sides. *Do we need so many apartments?* First they decimated the forests for agriculture, now agriculture for concrete jungle. The city seemed to be already bursting at seams. She drove into the parking lot of the Rock Garden.

Great! An architect can never really get done with this one.

They bought two entry tickets and bent themselves to climb through the small archways. The beams of the setting sun bounced off the shiny white surface of the broken tiles cladding the gates and as they advanced, rows and rows of figurines on raised platforms emerged into view. There were battalions of women in saris made of broken bangles and men carrying discarded sinks on their heads that doubled up as planters, monkeys the right hue of burnt sienna made with broken pieces of baked clay diyas, discarded by the hundreds after Diwali—ready for a show, cows made of mosaics of broken white tiles, looking holy and staring balefully. She dropped a coin in the wishing well and smiled. He drew close to her and said, 'If wishes could materialize from dry, forlorn wells, frogs would rule the world—*Je rabb milda nahtyea dhoteyan… te rabb milda daduuan, machhiyan nu,*' he quipped, modifying Bulle Shah's *qafi.*

Then they came upon the mud house of the creator, which

endlessly fascinated Nanaki—she so wanted to have a getaway like that. It was a hermit's hut with a grinding stone kept outside the doorway. And they walked further. They then came into a winding narrow pathway that cut between two high stone walls studded with pebbles. Bit of a rough climb because of the ascent, Nanaki felt breathless by now. With her back resting on the wall, she pulled out her water bottle from her tote and gulped down more than half of it in big swigs. Himmat could not help notice how fine her neck was, as she gulped with her head up from the bottle at some distance. In the taut neck, he could sense the flow of water beneath the skin. Some droplets trailed from her mouth to her neck and glistened there. From her throat it travelled down in little gulps. He noticed. Her cuboid amethyst rose by just a millimetre as the water flowed beneath the spot. The depression in her neck. He wanted to touch it but exercised restraint. 'Let's go,' she said abruptly. He snapped out of his little meditation.

Armies on horsebacks then swam into view. The beasts looking more beastly, made out of discarded metallic waste. As the dying sun fell on the many jangling parts, they looked every inch, a daunting army. And then a curved wall studded with the discarded ceramic parts of old electrical fittings. A dome of fused bulbs sparkling in the sun. A bevy of village belles, their bodies studded with a thousand semicircles of broken glass bangles. All colours conceivable. Dressed to the nines. A village wedding. Musicians with discarded chrome drain pipes for trumpets. More baleful-looking men, all identical, with cactii growing out of their heads. Sly monkeys ahead, looking droll next to their stately neighbours. Their tails long and winding, made of concrete and scratched while the concrete was wet, giving them a nice hairy feel.

Now the castle behind the waterfall. A spray of water drops brushed their faces as they climbed the ivy-covered steps. A stench of algae hit them as they made their way towards the little fort of gunnybags where the photographers accost you for a photo or two. Like it was a Taj Mahal. Of the hoi polloi. They brushed past a newly married girl, striking a pose against a stream, hand on hip, and the young man, doting husband, in the euphoria of new love, falling all over her. Her traditional red bangle set announcing to all and sundry, her 'just-married' status. Like a placard. A pretty placard, a jangling, pretty placard, on hennaed hands. Her oiled hair parted in the middle with a furrow of vermillion sindoor. And she laughs full throttle. The sun upon them, the sequins on her synthetic dupatta reflect a dancing pattern on the rock wall. Laughs again. Cupping her mouth with hennaed hands. They exit efficiently, the garden echoes with their gay prattle before a stillness finally descends.

Nanaki paced up to reach the distant part of the garden. They crossed the open-air auditorium where she remembered having watched *A Midsummer Night's Dream* long ago with her grandparents. The troupe had travelled from Mumbai to perform when she was a little girl. The memory was crystal clear.

'Imagine sitting under a starry sky and watching Shakespeare,' she looked at Himmat.

'You know, when I was a student, this was a mandatory trip, almost a pilgrimage. I even volunteered to lead so many foreign students who came to study just the Rock Garden. I would come down to Chandigarh with the study groups. Mostly art students from Europe. But you know, Nanaki, what to me is the most fascinating part about this creation?'

'Hmm?'

'That it was a secret. A secret garden for a long time when it began. It started, in true artistic flush, like a creation you want to protect from prying eyes. Like a baby, the first three months are a secret known only to the immediate folk, they are superstitious about announcing it too early. Perhaps it is the desire to protect it. Mere knowledge of its existence would mean its destruction. Sometimes it happens that our ideas are way too much for society to even hear of, and unveiling them prematurely only means their destruction, they are promptly nipped in the bud, but you keep them away from the prying eyes and nurture them in a safe place, slowly, lovingly and then they begin to erupt soft green shoots that are barely visible and then they grow, millimetre by millimetre, and then they spring forth with a light trapped within. By now they want to just grow because this has become their nature. They will, because it is them, no other reason. Nek Chand collected his materials, carting them from junkyards and cottage factories on his cycle, dumping it in this wilderness and working on it every single day, sun or rain, making these fantastical objects, the beasts and the dancing girls, the ferocious ones, the pretty ones, the simians, the horses…all welded as the inhabitants of his own city, a city within a city, a secret town, a phantasmagoria. It started as a secret and then when it was let out, the babus of your very bureaucratic city tried every trick in the book to pull down this *defilement*. Where was it planned? What was it? Who is this man? But when it began to attract international acclaim, they began to appropriate it by and by. At last something circuitous was allowed to take route in an otherwise drawn-on-the-board city. Some semblance of an anarchy let loose against the terror of the apple pie order.

North-South, 90 degrees, uniform facades, so many doors, so many windows, no more, no rules, rules, byrules, etc. Here was a disruption. A spoiler. A *nazar battu. Evil eye.* But to tell you the truth Nanaki, I have never really felt at home in your town. How this town has grown into an irascible, ill-mannered teenager! It is supposed to be the capital city, but all it has for others is a rich relative's contempt. If somebody wants to know what North-South disparity means they ought to visit your city. It is a trap you created for yourself.'

'Thanks for enlightening me, Mr Kaleka sir. I happen to know it for the most part. Professional hazard, we'll keep relating stories we already know. But then there is a way to look at a city from the inside too. That's another story. I'll tell you that story. Now, I was wanting to hear a story that I don't know. Himmat's story. Tell me about yourself. Apart from your Sir JJ School, I hardly know anything at all about you.' Himmat stared back at her. It was a look Nanaki could not comprehend. Despite the smile, it was a look of being found out, after dodging the pursuer for long, a look that said must you ask and yet succumbing to the inevitability of the question.

❧

VI

What Light Through
Yonder Window Breaks

The year was 1984. It was difficult.

In more ways than one.

One fine evening, my mother who had been married to my father for ten years just walked out of that door and never came back. Never. Come to think of it, I did see her step out but, had merely looked at it, in my glorious ignorance, as one of the many everyday comings and goings. It was twilight when my father remarked from over the newspaper that she hadn't returned. I sat on the lobby carpet, bent over a new Scrabble set. I was so self-absorbed, completely oblivious of the goings-on. Yet mother was needed soon enough. Twilight turned to night and there was no sign of her still. Father was getting restless. My heart was getting heavy. He called up his sister as she was one relative my mother visited occasionally. But Parneet bhenji drew a blank.

Ethe? Here...no. In fact haven't seen her in days. When she returns, ask her to see me soon, I've kept some phulkari dupatta samples for her.

Now father, who was from an old landed family of Patiala was wont to keeping a poise in most situations. In fact he was genetically wired to, was overtly alright but soon had begun to pace the length of the garden. He did not say it to me, but I knew he was disturbed for one. But too timid to ask him what the matter with mother was. From the jaali at the one end of the garden to the big falsa tree on the other, he paced the verandah multiple times. I looked at him from inside the room.

I had heard strains of discord and fierce arguments on many a night through the corridor that separated my room from theirs'. I had always, for as long as I could remember. My mother's free spiritedness had always been up against my father's feudal control. Now I understand how different they were. Their fights got worse. But then how much could a child understand? But as soon as I would hear father's belligerent booming voice, it stirred deep fears in the pit of my stomach. Like some sickness churning inside that would throw me off balance. And I still feel that old fear well up in my gut at times. A rush of bile. But then, all that would not really matter when Mother would hug me and put morsels into my mouth. I would not think of it then. Everybody warned her she was spoiling me silly. They warned her against too much indulgence.

She would give me a good scrub on Sundays and a long warm head bath. I was a boy with unusually unruly hair. She would first work a pack of curd into my locks and then run it through hot water and finally use Kesh Nikhar soap to rinse it all off. She would then sit with me in the sun running her supple fingers through my hair, disentangling the curls while the heat of her fingers moving circuitously through the hair would dry them out. She would ensure that there was no sign of dampness on the scalp before taking warm sarson oil in a steel bowl and applying it bit by bit into the dry hair and then portioning them to dress them into a jooda. I would cry at this ordeal each time. Meanwhile she would distract me with a tale or two. I would get involved with the story and forget the tediousness. She would then tie me a patka—a half turban. She had got me matching ones in bright colours for most outfits.

The following morning was a Sunday. Like every Sunday, I pretended to be very still in my bed with my eyes tight shut to give mother the impression that I was still fast asleep. All to avoid the ordeal of the head bath. I did the same. I would keep lying in the bed at least till ten. In the meanwhile mother's voice would repeatedly warn me from outside the door, each time she crossed, she would call out to me to wake up. But that Sunday there was no call. I got tired feigning sleep. So I rubbed my eyes and shook myself from the delirium. Suddenly last night's happening flashed before me. Mom had left. So, has she not returned? Despite everything, there was this confidence that she would return. Don't ask me how and why, I just felt she would be home, not because she could not go anywhere but simply because I could not imagine it any other way. It was probably my limitation as a child. Of course she will come back. And so I had this tacit, inexplicable confidence. Perhaps it sprung from a deep source of trust build over years when your mother has leapt from anywhere to tend to your needs. Without the asking. You know no other way but to believe that. But now the strange feeling was turning into fear. It started as that familiar churning in the pit of my stomach. Added to it now was a new feeling: a bizarre fear of abandonment.

That morning dragged on, and soon day after day began to glide past with no news of her. Sometimes, I could not help it and cried bitterly in the privacy of my room. I was never encouraged to cry. So I would muffle the sobbing with a towel. My father would call me names at the slightest hint of a tear. When, as a toddler, I had once slipped on the driveway chasing a kite and sustained a nasty gash on the knee, my eyes had involuntarily welled up. Upon seeing me cry, my father had flown into a rage that was so hard to understand. His anger perplexed me. I began to fight my tears ever since. So when mother was gone, I really did not know how to react: it was the fear of loss combined with an anxiety to fight a display of my grief. I was to never know. Grief combined with embarrassment. For some strange reason, I was to be blamed for her disappearance. And if not that, I was made out to be on her side. On the errant woman's side. A sinking blackness filled me. Where could she be? I was lonely.

Father eventually got in touch with my mother's parents in Kapurthala. They seemed to be clueless about their daughter's sudden disappearance. My father visited some distant relatives where there could be a possibility of her landing but each time came back more hopeless. He combed through the prominent gurudwaras around town and also the Harmandar Sahib at Amritsar but drew a blank. A year rolled by with no news. At last my father sought the family's counsel. My mother's parents, my father's older cousin and my father's mother all sat together and discussed the problem threadbare. I quietly stood outside the door, listening to the snatches of conversation. Again that fear. And estrangement. It was decided to wait for six more months, after which we could have the Akhand Path ceremony to presume her dead.

It was on my mother's disappearance from our lives that made father realize the role she played in my life. The litany of tasks, small and big that were part of the motherhood trial day after day after day. Work, inexhaustible work. So when it was time for a head bath, he clumsily wrestled with it for a while before giving up in a huff. A helper, Ramkali, was then sent into the bathroom to give me the final rinse. She squatted next to me and I remember, the bitter sods of Kesh Nikhar soap entering my eyes as her chapped hands vigorously worked the soap into my hair. The soap was piercing my eyes and before I knew it there I was, on the bathroom floor, bursting into tears, shouting at her to get out and wanting my mother back. I wanted her badly. All I could think of was her. For once I didn't care if father heard me.

ᘒ

I began to feel blurry with my distant vision. I was taken to Dr Gurupdesh Singh, the oldest ophthalmologist in town. Father and I waited for our turn in the waiting area and the sterile, ominous air of the clinic was made even more insufferable with the chilling description and illustration of eye disorders on the Ophthalmological Association posters meticulously lining the corridor, lit up with fluorescent tubelights. We had all the time to read. My heart thudded. My name was called. I entered the room with some circumspection. The old doctor wore a starched turban and his white beard framing a poker face. He was stiff, his skin like parchment and the folds of his neck sitting immobile on the starched collars of his immaculate white shirt. His eyes looked through his pince nez and he asked me very sternly to read from the vision chart. I could read for the most part but got stuck in the last two lines. He fixed a bulky contraption on my face and began to change the lenses in quick succession. Seemed foreboding. By the time I walked out I had a prescription for myopia as well as a deep-seated, lifelong fear of eye examinations. And this ritual was repeated each time I came home and the fear deepened as my myopia continued to increase by half a number on every visit.

There was some unusual bit of planning emanating from father's end. I could sense it in his movements. A big white envelope arrived through mail one day with a crest printed on it. It lay there on the dining table all day and I looked at it each time I crossed it. Father got back from farm and summoned me to his room. I was informed that I would be appearing for an exam to join the Lawrence School at Sanawar. Now this bit of news was very sudden, but the way it was communicated was like a decision that had already been made. In my best interest, so I was told. The day to leave home was here faster than I had anticipated.

He communicated to me also that since I would be joining boarding, it would be convenient to take a hair cut. And besides, the environment owing to political kharabi could threaten me as a Sikh boy outside of Punjab. These matters were too complicated for me. Besides, I did not seem to have a choice in the matter. I complied. I was taken to a salon, a sight that had been alien to a boy from a Sikh family. The barber came and cursorily took off my patka. I could see him in the mirror examining my hair, like it was a vegetable to be chopped. He held the curly mop in his hands and turned it up and down. It was at that point that I wanted to just flee. But I was too much of a coward to do it. Before I knew, the unruly obstinate curls, all fell around me in clumps. Lifeless things. Accumulating in two heaps on either side.

The day I was to leave, something troubled me from inside. I took a picture of my mother and put it in a tiny copper frame and hid it under my clothes. Between me and my father very little was now said of mother. He had begun to write her off and my attempts to broach the topic were met with an obstinate silence. Hectic packing activity resumed the following week and *my father drove me to Sanawar and handed me over to the headmaster. Two weeks and my life had irrevocably changed.*

The first prolonged break from school came around Christmas. I was to return home and like the rest of the children, I waited for my name to be called out. I was running a mild fever. One by one students' parents started arriving in the lobby. My name was called out and I took leave of the warden, expecting to see father, but instead he had dispatched the driver, Balwinder Singh to pick me up.

There was an eerie silence in the car and as we crossed the Himachal border and entered Chandigarh I felt something had changed since the last visit. Chandigarh was a grey desolation. I mean the city had always seemed dull to me as compared to Patiala, but today the silence and despondency had a different quality. It looked emptier than I remembered. We passed several temporary checkposts made of gunnysacks, with CRPF men in position, wielding AK-47s. They wore camouflage uniforms and combat helmets with leaves and twigs sticking out. The streets were deserted. We were flagged down by security personnel as we crossed the university campus. Balwinder went white in the face. After some cursory questioning the policeman asked him to park on the side and wait till further clearance. When the driver asked him what the matter was, he was told that a curfew had been clamped, owing to a possibility of anticipated violence. Things had become worse since the storming of the Golden Temple and the subsequent gunning down of madam the previous month. Nothing more was said. So we stood there, me and Balwinder waiting.

It was really the middle of nowhere and all there was in this wilderness was an equally deserted petrol pump, behind which there was a decrepit white apartment, part of a small ghetto,

Badheri, which at one time had been one of the scores of villages before its land had been acquired to carve out Chandigarh. My gaze was arrested by the face of a child—I could not make out if it was a boy or a girl, with its nose pressed against the window pane of one of the apartments that rose out of what looked like a dilapidated village. A dead bat dangled from a high-voltage electric wire running overhead. The wide-eyed child just gazed out.

We were finally let off. On the way back, Balwinder told me of his younger brother Baljeet, who, at just twenty-two, had been picked up by police for questioning for suspected links with terrorists. That was not the case, but they kept him in custody for a good week's time and inflicted unimaginable tortures on him. When I wanted to know the details, Balwinder promised to tell me when once I was a grown up.

'Thode jehe wade ho jao, chhote sardarji—grow up somewhat, little sardarji.'

By the time we drove past the old bus stand into Patiala, it was already twilight. I thought father would be beside himself with worry because we had taken way longer getting home. My fever was spiking. The car entered the kothi and a feeling of comfort enveloped me. Subconsciously I expected to see mother but soon reminded myself that that would not happen. I took long strides cutting through the colonnaded verandah, into the hallway leading to father's room. For a minute I thought I was in the wrong house. From a distance, I saw a young lady sitting on the bed with her head thrown back on the pillow and her legs sprawled. I saw her from the edge of the door, dressed in a vermillion salwar kameez, her unusually fair arms and hands sporting henna. My mother's bed. I ran out into the garden. My father, who was at that point in the bathroom came out and hugged me. It was an awkward hug. He explained he had remarried two days ago. 'Really a simple gurudwara ceremony.' From the edges of my eyes I could see lacy undergarments on the cloth stand in the back garden. I wanted to throw up.

I had come home to a foreign country. That night I lay on the bed and heard a distant rumbling of AK-47s through the night.

∞

Our immediate neighbours, the Sharmas, made the decision of relocating to Delhi. Theirs was an old house: Mr Surinder Sharma's great grandfather was Lala Hardyal, who had served the then Maharaja of Patiala as a physician three generations ago. In fact the piece of land on which the house stood had been gifted to him when his intervention had saved Maharani Sahiba's life after a protracted battle with tuberculosis. This was a part of the family lore, their identity as Patialvis. Their son, Sarjeet, everybody called him Sherry, had been my classmate at YPS before I moved to Sanawar. We continued to meet and my total alienation at home was somewhat assuaged by this family. There was a time we were so thick, we were in and out of each other's house all day. To interrupt play would be abhorrent and we would eat wherever food we chanced upon. On many late afternoons, with his mother fast asleep, we would rustle up something from leftovers to allay the legendary teenage boys' hunger—two eggs thrown into a shallow pan with a generous amount of white butter and mixed with a cup of leftover boiled rice. Or quickly made Maggi. Or panjeeri lying in the big steel container. We would have the contents emptied into two bowls and sit out on the outer staircase and eat.

Some sleepy afternoons we would smuggle seedy magazines

from Nandu's corner shop. He sold groceries, threads, odds and ends. The outer entrance of his shop was lined with varieties of dal and rice in open sacks. The smell of freshly fried samosas from his neighbour Jang Halwai constantly hung in his shop. The halwai's kadhai would be laid out on the sidewalk with rows of samosas waiting for their batch to be lowered into the humungous, smoking vessel gone black over the wood fire. Nandu's sacks with rice and dals were arranged on his part of the sidewalk. Next to his scale, which was suspended from the roof with a robust iron chain, was his rusty money box with two drawers. He sat on an old mattress covered with an old gunny sack. It had become two shades darker with the constant oil spillage from the tin container. This was where he hid the seedy magazines, which a wholeseller, his friend got him from Ludhiana. With shifty eyes he would lend them to us, anxious boys, on a charge of a rupee for two days. In that price and through a thoroughly unsexy mediator, we discovered our sexuality and its attendant thrills, our boyhood imaginations exploring territories throbbing with possibilities.

On some afternoons we would cycle down to Gurudwara Dukh Niwaran Sahib where Sherry would grab a saffron scarf from outside the entrance to cover his head. We would pay obeisance, and soon end up in the langar hall where we would try our woolfy teenage appetites in 'who-can-eat-more' competitions, gorging down chapattis by the dozen with dal and runny gobhi aaloo sabzi, much to the disdain of the langar bhaiji.

Upon my return, I saw Sherry's stately, though now decrepit, house being pulled down by a builder. Two JCB machines stood at the gate amidst a flurry of activity. There were labourers atop the terrace of the house hammering the structure into rubble.

The colonnades of the house were reduced to debris and the cement jaali used to run the length of the terrace parapet was lying discarded amongst the mango trees. I wanted to scream and tell them to stop. But like most things at that point, it was spiralling out of control.

There would be intermittent gunshots piercing the vacuum of those dreary nights and one would read about people having been gunned down in the morning newspaper. That evening a curfew was clamped in Patiala city. A prominent journalist had been murdered in broad daylight by terrorists. Things were getting murkier. The clampdown proved much longer than anticipated. We heard of two more Hindu families relocating to Delhi. Our kitchen ran out of supplies. We had consumed the last drop of milk. And then we managed with Milkmaid. It was delicious at the start, but after two days in a row, Milkmaid began to make me sick. So sick. I threw up one morning trying to have the concoction for breakfast.

∞

Two days before I was to leave for school, father stormed into my room. My mother's dead body had been found. Apparently she had been knocked down by a speeding bus in Anandpur Sahib, where she had been living in one of the gurudwaras ever since she left home. What I saw in my father was not grief of having lost his wife, rather an affirmation of a loss he had anyway accepted. I could sense that his principal emotion was one of relief. He pragmatically took on all the rites. My grandparents came down from Kapurthala with my mother's younger sister. They all made a beeline for me, but I had no heart to meet anyone. One after the other, days were whizzing past me. I was just a spectator. They brought her home. They egged me on to pay my last respects. I shied away and got a glimpse of her pallid face. There was a hasty cremation and I stood watching the pyre from a distance. In the front was my father with his new wife. I just could not take it anymore and fled midway. I sleepwalked through the subsequent ceremonies and was, by now, looking forward to getting back to Sanawar at the end of the break. The school now seemed like a sanctuary. However, before leaving I tied a turban on my own accord, which I continued to sport despite the cut hair. There is a custom in Sikhism whereby upon the death of the father, the son, no matter how young, is made to tie a turban as a mark of his taking over the father's role thereon. For me, I felt the turban was my first rebellion against my father's arrogant impositions, which he had inflicted on me all along. It was also a spool of bandage on the raw wounds left by the unnatural loss of my mother. And somewhere I had taken charge of my life. Father was there but, then not really. I had understood the bare truth. I was alone hereon.

Things were better thereafter. Acceptance is a great gift: the courage to see clearly, to see the truth in the face. At times one can grow only with acceptance of incontrovertible truths that cannot be wished away. Acceptance then does become the first rung in overcoming misfortune. At times, it is an alternate view of things and it expands your mind in ways you hadn't known. I just understood it one fine morning. And then I was alright in the six years I spent in the boarding, going home only during the mandatory holidays. For me, there were no night outs, no local guardians. The transfer for my annual fee and other expenses was made promptly every year. I involved myself more and more with the on-campus activities, volunteering to do jobs that required my presence in the short-term off periods when no one else would be available. I had nowhere to go.

This was the time also I discovered my inclination to arts and design. The colonial stone structure of the school building would captivate me endlessly. On Sundays I would perch myself in the front lawns of the school, lie down on the grass and just gaze at the spirals rising into the blue skies. If you have seen the pure azure of mountain sky, you would know what I mean. I would pack my water colours and do nature—architecture studies on Sunday afternoons. I was filling up more cartridge sheets than ever. Honestly I was surprising myself. My decision about architecture as my calling was sealed early on. Swiftly I moved from rung to rung and, as things worked out, landed at Sir JJ in Mumbai.

℘

It was late for the long haul to Patiala but Himmat started back and Nanaki looked at him, riding out of the parking, his silhouette melting into the cold blackness.

Later that night, she lay in bed staring at the ceiling. While she too had grown up without parents, she had been too young to understand loss in a concrete way and had been adequately compensated in love by her grandparents. Himmat's misfortunes went deeper—he had been stripped off protection one by one and utterly abandoned. Himmat's face swam before her and she pined to reach out to him and wished he lay next to her. She wanted to kiss his eyelids. She wanted to make love to him at that instant and such was the surge of desire in her bare body, it seemed to her she was floating. She wanted to lie next to him, embracing his cramped body, waves of delight rising inside. She felt drawn to him in ways that baffled her, and in those moments locked in her room, all she wanted was to entwine with him limb on limb, to caress his chest and shoulders, rub her lips on the length of his body, she wished to just lock her body tight with his. Summer breeze was blowing in from the window that opened into the garden. Spring was gradually giving way to summer. The seasonal flowers were half wilting. Suddenly, a heady burst from the wilting petunias came riding on a breezy wave into her room. The rising desire and the floral burst created a strange intoxication. She slipped out of her nightgown and discarded it on the floor. Her hand lingered on the length of her bare body, finding that deep dark hollow enlivened right now. She found the place nestled in the many folds that was beginning to respond to her feelings. My God! This had enlivened her in completely unknown ways. She did not know of the reserve of this creative energy that was lying latent within her. A tremble travelled the length of her body. She lay in the river of calm and drifted to sleep.

༄

Nanaki needed to get an extended study leave for a project on Punjabi durries. She required at least a month's time to enable her to take field notes and visit weavers across the state. She had been able to secure a National Arts Commission grant and wanted to start on the project without further delay. She had moved the application and secured the Director's assent before submitting it for further action. Normally such applications took a fortnight to process and an order would be handed over to the applicant. It was already close to a month now. She met Prabha, the clerk dealing with these matters in the office. The normally enthusiastic lady seemed unusually thrifty with words, all the while absorbed in a file from which she would not look up. Nanaki felt she was clearly avoiding her gaze. She stood there for a good ten minutes before she got the lady's attention. By this time she was already a bit flustered.

'Prabha ji, my application for study leave. Can you please tell me when I can get the order?'

After a good ten minutes, Prabha looked at her peering over her bifocals. 'Madam, we have sent it to the finance branch but have not heard anything.'

'Have not heard anything? Normally this kind of routine application does not take more than a fortnight. What's the matter? Especially when it's already signed by Director sa'ab.'

At this Prabha kept her pen down and gave her a blank look.

'Ask me, madam, in two days,' she said, playing non-committal.

Nanaki came out crestfallen. There was definitely more to all this office harassment than met the eye. They could not deny it to her, but they were doing what they did best—harassing her to the point of inducing a vague fear of the immanent authority that you eventually have to recognize. So all her little jobs had begun to suffer. She suddenly realized how so-called modern institutions could also transform into narrow fiefdoms where dissent has no space. Because they cannot flog you physically, they will beat hollow the source spring of any enthusiasm inside you. They will make you feel stupid for insisting on paying a humungous price for very 'lay' things. They will create a regime of oppression around trivialities. Your days will be consumed with inanities. So you will eventually fall in line. It would not be worth the while. They are too wily to say it directly, but they will extract their pound of flesh. You will not even know and there you would be, struggling. Things that ought to be handed to you because those are your rights would be made inaccessible and reaching them would be tortuous. That is their way of getting even with you. They have the power. And come to think of it, the face-off hasn't even started. This was just the tip of the iceberg but could be enough to ward off most people. Nanaki didn't want to think ahead, so she concentrated on what needed to be done for now. Simple.

∽

Nanaki felt drained, bureaucratic hassles were just not her thing. It was all a colossal waste of time. She felt somebody had blocked off all the light. She was suffocated. She knew these people would not leave it at that. They will try to do everything they could to dissuade her from pursuing Joginder's case. A dilemma was cracking open and like a sinister pest digging holes of faithlessness. She felt weak. Her head was reeling.

She did not know what would come of all this, but she understood that she needed to take it on. Having figured out the path she now needed to walk on it and not abandon it midway. She would have to go the whole hog. No matter what it took. No matter where it led. It is possible it will bring her to a dead end. It is possible her little road will hit a wall. This were all within the realm of possibility. Despite this knowledge she would have to go on. What she needed was the courage to embrace a new experience at this point. Not with trepidation, but completely. It would show her the path. Bit by bit. Every day. Within the treachery of the many dead-end-tunnels, she will eventually see light. She will follow that trail.

∽

Nanaki was scheduled to meet Nafisa in ten minutes. A journalist with *The Spectator*, she was a friend of Neil's. Nanaki waited for her in her office. It was a modest room she shared with Prof. Chopra, who was on a long leave. There was a knock on the door and Nafisa entered. She was rather diminutive and wore a college girls' short kurta with jeans. Her curly mop, almost like an afro, framed her dark oval face. She could easily pass off as a college student. She had been with the newspaper for two years now. Earlier they put her on the general beat but now she was focussing on Art and Culture. Neil had had a chat with her about her possible help in the matter.

'How we would request you to help us is by writing a comprehensive story on politics we are faced with here.'

Nafisa looked at Nanaki for a while and no word passed her. She understood their problem but whether she trusted Nanaki on this account, she kept under wraps.

'I will look into the matter and would really want to also meet other concerned parties,' she announced. Think I want to meet the lady in question and also the old subedar gentleman. It will take me some time. For now I am really racing against time for another big story I am currently doing on the Anandpur Sahib foundation. I have this weekend to file it.'

Nanaki was disappointed. She was expecting to see a ready affirmation from the journalist's end but soon realized that her idea of bringing out the truth of the matter through the route of the newspaper too was going to take time. Nafisa was non-committal at this point and that made her think of possible pressures that could be exerted on her, or for all you know, have already been exerted on her. She wanted to be hopeful, at least she had promised to engage her with the issue, but in all fairness, being realistic was a better bet for now.

She went to the college branch of State Bank of Patiala

to withdraw some cash. She filled in the withdrawal form and stood in the line awaiting her turn. The lady behind the counter was a wispy, sprightly twenty-something. She held a wad of currency notes in her hand and with deft fingers did a quick count. She then thumped it once on the counter and ran it through the currency counter. The wad was accounted for, like lightning. She picked it from the machine in a quick swipe and flung it into the drawer and entered ₹10,000 in her grimy register. Nanaki felt the woman had so much power, her absolute authority in dealing with currency wads, and absolute certainties like that.

❧

This time Nanaki and Himmat did not even give the taxi a thought. They decided to take the bike to Kasauli to try out Joginder's embroideries before handing them over to be framed. Nanaki was happy with the price settlement reached with the subedar. Himmat had pushed the envelope with his firm in negotiating for an offer of five lacs for the big panel and a couple each for the smaller panels. At least one part of her job was taken care of.

She held him from behind and it felt like the most natural thing to do. Himmat seemed familiar, their bodies drawing close, like reflex. She threw her body on his back, closing her eye and knowing that the world was passing her by in a blur. Himmat's gaze firmly on the road ahead, he had the same lack of self-consciousness that had initially attracted her. She knew a lot more about him by now and that knowledge lent her a quiet comfort. She could ride like this with him at the wheel, and not bother with arriving anywhere.

The work per se did not take very long. Nanaki felt that in

all honesty this trip could have been avoided. But then there was more to Himmat now than work. They thought of taking a walk in the Mall before hitting the club or some place for lunch. At least that was the plan.

They crossed the Louis Pasteur Institute and the ascent started—first gradually and then it rose sharply. They crossed a mountain side covered with seasonal wildflowers—one does not come by those varieties in the plains. She asked Himmat to stop for a while as she climbed up from one end to gather a bunch along with the lush ferns with scores of fiddleheads that were aplenty in the upper reaches. With the glee of a child, she soon returned with a rather lavish bunch. She was almost frolicking and in this moment the two could have been school children on an excursion without a care in the world. As they moved, a curtain of rain-bearing clouds just materialized out of thin air. Before they knew, it was pouring. Mountain rain is like that. It can catch you unawares. The occasional car that earlier crossed them also ceased and the road soon became a muddy slush. In no time, riverines of mountain mud were flowing down the hill on either side of the road. Himmat almost slipped, which could have been disastrous, considering that a part of the road had caved in at the edges, invisible under muddy swirls. They came upon what looked like an abandoned structure. They ran for cover through the little arched doorway tucked in the other end of the wall.

It was clear that this place had been abandoned for a while now. Neglect was writ large everywhere. The old wooden floor had come undone at several places, with some showing glaring gaps between slats. The ceiling was unusually high and on closer inspection, Nanaki observed a row of small glass ventilators running the length of the walls on all sides.

The stained glass icons on the windows had become cloudy with age.

Nanaki was not too sure if stopping here was a good idea. What if the rain did not stop any time soon and by the time they decide to return it got worse and darker and the roads slippery? At least for now they could see clearly if they chose to return.

'Think it is better for us to wait and if it does not stop, we start back in say, fifteen minutes,' Himmat negotiated a middle path.

'OK', by now her collection of flowers and ferns had been washed away and all that she held in her hand were a bouquet of stubs.

The hingeless door was now buffeting with the wind raging outside. Himmat held it and in a swipe and bolted it shut pushing out a gust of wind. With the wind and the rain pushed out, it was suddenly calm inside except for the occasional peal of thunder.

Nothing was said. Himmat hugged Nanaki like it was the most natural thing to do at that instant and she huddled close to him as they stood next to the alcove on one end of the room. He pulled her face close and kissed her languorously all the way down to her neck. His expectant mouth moved all over her face and then down into the depression in her neck. Her cuboid amethyst brushed against his nose and he led her towards the wooden bench in the corner. Soon they were lying down on a bedding made with their clothes spread out on the bench. It was narrow and just about enough for Nanaki to half lie down with her legs dangling on one side. A draught of chilly wind pushed in through the several cracks in the walls, piercing their naked bodies. He pushed her to make room for himself beside her, entwined his legs around her thighs and tightly secured his arm around her. He caressed her taut breasts and soon enough their bodies were throbbing against each other. Snatches of their heavy breath echoed in the empty corners. The roughhousing threw open her plait and her hair was now hanging loose and falling about her in disarray. Himmat could not stop kissing her. They held on to each other tightly, heaving for what was a long time. A street light from outside created a yellow glow on the ventilator. A calm now began to spread in their bodies like a river, moving quietly. For long they lay side by side, in silence with Nanaki's dress as a covering.

It was getting dark. Himmat realized that his turban had come undone. He did not mind it in the least. Just a tad inconvenient to tie it in these surroundings. Had to be stretched into shape before tying. Nanaki held the turban at one end, Himmat at the other. They began to roll it, Himmat gathering it in little laps, moving towards each other. As they met, he planted another kiss on her lips.

೩

That Nafisa had been hard at work became clear the following Sunday. She had sought out details about Subedar Joginder Singh from Nanaki and met him a couple of times in the past fortnight. About her having approached Gurkanwal Kaur, Nanaki wasn't sure. But she had called up Joginder to find out how the meeting went with her each time and the man seemed willing to talk beyond his usual recalcitrance, which in itself was encouraging. Nanaki knew Nafisa was on the job, but exactly what direction her writing would go was beyond her, nor did she want to ask her and in the process influence her.

Nanaki empathized with the young professional and wanted her to concentrate on the job. She could gather by now that Nafisa would satisfy herself before filing the story. She took two weeks, which was long by journalistic standards and just in the nick of time for Nanaki and Neil.

Nanaki got up Sunday morning and sat up with the newspapers on the bed next to the window with the utterly unexpected spread on the supplement page. It was their story, carried over a generous three quarters of the page, supplemented with coloured photographs of Joginder's big pheasant panel and other embroideries. But then it was unexpectedly in the *Herald*. The byline read Nalini Chunawalla.

Hmm. She either has the good sense to pick the most interesting of Joginder's works or has been guided by a well-heeled critic. Nanaki was bubbling with excitement by now and began to scan the article line by line, word by word. The article was unsparing, rather ruthless in its criticism of the bureaucratic control of the art institutions. It clearly pitted Joginder next to Gurkanwal by showcasing their works. The argument was clinched by a small 'Expert Speak' box at the bottom in which no less than Dr Venkat Subramaniyam, the authority on textiles from the National Museum was quoted. Dr Subramaniyam had taken a very favourable view of Joginder's art labelling it as an experimental mix of old phulkari stitches and world classical embroidery techniques. He hailed it as an evolved vocabulary in thread. Gurkanwal's pieces, on the other hand, were written off quite candidly as tacky, impostering, not to be confused any which way with art. The two, in his view were not in a position to be compared. Nanaki felt embarrassed at having initially doubted the young journalist's resolve in handling the issue. She had looked at her askance, doubting if she would get it right, if she would show the courage and the consummate understanding of grappling with the issue. But Nafisa had revealed tricks up her sleeve she could have never suspected. Now the young girl had gone all out. This could have been risky.

Nanaji read the article while lying on the cot in the sun. His wrinkled skin looked even craggier on his bare chest. When he picked up the apple slice from the bowl Beeji left him, she could see his hand shaking and the action that had hitherto been effortless, looked laboured.

Navneet suddenly burst upon the scene from the vernadah. She sauntered in, asking for Beeji. She carried a bulky shopping bag in her hand, bulging from all sides. Nanaji was unhappy with the sudden interruption and had to cut short his sunning by sitting up and slipping into a vest.

'So, Nanaki, what's happening? I was expecting you to pick up the kurta design, but it looks like you are super busy.'

'Actually kind of, caught up with a project and then college work.'

'Why do you take so much tension, dear? Look at Preeti.' At this Nanaki gave her a questioning look, she could not place the reference.

'Oh Preeti...you don't know Preeti... Mrs Varma's daughter-in-law. Our neighbouring house. Yellow kothi. Yes, you girls should be meeting. Now what I was saying was Preeti also teaches at a government college and she is always back by one. She takes good care of herself... I mean facial, pedicure, manicure, hair...always tip-top. And she keeps placing orders with me...never less than three suits in a go. Girl is really well-maintained. I stitched this yellow A-line for her. I can show you hers'...in case you want...it's really *in* this season.'

Nanaki just smiled.

'Actually I keep busy so I just pick up stuff from Fabindia… so much more convenient.'

'Yes…but what keeps you so busy? I thought teaching job was good for women…they can manage home and family easily. Look at Preeti…she does it. And come to think of it, you are yet to have family responsibility.'

At this Nanaji butted in. He thrust the newspaper towards her. 'Nanaki is fighting bigger issues, Navneet. Look at this.'

Navneet looked at the newspaper and gave up in a jiffy.

'*Samjha deo*—tell me about it. Make me understand this. I read really slow.'

So Nanaki, much to her chagrin at having been put in this position explained, whatever she could muster about the college issue.

Navneet listened big eyed, her mascaraed eyelids batting now and then. She lost interest soon after. She pooh-poohed the matter with a swipe of hand.

'All this is OK. But why take such tension when the issue does not even affect you? You think too much. Take care of yourself also. *Philosopher dhee jam pai*—Uncle has a philosopher daughter here,' she offered it almost like a condolence to Nanaji.

Beeji came out wiping her wet hands on her apron. She had been kneading dough. Navneet spread the contents of her bag on to the cot. It was cloth material of various dressy kinds. She began to persuade Beeji to select for herself. From a distance Nanaki saw Beeji shaking her silvery head multiple times. Nanaki knew that it would end in Beeji picking up something out of courtesy and then what would follow would be an elaborate pantomime with Beeji insisting on paying for the purchase and Navneet equally vociferously insisting on giving it to her gratis. Beeji would be prompt with getting the money out and pressing it into Navneet's hands—who would shoot back a scandalized look. '*Bilkul nahi...bilkul nahi*—absolutely not...out of the question,' she would tell her. 'I will not accept any payment from you.' Beeji would display 'rightful' anger and eventually end the matter by telling her that she was accepting it this time but never again.

ॐ

Nafisa left the story at the editor Subhash Chopra's desk early next morning. She still had some unfinished business with the Anandpur Sahib report and set off early morning. Her day turned out to be tiring what with a flat tyre and then the wild goose chase with some officials whose bytes were essential to the story. She reached home really late and got a call from her colleague, Karan. He explained to her about his meeting with Chopra who, he guessed would try to scuttle her attempts of going ahead with her story. He said he found his objections vague, which was always the case when your criticism is not based on facts but is a result of outer influence. Nafisa was crestfallen. She had hoped for some positive feedback because she earnestly felt that it was a good story. In fact, it had turned out to be more than a story. The seamier side of art institutions was now visible to her and in that flush of idealism that had seized her, she had wanted to do her bit in exposing the corrupt nexus. But this reaction was totally unexpected and she felt a pang at how utterly unwarranted it was. She was ready to storm into Chopra's office to demolish each of the objections he had, till Karan offered another perspective. He was senior at the office by three years and had a wider experience of these situations. He explained it to her that Chopra's objections had nothing whatsoever to do with the merit of her reportage and research; it had to do with his political compulsions.

'Like what?'

'Like the people you are ruffling have placed big stakes in the matter. It goes much deeper than you can imagine. For them, it means they have to forgo a chance at grabbing a place in hallowed portals. For the chief secretary, it is his ambition and for the Director of the Art College, it is purportedly a case of quid pro quo—in exchange for the gallery space he is being offered the chairmanship of the Art Council upon retirement. His retirement is due next August. He doesn't look it though.'

'Oh!'

'And there's more, the chief secretary is also related to the chief minister who you know is a major donor with our publication. Outwardly he cannot do it, there is a conflict of interest, but this monetary control of our paper is a story everyone knows.'

'Oh God! So there's one brewing right under our nose and we look elsewhere. What is this sham, Karan? You spend years in the classrooms learning about the power of the pen, and it all ends up like this. I wish they taught us about how to take on goons in the profession. About the inevitability of impasses such as these when fairness is pressurized to surrender before vested interests. I wish they taught us how to be your own in these circumstances. Instead, this is what most people begin to accept with time. Is this what being "experienced" means?'

'Relax, Nafisa. He has not refused the story totally. It's just that I see it coming. He was nervous. You know what I mean.'

'And come to think of it, I, in my naiveté, was expecting that they will notice the effort I have put in with this one especially *by tracking down the expert and digging the details from the subedar, who was so reluctant. And one thing, Karan, I know this story has potential.'*

'Precisely the point.'

'And I can also see how Nanaki is pitted against a wall. Someone is hell-bent on pressurizing her to give in. They will not even be seen, they will do it by disempowering you. You will feel you have no locus standi. They will degrade your work and make you feel unimportant. That is what they do. Typical.'

'Hmmm...'

'But I like this fighter streak in the woman. I mean she is so intrinsically driven. She is convinced about what she believes in and is merely doing what she thinks is right. Without fanfare. That is a great power these days. When most people can't seem to tell what is right from wrong, let alone do anything about it. Why has this strange stupor got to us, Karan? You know there are times I am outraged at things when you see them up close, but no one seems to be feeling it and I feel I might be overreacting. You know I do go OTT.'

'Chill, Nafisa. Please continue getting outraged.'

'Yeah, I mean I feel, we will all be hollow dead if we didn't. In Punjab it's like you have got so used to perversions that you've stopped noticing it and the measure of your social standing is your ability to manipulate procedures to milk them for your use. And everyone, everyone is on the bandwagon for their pound of flesh. It's getting sick... It's like the Chinese addiction to opium made them hollow, in that case the British were making a profit...here, we are just killing ourselves.'

'Chopra would get back more emphatically to silence you. So beware. Let's just take it as it comes.'

Karan hung up.

Nafisa could hardly get any sleep. Her mind went in circles. She marvelled at her own naiveté—why she was the twenty-something who had done an elaborate interview with Prof. Chaudhuri only last month and how impressed she was with his ideas. But so soon had found him to have feet of clay. And now the facts she had unearthed were enough to disgust her for a long time. This nexus business was closing on her from all sides. What could she—an ordinary middle-class girl possibly do? She was the only one from her family to take up journalism—her father, a mid-level bank official with Oriental Bank, had so wanted her to take the PO exams and get into the secure world of banking. But Nafisa's love for writing steered her in this direction. Though at that point it only meant the ability to string pretty words together. And she had done well for herself by landing a campus placement while still being in the final year. These people were way too important. What could she do? I can write, yes, I must. That's my only way and that is the way.

It was barely six in the morning when Karan called.

'Nafisa, the story. Email it to me now.'

'What? Really? Great…right away.'

'Only thing, it'll be in the Herald and under a pseudonym. Are you OK with that? They said they could not carry the photos, but I have pushed the envelope.'

Better for it to see the light of day than languish in cold storage or come out when there is no use.

৯

On Monday morning Nafisa and Karan were summoned by Chopra in his office. The boss was clearly miffed at this circumvention by the subalterns. The fumes of anger from his head entered his nostrils and came out as a watery trail. He sniffed as he spoke and his anger was spilling out.

'Go away, go away,' Chopra said, pushing a Vicks inhaler up his left nostril which was red with constant wiping.

They met with nothing but blankness.

Karan and Nafisa were duly informed of a transfer order to Bathinda branch of the paper. While they both emerged downcast from the editor's office after the fireworks, they had just witnessed their own power, even though 'by hook or by crook.' They could not be fired, so the office did the next predictable thing: they were transferred to Bathinda. That was hardly an interesting proposition to begin with but something changed in the way both began looking at their profession. Overnight it had become more than a job—it had become a career choice. These were stories that would define their path as journalists, as people. They were happy to be a team and heading out together and more importantly, it was a land with a lot of potential for some serious reporting on the political machinations rife there. It was the hinterland, the turf where major players worked their manipulations, lots to take on.

As they hurtled down the office stairs, Karan tried in vain to download the epaper version of the Herald. As they came out into the parking lot, Nafisa jibed, 'Throw this stupid phone of yours, always playing up. I've told you once, I've told you a hundred times—get a better phone. You'll not goof-up. Or maybe it's to do with better connectivity. Bathinda will give you better connectivity.'

They stood in the setting sun, guffawing.

❧

Professor Chaudhuri's Ambassador halted in the college porch. Nanaki was still in the studio with her first year History of Textiles when he walked passed. His peon Sadashiv was trailing with heavy files and trying to match step. Nanaki could feel a flurry of activity and commotion as he crossed. From the studio she could make out his brusque manner and it seemed somebody on way had already been ticked off. The meeting was scheduled to begin at 11.30.

Nanaki was the first one to reach the conference room, but in no time all the members had taken their seats. The agenda of the day was announced and Chaudhuri was firmly in his seat—unflinchingly, unambiguously in his seat. His sense of self-importance always grew by a few inches on these occasions.

'So, Chander, all well at your end?' he enquired of a young faculty member.

'All well, Sir' was all the young diffident chap could muster in the few seconds. Chaudhuri decided to expend on the hapless man. Clearly Chaudhuri was not interested in his welfare. It just made for a nice display when you have a young man grovelling all over you. As if you owed him his life and thankfully there were many such who would oblige him to create a spectacle. A spectacle of power. You see them falling at the feet of politicians and now the odious practice had begun in institutions as well.

Chaudhuri was now securely ensconced.

He began his address: 'You all are more than familiar with today's agenda. Not a very winding one, we are simply here to accord our assent to the proposal that has already been floated to you all in the previous meeting about the inclusion of two artists in our art gallery. One is Mazhar Khan, the artist of international renown and the other is Gurkanwal Kaur, who has extensively exhibited her embroidery work in the region. Her competitor is one Joginder Singh. I am afraid I do not know too much about his credentials but yes, he has *never* exhibited. Never.'

Nanaki was amazed at the poise with which people could manipulate information. Chaudhuri was consummate in these arts and she could not help notice the stresses, elisions and composure in his speech. They bend people and circumstances and hammered them in or out depending on their motives in a given situation, and eventually explained it all by doing the same with words. Words, empty words.

There were five members in the meeting and Nanaki knew she had no chance pitted against the likes of her boss and the representatives of the administration and university VC. The former was clearly in his pocket or rather, he was in their pocket and the latter would have been convinced by now. Nanaki was realistically not hopeful because her few attempts to meet the VC in this regard had been met with cold indifference. Earlier she and Neil had decided to record dissent formally in the meeting, whether or not it was to any avail.

The moment of truth was now upon them. The Director asked all concerned to vote in favour of Gurkanwal by raising hands—the others would be counted as votes for Joginder. Nanaki and Neil looked away while the Director and UT administration nominee unequivocally raised their hands. Nanaki looked up and saw two hands. The VC nominee funnily was desisting from the same. At first, Nanaki thought in her absolute certainty that they would lose, she had not noticed correctly. But she looked again. No, only two hands were up.

'Yes, Bhatia, hand please,' Chaudhuri prompted him.

'Sir, later, I am not with this motion,' Bhatia, the VC nominee, said wihout batting an eyelid.

Chaudhuri could not bring himself to say much after that. He asked Senior Prof. Mehta to conclude the proceedings. The meeting ended rather abruptly. Chaudhuri rushed out, affixing his initials where required. The samosas were not touched.

Chaudhuri had a really bad evening. He went home surly and vent his anger on his wife and then the poor dog. How, in the course of the day he had gone from smug joviality to a sullen silence to seething anger was anybody's guess. This was the most unexpected turn in the events. It seemed the VC, upon reading the comprehensive story in the *Herald,* had indeed changed his mind.

'It would have been a travesty,' he said to Chaudhuri later, explaining his turnaround.

෨

Marasi 1: How are you? Kiven?

Marasi 2: This blessed bukhaar is troubling the whole tabbar family. They say these days the fever and cough take much longer to heal than they did in the good old days.

Marasi 1: Aaho, that's true. Shown to the daktar?

Marasi 2: Yes, still taking long.

Marasi 1: Aaho. Bande made, keede tagde—frail men, robust germs. Feed your folks lassi—that should do their guts some good.

Marasi 2: Not that lassi is any pure, or milk, or malai. Not water, not air. All spoiled at the source. Khuraak hi madi ho gai—our diets are pure no more. You know, to be honest, can't even trust the daktar these days. You go to one of those shops and you will know what I mean.

Marasi 1: Tell me more.

Marasi 2: Nothing. Nothing to be told. Nothing worth telling. What to say: Lassi reminds me, the buffalo died too, she was an old one, bad news all around.

Marasi 1: Then hear me out brother, you know Pammi? The halwai's daughter, Pammi?

Marasi 2: Aaho, aaho. Yes what about her?

Marasi 1: She cleared papers. Very difficult papers. She was a bright one. About the sarkari school and college she attended, the lesser said, the better. Self study. They say she will become DC.

Marasi 2: Achha... Then it is celebrations for the village. Pind di dhee—village daughter—becomes afsar.

Marasi 1: Aaho. And they went to the dahda peer's dargah for thanksgiving. I tell you, brother, for us folks, this is the only way. I have a feeling it is now the time of the daughters. Provided they care for their own people. Otherwise Pammi could very well go down whatwashisname Balraj Singh's way. The man refused to recognize us once he became afsar in the city. We could not enter his sarkari kothi in Chandigarh. Paisa sakka ho gaya—power and pelf became more important.

Marasi 2: Achha? No, what did you go to him for?

Marasi 1: Needed some help with my old man in the big city hospital. That's all.

Marasi 2: Tu rehan de. I do not believe you. Must have crash-landed at his place. They don't have time for the likes of you. Nikamma, nikhattu, good for nothing. (Slaps him with the leather belt.)

Marasi 1: And you? Are you done with vadai harvesting?

Marasi 2: What are you? DC? Enquiry Officer? Will not tell you.

Marasi 1: Tell me.

Marasi 2: Will not tell. No.

Marasi 1: Chhad—leave it. Let's go and see off Pammi. Leaving for training. They WhatsApped me on Pind group.

Marasi 2: Let's go. For a change no need to buy laddoo. Halwai di dhee hai—daughter of a halwai. We might get some—whatsit?—return giffit. (Guffaws.)

(They walk off.)

∽

It was long overdue. Nanaki had promised Himmat she would visit Patiala with him on the next available weekend. In an hour's time they were cutting through the surrounding villages of Fatehgarh Sahib district. Nanaki wanted a leisurely ride through the several forts and village gurudwaras that dot the area. There was Gurudwara, Pehli Patshahi, located about five kilometres into the highway, which she wanted to visit on the way. Himmat was upto it. She chose her mother's ivory jamavar shirt and cream silk pyjamis for the occasion—and paired it with Beeji's kundan studs and beige leather juttis. She was feeling inordinately indulgent today though going biking in that gear was impractical. But then practicality had never been her upmost trait. She let her hair loose with a tiny gold comb holding a stray flick in place.

A dirt track veered from the highway into the adjoining fields and a ceremonial gate pointing to the direction of the gurudwara loomed into view. The track of the gurudwara was festooned with overhead silver buntings. They made flapping sounds as they rode under the silver canopy. The still waters in the acres of paddy fields exuded a silence. It was the kind of afternoon silence, when you can hear the gnats. It was not the service hour at the gurudwara either. The pale-yellow gurudwara building looked old and worn out at places. Two wizened banyans stood at the entrance, their aerial roots swinging in the breeze. A grove of ancient mango trees filled the backyard. Near the outer wall lay a wooden cot with a sleeping infant. It was covered with her mother's dupatta. Probably the *sewadar's* child.

There was another shed-like structure which said 'langar' in Gurmukhi. Nanaki gave a pleading look to Himmat and rubbed her hand on her stomach. They entered the long, dark hall through clunky wooden doors. Hundreds could sit together on the jute mats and eat in a go. In the farther end of the hall, steel utensils were stacked in huge cast iron trolleys. The utensils, hundreds in number were stacked there, the clanging of the steel intermittently echoing through the empty hall. Himmat took out a pair of plates from the trolley, spoons and bowls and settled on the floor with Nanaki. They sat down and in no time two young men emerged with food—one held an iron bucket with dal and the other a wicker basket of chapattis. It was a delicious meal, probably because food was cooked at a slow pace and sometimes dal was simmered overnight on wood fire, allowing it to seal in the flavours.

The hall was practically empty. Still they lingered on. It had begun to rain. They decided to stay put till it let up. Himmat saw her sitting across him on the floor, cross-legged, her eyes closed and head covered. A stray raindrop suddenly hit her on the cheek, she opened her eyes and smiled at Himmat.

They were going home.

∞

Acknowledgements

Writing a novel is alchemy; sometimes the debt one owes to people is too subtle even for oneself to realize. At other times it is humungous—it envelopes one's reality in such an all-encompassing way that it too becomes invisible. In that space is my family—parents, siblings, my husband and my son. They sportingly put up with all the typical writerly hazards.

I am indebted to special individuals whose judgement I relied upon at various points—Ms Neel Kamal Puri, for her thorough engagement with the manuscript; Dr Neelam Mansingh, for her vital feedback when the novel was in nascence; Prof. Pushpinder Syal, with whom I have had the luxury of no holds barred exchanges, often ending in delightful insights; Mr Karthik Venkatesh, whose prompts were very valuable in the initial stages. My thanks also to Mr Amandeep Sandhu for egging me on, Mr Kanishka Gupta for his encouragement at various points, Dr Pawan Sharma for his enthusiasm and Prof. Avnindra Chopra for his constant support.

Thanks are due to the editorial team at Rupa, who were passionate and patient with the manuscript and whose steady discretion steered the novel to its present form.

Made in the USA
Las Vegas, NV
17 August 2021